The Sweethearts & Jazz Nights

Series of Sweet Historical Romance

The Complete Collection

Jessica Eissfeldt

The Sweethearts & Jazz Nights Series of Sweet Historical Romance
Jessica Eissfeldt

ISBN 978-1-989290-09-5

ALSO BY JESSICA EISSFELDT

Sweet Historical Romance:

Sweethearts & Jazz Nights
Dialing Dreams
Shattered Melodies
Fancy Footwork
Unspoken Lyrics
The Sweethearts & Jazz Nights Series:
The Complete Collection

Love By Moonlight
Beneath A Venetian Moon
Beside A Moonlit Shore
The Love By Moonlight Series:
The Complete Collection

Sweet Contemporary Romance:

**Prince Edward Island Love
Letters & Legends**
This Time It's Forever
Now It's For Always
At Last It's True Love

Dialing Dreams

A Novelette

Jessica Eissfeldt

Dialing Dreams

A Novelette

The Sweethearts & Jazz Nights Series of Sweet Historical Romance

Jessica Eissfeldt

*Inspired by the song "Operator,
Please" by Matt Dusk*

Chapter One

BELINDA THOMPSON COULDN'T STAND ONE more moment of this. What was she doing here anyway, sitting at a switchboard at midnight, humming jazz melodies to herself? Melodies that she'd practiced through all four years of high school vocal classes. And then sang for hours more in the kitchen at home, with her heart full of hope and dreams. So shouldn't she be enchanting audiences and singing songs, not answering calls and connecting wires?

But the sound of her father's hoarse cough echoed through her mind and tugged at her conscience. She would not abandon him. She straightened up. She was all he had. She might not want to work as a telephone operator at the Hotel Whitcomb but she could still choose how she acted about it. She would do it—for him. Taking comfort in that, she began the jazz tune again. But it faded from her lips when a call came in.

"Operator. How may I transfer your call?" She cringed as a male voice slurred a greeting.

"No...no tra-transfer. Please, can we just...talk?"

Not only drunk, he's desperate, she thought. Yet his velvety baritone intrigued Belinda in spite of herself. "I'm sorry, sir. You have to tell me who you want to connect to."

"Room five oh...five. Yeah, that's it."

Belinda studied the tips of her polished nails. "One moment, please, while I—"

"No, no, no. No. No...need. I don't...*actually* want to talk to her."

"Sir, who *do* you want to be connected to?"

"There isn't a number. I want...to talk to someone like you."

"I need to connect you. Or I really can't continue this conversation."

"Operator, you sound like a nice girl, and I...need to talk to a nice girl. Claire wasn't—"

A little unnerved, she spoke over him. "That's not my job."

"All right. All right. I...won't bother...you."

The line went dead.

Belinda frowned then shrugged. She glanced at the clock. Time to go. She collected her purse and slid on her trench coat before cinching its belt. She pinned her hat in place and pulled on her gloves before locking up the tiny switchboard office on the hotel's main floor. With a sigh of relief, she walked through the marble-floored lobby, waved a goodbye to the doorman and headed up Market Street, her seven-cent fare in hand. The

cable car's rumble and screech told her she'd arrived just in time to jump onto the Powell-Hyde line and head for home.

A LIGHT DRIZZLE SPATTERED THE phone booth the following Friday night as Nick Hart ducked into it on impulse. Couldn't sleep anyway. And a walk usually cleared his head. He stared out into the darkness enshrouding the Bay Area as the lights of San Francisco winked back at him, as they did every evening across from his place on the waterfront.

Not so long ago, things were going great. His third record was selling well, and he'd gotten his polished shoes onto the crooner stage at last. But this whole thing with Claire had begun to fall apart. He'd put his soul on hold[1] for her. Showed what a fool will do for love. He frowned and shook off the raindrops that clung to his fedora, placed it back on his head, and tugged the brim lower.

Eying the sleek black handset, he ran a finger along it as he pondered last week's drunken call to the Hotel Whitcomb. Was he that desperate that he'd actually tried to get sympathy from the operator? Even though she'd been annoyed with him—he hadn't been too drunk to remember that— he couldn't quite forget her satiny voice.

He winced as he recalled the bottle of Jack he'd downed. He wasn't normally a big drinker, but, God, sometimes he still missed Claire. Could he do anything about her leaving, though? No. Not a damn thing.

Yet why did he feel this need to figure out what had gone wrong? He contemplated the view for a second time and sighed as he fidgeted with the change in his pocket, then reached for the phone— this time sober.

He couldn't quite forget her satiny voice.

"Operator. How may I direct your call?"

It was the same girl! Nick's heart quickened. He cleared his throat, somehow suddenly struck speechless even though it was Claire he thought he was supposed to be asking for. Or had he actually called back in hopes of talking to the operator again?

"Hello? How can I transfer your call?"

"Yes, er, hello."

"Who may I connect you with?"

That voice. Exquisite. Just exquisite. It didn't seem as if the operator recognized him, though. "I don't know why I'm calling[2]," Nick said, watching a raindrop slide down the glass door.

"A transfer, please." This time she sounded impatient.

"Room five oh five—no." Nick drummed his fingers on his leg. What was he doing anyway, out here in the rain? Being ridiculous. Calling Claire when she'd taken up residence at the Whitcomb wasn't the way to let her go. Hell, it'd been over a month now. How much longer was he going to wallow in the muck of misery? It certainly wasn't the best place to get clean. Better to stand up and be a man about it.

Claire obviously didn't want to talk to him, so why was he wasting any more of his time on her? Perhaps the Fates had shown him another way—were pointing out a different path. And who was he to argue with that? "No. You know what? I do know why I'm calling. It's because..." He needed someone to listen. To his side of the story. "I know you're not a doctor.[3]" He hurried on before she could hang up. "But you could do me some good.[4]"

"Excuse me, sir? I'm the operator."

"Exactly. People call you all the time. So please. You have a minute, surely?"

She sighed. "Quite a few minutes, actually."

The story, corked up inside for so long, finally spilled out of him. "You see, my gal left me. Claire was her name, and she just...bam! Vamoosed. Well, I'm not saying I really helped the situation. Being gone all the time. That's the thing, though—I thought my life was going so well. Like I had the world on a string..." He chuckled. "To quote a piece of that show tune title."

"Oh! 'I've Got the World on a String' is one of my favorites!"

Her voice singing the rest of the verse surprised a smile onto his face. And for a few moments, he just listened. But then, as the familiar melody coursed through him, he found himself singing along, the tune nudging away the loneliness, loosening the bands of discontent. Before he knew it, he'd sung the entire second verse and the chorus with her.

"Say, that was fantastic. You've got a great ear!"

"Gee, I...Thanks."

They lapsed into silence again and Nick felt sadness sneak into his thoughts once more. "So Claire left. Said I was, er..." He paused. Tried again. "Said I was untrue to her. Which I wasn't. Said I was playing fast and loose with some business deals." He scratched the back of his neck. "Yeah, okay, so I made a few impulsive career choices, but, you know, it was all completely above board with the record company."

"Record company?"

"I'm a singer. Name's Nick Hart."

"Mr. Hart! You—you're Mr. Hart?"

"The very same, miss. Just got back from Vegas, as a matter of fact."

"Vegas? That's swell!"

Nick grinned, feeling his natural optimism return. "A fella like me is mighty lucky to bring joy to so many others. I love what I do."

"Maybe"—she hesitated—"Claire didn't understand that. Maybe she left because she missed you. Because I'm sure you must have spent a lot of time together at the start? And then if you were away performing, well, all that time back home by herself, she probably felt lonely, and it might've gotten her to thinking you were up to something—" She interrupted herself. "Oh! I need to answer this other line. Please hold."

Nick waited, wondering what it would be like to stare at a switchboard for hours on end. He mulled over what she'd said—she could be right. But then his mind drifted back to Claire. How could she think he was cheating? Just because he'd be zooming off for gigs or recording at the studio didn't mean he was seeing anyone else on the side.

The light drizzle turned to a heavy downpour. Claire hadn't really seen him for who he was. He hadn't been around enough for her to find that out. The girl did have a point.

And Claire hadn't really understood what he'd truly wanted or needed. Hell, neither had he—not at first. Because he'd been so caught up in what he thought she wanted him to be that he hadn't taken the time to step back and see the lack of true connection between them.

He gripped the handset. Maybe Claire's walking out, marked by nothing more than the staccato clicking of her receding heels and the lazy lingering of her powdery perfume, had been his deliverance.

He exhaled. Had he truly been in love with Claire? Sure, she'd been a great girl—fun, interesting, beautiful. But there—bare and exposed within the depths of his soul—lay the truth. He'd wanted something more. Something deeper. A woman who could understand what it meant to truly live life. A woman with a dream.

He heard the girl reconnect their line. "Do you have a dream?" Nick asked, unapologetic, as he fidgeted again with the change in his pocket.

Silence.

"Hello?" Nick said, wondering if she'd disconnected him.

"Uh, I'm here," she responded, her voice lowering to a whisper. "A dream?"

Nick waited.

"Well..." she stalled.

"Come on, you gotta have at least one."

"I want to be a singer." The words came out in a rush.

"How about that!" He grinned. "See, people need 'em, you know?" His voice grew deeper with conviction. "Something to keep that fire in the soul burning. Otherwise everybody just walks through life dead to the greater potential all around."

"Oh yes!"

Huh. In the minutes that he and the girl had been talking, they were more in tune with each other than he and Claire had ever been in all the months they had been together. Nick held his breath, then let it out. "Everything you've said about me and Claire has been right on the money. You must have a great relationship."

"I, um, actually my father's all I have now...I'm an only child. My mother died, and my father's an invalid, and I need to focus all I can on helping him. He can't work, and now I'm talking too much and...Oh, no! I have to go. My shift's over."

"Wait!"

No reply.

"Goodbye, then." But the dial tone was his only response. Nick replaced the handset and left the phone booth. He lit a Lucky Strike and contemplated the glowing end. So she wanted to be a singer. He put the cigarette to his lips and inhaled, the corners of his mouth quirking upward in remembrance of his own early aspirations. Great dream, doll, great dream.

He smoked and walked, a renewed sense of purpose filling him. His brisk pace soon carried him back to his place.

But when he let himself into his silent, dark apartment, a wave of loneliness hit again. He shook his head, forcing the feeling aside as he unbuttoned his now-wrinkled shirt. He flopped across his bed, soon falling into a dreamless sleep as the smoke from his snuffed-out cigarette curled up into the darkness.

Nick blinked awake as the next day's late morning sun streamed through the blinds. He rolled over to shield his eyes from the glare. God, he needed to get back to rehearsing. He was already too far behind schedule, what with that big performance at the end of the month.

He sat up. Taking time off to heal a broken heart wasn't exactly an option with showbiz. Nick bathed and then dressed purposefully in fresh clothes before fixing himself some scrambled eggs and coffee. He wasn't going to feel sorry for himself any longer, he decided as he ate. After finishing his breakfast, he grabbed his fedora off the coatrack and walked out the door, hopped a bus, and headed downtown to the studio.

Chapter Two

"OPERATOR. How may I direct your call?"

"It's Nick Hart here."

A flurry of butterflies swept through Belinda's stomach on wings of joy and trepidation. He had taken the time to call her—again. They'd been talking for more than a week now.

And with each conversation, slowly, slowly, she had begun to see it: his character was embedded in his music. And because of his music, she could trust him. Sure, some may have called that trust naïve. And maybe it was. They had never met. But to her he spoke the truth each time he sang: deep loss in every note of those heartbreak songs; steadfast devotion in every line of those love songs. A man who was that real in his art would be that

real in his personal life, would be that real in his daily life. She just knew it.

"Say, Miss Thompson, umm..." Nick paused. "I've been thinking. I like the way you carry a tune. Why don't you come downtown here the day after tomorrow— Tuesday? Check out your voice. I *am* doing a show the end of the month, so who knows?"

Belinda stared at the switchboard in disbelief. It was too good to be true. Then again, he wore his heart on his sleeve every time he picked up that microphone, so why wouldn't he be speaking the truth when he showed interest in her voice? And maybe, just once or twice in a lifetime, shiny pennies like this one dropped down from the sky and into her lap.

Still she sat, immobile. He was the one with the amazing voice. All his albums were marvelous. Yet he seemed to think she had potential. Excitement rippled through her. But then she felt her mouth go dry. Guilt soon followed. She couldn't go gallivanting off on some lark. What about Father? To go to work was one thing, but to go to a recording studio just to sing? She'd be abandoning him.

"I don't know." She studied her reflection in the darkened window and twisted a brunette strand of hair around her finger as she watched her eyes fill with worry at the sudden chance at freedom.

"It'll be a blast!"

She chewed on a cuticle. She'd be a disloyal daughter if she went through with it. And selfish.

"Let me ask you something," Nick said finally. "Are you an artist?"

"Uhh..."

"Just remember, if you're an artist—and Miss Thompson, I'm certain you are one—your art comes from inside." He paused. "From your heart, I mean."

He continued. "You have to make your choice from that place too. Although," he added, "what can it hurt? Listen, I gotta run, but I'll give you my studio number. Call me there."

Except she hadn't. And now it was

Monday evening.

The clock's ticking seemed louder than usual. How many times had she sat at this very switchboard, fighting tears of regret, tears of boredom, tears of frustration at not having a chance to live her dream? And now that it was here? How could she give in to fear again? But she couldn't help her emotions. She just couldn't. Her dream continued to beckon, though, its light shining through a crack in the wall of her fears.

Maybe he had a point. She shifted in the chair and reached for her handbag. What could it hurt, she mused, as she slid a silver tube of lipstick out and carefully applied the crimson shade.

Perhaps she could ignore her fears. Be brave for once. She put the lipstick cap back on with a firm click. Yes. She didn't have to listen to her doubts.

And it was true that Father had been feeling better in the past few days. She could probably slip out for a little while. Besides, she'd finally get to meet a real jazz musician. None other than Mr. Nick Hart.

With a shaky hand, she dialed.

TUESDAY AFTERNOON SUNSHINE BATHED THE low brick building in a warm glow. Belinda double-checked the downtown Geary Street address and took a final glance at her trim figure reflected in a nearby window, relieved that her veiled burgundy hat and pinned-up hairstyle were still in place after the windy block-and-a-half walk from the trolley stop.

She pulled open the door and stepped inside the foyer. The click of her heels on the black and white penny-round tiles sounded far more confident than she felt.

She closed her eyes a moment, gathering strength, and allowed a small smile of triumph to form. She was doing it—taking one tiny step toward something she'd held so dear. Whatever the result, she was here now. And that's what counted. She opened her eyes. Touched her mother's pearls once for luck. Then, placing her palm on the reassuring solidness of the polished oak handrail, she began climbing the three flights to the recording studio.

What would Mr. Hart be like in person? She thought about his records in her living room. Heat rose to her cheeks. Who was he beyond his smiling album photograph? Her heart surged. Beyond his silky timbre? Her lips curved upward in anticipation of finding out just that. She reached the door at the end of the third-floor hallway and tapped on the frosted glass.

The door swung open. And there he was.

"You came." The warmth of his firm grip enveloped her gloved hand.

She caught her breath. His voice had been splendid over the phone, but my oh my, in person it was positively divine.

"I did." But frivolity had no place beside duty. She cleared her throat, trying to dislodge the guilt forming there. She couldn't allow herself to stay long. She had to focus on Father, not on herself. No matter that he'd been doing better today. And so, guilt forced a lie past her lips. "I can't leave my father alone too long."

"Of course." Nick stood aside to let her pass. "We'll get right on it, then."

Belinda took off her hat and saw the upright piano in the middle of the room; removed her gloves and noticed the music stands by the piano; smoothed down her crepe blouse and spotted a pile of sheet music on top of the piano. And with those small actions, the guilt she'd been feeling only moments before began melting away, replaced by tingles of excitement.

Because there in that high-ceilinged room, with its scent of lemon floor wax and its large, clear windows streaming in daylight, she'd stepped into the vastness of herself. A grin spread across her face. She could feel it all—the potential, the possibilities, the hope. Just—there. Like...magic.

The warmth of his firm grip enveloped her gloved hand

And so, Belinda walked to the center of the room.

By the time she perched on the wooden stool Nick had placed in front of a microphone, crossed her ankles, and adjusted her pencil skirt, the guilt had vanished.

"So." Nick loosened his tie and rolled up his sleeves. "What would you like to sing?" He took a seat at the nearby piano and she caught a whiff of his spicy cologne.

"'I've Got the World on a String.'" She watched his brown eyes light with what looked like approval.

"Great choice. I sang that for a charity gig I did last year. Raised a pile of dough for a soup kitchen. It's one of your favorites, right?"

Belinda blushed; he'd remembered. She stole a covert look from under her lashes at his handsome profile, his dark hair neatly slicked back. While he rustled through the sheet music, she willed the butterflies to stop flitting in her stomach

and tried to ignore the sound engineers and the man whom she assumed was Nick's manager working across the room.

But as the smooth intro began, its rich fullness eased through Belinda's nerves and the first verse slid from her lips effortlessly. The sleek notes washed over her as she swayed, lost within the melody. Five, six, seven, eight. She counted beats to herself, eyelids closing, lips parting in anticipation of the chorus.

Her light soprano flowed over the deeper valleys of Nick's baritone when he joined in. A surge of pure bliss ran through her. Perfect harmony. She grinned. Her gaze found its way to Nick, who smiled back, his expression flooding her with delight. He must feel it too. She saw the answer in his eyes. He knew this sensation, had this passion for jazz just as she did.

When she opened her mouth for the next line, though, no words came out. She froze. How could she have forgotten what she'd memorized by heart? Perhaps because her heart had been pulled by the attention of this man who had opened a window of opportunity for her.

Nick lifted his fingers from the keys. "...really got it."

"Oh, um—what?"

He laid his hand on her arm. "I said you've really got it. Skill and talent—in spades."

"That's very kind of you to say."

"No. It's not empty flattery, Miss Thompson. You see..." All at once, he broke eye contact and trailed his fingers along the black-and-white keyboard. "I won't lie. When I first started out, I had no support." His voice lowered. "And people kept turning me down." Now his voice was a just above a whisper, almost as if he was talking to himself. "They laughed. Told me I'd never make it and said I could be tone deaf. It would've been so easy to believe them." His jaw clenched. "But somehow I knew they

were wrong.

"And so I want to give you a chance, plain and simple. The kind of chance"—he cleared his throat and shifted on the piano bench. It creaked slightly underneath him—"that I had to claw and scratch for." He turned to look at her again and she saw, in a shaft of sunlight, his brown eyes burnish to amber.

Goose bumps rose on her skin. He was so much more than she'd thought. Or imagined. His essence shone through him like the steady glow of a candle flame— the kind of flame that gave others the courage to shine too. Why, she could tell him anything. She wanted to tell him everything. His openness and humility seemed to pull her into some higher realm of herself; he was not afraid to be great, she realized. He was simply himself.

"I'm just saying, how would you like to swing by here a few times a week? Not for lessons, but for a place to be around music, to practice whatever you'd like, maybe even go over a few numbers to-gether?"

Before guilt and doubt could jump in, she blurted out, "Yes!"

♫

THAT NEXT SATURDAY, THE SOFT twinkle of classical music drifted past Belinda as Nick held the restaurant door open for her, its heavy brass handle gleaming in the fast-approaching twilight.

Belinda stepped through the doorway and onto the carpet, her best shoes seeming far too ordinary now as she glanced at them contrasting against the bold blues and golds of the Aubusson carpet. No. She lifted her chin. This was her first date with Nick. He'd asked her out, picked her up, brought her to dine here. She smoothed down the skirt of her navy blue cotton sateen dress. Of course she wasn't out of place. And she was doing the best she knew how. So there.

"Your best table, please." Nick said to the maître d' before offering his arm to

Belinda. Her lace glove nestled against the tailored sleeve of his light gray dinner jacket as if it belonged there. And perhaps—her teeth caught her lower lip at the sudden thought—it did?

They were shown to a candlelit corner, the semicircular booth curving around them like an embrace as they sank onto the red-velvet buttoned upholstery.

Nick opened and then handed her one of the heavy leather-backed menus, his cufflinks catching the light. "With all the practicing we've been doing," Nick began, "I never had a chance to ask you—what started you out on your dream to become a singer?"

Belinda studied the pattern of the heavy white damask tablecloth while tracing a fingertip along its edge. "It was Mama. You see, she loved opera and had studied music. She even briefly sang with"—her voice lowered to a whisper, and Nick had to lean in to catch her next words—"the Metropolitan Opera in New York."

Nick gave a low whistle. "Now I can see where you get your talent."

"Thank you. But that was before—"

The waiter had come to their table. "Good evening, Mr. Hart. Miss. What shall we be drinking with the meal tonight?"

"The usual, thank you, Steven."

"A scotch, very good." He turned to Belinda. "And for the lady?"

"Um, a glass of red wine, please."

The waiter departed.

"You were saying?"

"Oh, it was all before I was born. She gave up the beginnings of a singing career to marry my father. And then she"—Belinda cleared her throat—"she passed away in forty-four." She blinked rapidly. "Hard to believe it's been two years already." She sniffed, fumbling with the clasp of her handbag. "A few months after that, Father had a bad accident. It was right before my birthday—he'd taken an extra shift at the munitions plant to get some money for presents. I'd asked for a new dress and...a songbook."

She kept her eyes on her handbag. "He was helping replace some machinery parts. Workers on the walkway above him were transporting some steel plating when a chain snapped and the plating fell. He couldn't get out of the way fast enough; both his legs were crushed," she whispered. If only he hadn't taken that shift. She bit her lip. If only she hadn't asked for that dress and songbook.

"Needless to say, he couldn't work. Then there's that cough he'd gotten from breathing in all those smelter fumes at the plant." She shook her head. "So I took a job to supplement what he receives from the Workers' Compensation Board." The purse finally opened. "But I didn't mean to go on so." She dug around inside.

"What you're doing is commendable," Nick said softly. "And I'm sorry about your parents." He moved his hand across the table. "Here." He gave her his own handkerchief, the initials N.H. threaded silver through the fine linen.

Their fingers brushed as Belinda

reached out to take the neatly pressed square of cloth, her voice husky. "Thank you." She took a deep breath. "I'm still adjusting."

Nick's hand, strong and gentle, closed over hers. For a moment, neither spoke, the only sounds the hushed tones of other diners, the clink of silver on china, and the notes of a Beethoven concerto woven into the silence suspended between them.

The waiter returned with their drinks. Belinda took a sip of her wine and felt herself begin to relax.

Until Nick spoke again.

"Miss Thompson," he said, "I'll be frank."

Her fingers tightened on the stem of the cut-crystal wineglass. Had she done something wrong? Heaven knew she had been dead tired as of late. All those early mornings in the studio with him while Father slept. It was the only way she could justify any of this to herself. Barely. Then of course the daily errands and her four-to-midnight shift at the Whitcomb.

She tensed, remembering every wrong note she'd hit that morning. Was he going to say she couldn't come back? And if so then what? Her dreams would vanish into the mists that hung over the city. And then she would be left with nothing.

But she forced herself to stare fear in the face by meeting his gaze. "All right. Go ahead."

"I'd like you to do a number in the show."

She caught her breath as joy zinged through her; it lit up her eyes and spread a smile across her face. "Oh, Mr. Hart. Truly?"

"Yes." He smiled back.

But her throat constricted. It was too much. She clutched the edge of the table for support and clenched her jaw.

He leaned forward. "I've been thinking of a few different tunes that could work well with your voice." She saw expectations in his gaze.

And all at once, a deep terror shrouded in anger sprang to life inside her. She pressed her lips together and hunched her shoulders against it even as it began to surge through her, urging her to push him, push her dreams, push everything but safe numbness—away.

"But there'll be a helluva lot more practice," he added and took a sip of his drink. "The show's coming up at the end of the month." She watched his enthusiastic expression.

"We need a few slow numbers in the set. And there are some crowd favorites we usually do, like 'Someone to Watch over Me.'" He smiled. "And so I was thinking," he leaned forward, "you could do that one. It gets a good response from the audience, and it would really fit your range. What do you say?"

Of all the songs in all the world, he just had to pick that one, didn't he? Her chest tightened. She'd never mentioned it to him. She'd made sure of it.

She balled her hands into fists in her lap. He had absolutely no right. None. To ask her to perform that? On top of everything else? It was unthinkable. He couldn't force her to open herself to that much vulnerability. Not onstage. She just couldn't do it. She wouldn't.

That was Mama's song, the very one Belinda had listened to over and over all those nights after Mama's death, consoling herself with those words, the melody almost a lullaby, soothing, caressing. Nurturing the smallest hope that somehow, someday she might be able to move through the grief and into the light—to perhaps heal at last. And now he asked her to sing it in his show? What nerve. Her eyes narrowed.

"How dare you!"

The words hung in the air between them with the sharpness of a slap, impossible to take back but impossible to ignore.

Nick's head jerked back. "What are you talking about, Miss Thompson? You'd be perfect for it in the show." He studied her. "I meant what I said." He reached for her hand.

But she jumped up. "Oh, you think it's that simple, do you?" She put her hands on her hips. "Think you can just walk into a gal's life, sweep her off her feet with your sweet talk and your praise and your promises. I might be young, but I'm not stupid!" She snatched up her hat, gloves, and purse with cold fingers.

Nick jumped up too, napkin in hand. "Now wait just a minute. It's not like that at all. You're great!"

She moved away from the table without a backward glance.

Nick followed her toward the door. "I want you to have a chance to show this city what you're capable of. Can't you see that?" He caught her arm and whirled her to face him. "What are you running from?"

But the roaring in her ears drowned out everything as she shook off his grasp and stalked out.

NICK CLENCHED HIS FISTS. DAMN it. Upsetting her was the last thing he'd wanted on their first date. But before Nick could decide what to do next, the door swung open. In walked his manager, glaring at him. Anger shot through Nick.

"Christ, Dean! What are you doing here?"

"Protecting your public image."

"What the hell are you talking about? Just because I'm out with, *was* out with—"

"Some dame who has no business being in show business, let alone out with you. I saw the way you've been looking at her all week. Figured you two'd come in here. You're wasting studio space and company time on her."

"Hold on just a second." Nick threw down his napkin onto an empty table. "I have more than a fair stake in the label. Besides, my personal life is not a concern of yours."

"Oh, but I think we both know that it is, Nick." Dean crossed his arms. "You're a star, not some street yokel who can set his cap for whomever passes by."

Nick ground his teeth and shoved his hands in his pockets. "Listen here, Dean. It's—"

But just then the maître d' approached. Nick gave him a tight smile, lowered his voice, and headed back to the table. Dean followed. Nick slumped onto the seat and began rearranging the silverware; if only he could straighten out his jumbled thoughts as easily.

"Nick, you need to think about what you're doing. That's all I'm asking."

Nick picked up his glass, frowned down into it, and swirled the contents round and round. What *was* he doing? Suddenly he stopped and set the glass down. Doing? Doing? He was a singer, an artist.

He snapped his fingers. "Yes! You're brilliant, Dean!" Of course. He always wrote best with a little feeling behind it. "That's exactly what I need to be doing." He grabbed his fedora, put down the right amount for the drinks, and left.

IN HIS APARTMENT, NICK STARED at a blank sheet of paper on his roll-top desk. All he could see, though, was Belinda's face. Scared. Hurt. Angry. What was she so afraid of? Had he been too pushy, trying to get her to do something she hadn't really wanted to do? He ran a hand across his chin. That wasn't what he'd intended, to force her into anything or to push her away. He sighed. She probably hated him now.

His gaze drifted toward the rotating ceiling fan, then out to a last glimmer of light glinting gold off the bay.

Just like the water, Belinda held that same sparkle and gleam. If he'd realized anything over the time they'd been spending together, it was that. He could see it in her expression and when she sang. Her very heart flowed through every measure. He'd been right, back in that phone booth. Claire simply couldn't compare.

And with that thought, the lead of his pencil sailed across the page as words flooded into his mind, spreading through him, freeing him. A new melody and lyrics took shape, brought to life through those feelings he had been holding on to, all the hope, discontent, despair and defeat he'd felt in the restaurant, emotions that Belinda had poured through him.

And, he realized, as he made key, register, and meter notations in the margins of the lined page, it had not been him at all that she'd been reacting to. That shrouded pain in her eyes—she was sabotaging herself; certainly not something unfamiliar to him—especially when he thought about his own early days. And because of that, he could forgive her anger.

He returned his concentration to the ruled page where he scrawled the remaining lines. Finally, he put down the worn pencil nub, reread what he'd written, and sat back, savoring that familiar tingle of joy and satisfaction that came with creating. He folded the piece of paper and pocketed it in his suit jacket. Now off to the studio to set down the melody.

HE COULD SEE IT ALL so clearly after writing the song, he mused the next morning as the Powell-Hyde line took him into Belinda's neighborhood.

And though he didn't want to intrude on her or presume anything by showing up at her doorstep, especially at this hour, she hadn't come to their session that morning. And as to why, well, he had a feeling it had something to do with her doubts seeming larger than her dreams.

And as one artist to another, Nick couldn't let Belinda commit that kind of creative suicide. He had to at least tell her that. But not by phone. If he did that, she could just hang up on him. It had to be an in-person appeal. No matter if she rejected him for good. No matter if she never came back to perform with him. That wasn't the point. The bigger picture, not his ego, was most important. Because hiding never did anyone any good. It just kept the shadows in charge.

The cable car descended Lombard Street, and Nick looked down at the bunch of black-eyed Susans he held. Altruism aside, he realized, he didn't want Belinda to walk out of his life as Claire had. Nick swallowed. So maybe he had a bit of selfish intention, acting with his heart instead of his head, but maybe that was okay, because wasn't that what life was really about sometimes?

At the conductor's call, Nick hopped off onto the street where she lived. If she didn't want to sing, she didn't want to. Period. At some point, he might have to accept that. But not today.

THE SUDDEN RAP AT THE door made Belinda jump, and she dropped the milk bottle she'd been washing with a clatter. Who could it be at this hour? The sun was barely up. She wiped her hands on a dishtowel and leaned forward to peer through the sheer curtains above the kitchen sink and felt a wave of nausea.

But she knew she would answer the door. She crossed the room and turned the doorknob, ready to face her mistake and her shame. Living with those emotions for a full twenty-four hours had done nothing to free her of their grasp. Probably, dealing with them head on would. Her chin lifted.

"Miss Thompson." Nick kept his voice low. "Forgive the intrusion at this hour, but I can't let—" His words jumbled with hers as she spoke at the same time. "Mr. Hart, I want to—"

She took a breath to try again, but a laugh came out instead. Here they were, trying so hard to get everything right, when perhaps there really was no right or wrong. Maybe this whole situation had evolved into something that just wasn't meant to be quite this dramatic.

She'd been so gravely serious about it all. Acted as if he'd asked her to sell her soul to the devil. Or as if he *was* the devil. She laughed again. Besides, she certainly didn't see any pitchfork or brimstone around. Another giggle escaped her.

Though he looked puzzled, Nick joined in with a chuckle. "You're not angry?"

"No." Still smiling, she said, "I don't know what you were about to say before, but I've been a silly little fool." She stepped from the threshold to the street. "You were right in the restaurant." Belinda closed the door quietly behind her.

Nick turned to her. "See, that's what I came to say."

But then he stopped talking. Belinda watched him shake his head; several emotions moved across his face in rapid succession. "No." He took a breath. "Maybe I wasn't right." He spoke slowly as he met her gaze. "I had no business questioning you like that. And I'm sorry if I upset you."

She took the bouquet he offered as he continued. "You don't have to sing in the show at all. And if you did, you wouldn't have to sing 'Someone to Watch over Me.' I just wanted you to know that." He glanced at her with—was that a hint of shyness? "Because I wanted to, well"—he cleared his throat—"square things up between us."

She blushed. "Oh, but I know I overreacted because, tell you the truth, that song helped me get through my mother's death. You couldn't have known that, though." She looked over at him. "So, yes, I want to sing in the show with you."

"Yeah?" He seemed relieved. "How about a duet? I just wrote one, actually."

She smiled. "And this time I can promise you there won't be any running away."

♫

THE EVENING OF THE PERFORMANCE, Nick and Belinda stood together backstage at The Blue Mirror Club. He couldn't help grinning to himself. She looked gorgeous in her silvery dress. But his smile faded when he noticed the paleness underneath her stage makeup. "Are you okay?" He frowned and touched her arm.

She gave a light laugh. "Of course!" She swallowed. "Why wouldn't I be?"

"All right then. I'm going to do this first number, and then you'll come out, just like we've been rehearsing."

He moved onstage to the microphone and looked out over the tables; every chair was filled. He grinned at the audience's welcoming applause. "Thank you. Thank you for coming out. Got a great show for you tonight, so here we go!" He poured his soul into the song, toe tapping, fingers snapping.

As the final notes faded, Nick nodded to the wings. "For this next one, I'll be doing a duet." He paused for emphasis. "Please welcome Miss Belinda Thompson, everybody."

Except where the hell was she?

BELINDA FELT HER PULSE SPEED into triple time just as Nick announced her name. She couldn't run. She wouldn't run. She'd promised. But she kept seeing the audience. All those eyes, staring at her. Failure, they silently scorned her. Don't deserve to sing anyway. All those fingers, pointing at her. Self-centered, they accused her. All those voices, menacing: how dare you do this.

She bolted and pushed past Nick's manager to the backstage exit. Through the haze of her tears, she tugged open the door. The cool evening breeze brushed past her as she found a piece of safe, solid wall to lean against. Dabbing at her tears with her handkerchief, she gulped down lungfuls of night air. So much for promises. And for being brave.

The creak of hinges startled her as Nick leaned around the door. "Miss Thompson?"

"I'm so sorry," she said, staring at the pavement.

"Come back in."

She glanced over at him. "I'm terrified."

His expression softened. "Of what?"

"Of doing it badly." She laughed feebly, the ugly voices in her mind sneering. "And of doing it well. And Father..."

"All you have to worry about right now is getting back up there. Doing that one little thing," he said gently.

She shook her head, those silent voices growing more reproachful. "I-I can't."

Seconds stretched into minutes.

"Listen, doll." Nick frowned and spread his arms in a gesture of surrender. "Make up your mind. I have a show to do—an obligation to my audience. I've given you a chance. Several, in fact. But if you're not in, you're out."

Belinda watched, listless, as he ducked back inside, the door banging shut behind him. In the quiet left by his absence, those loathing voices swelled to full crescendo. She pushed away from the wall. She couldn't stay here. Not after she'd ruined

everything for herself. She ran down the sidewalk, hot tears marking time on her trail of failure home.

Chapter Three

BACK IN THE WINGS, NICK groaned and put fingers to his temple. "Hell." Belinda had gone. He winced—he'd seen to that.

His eyes slid to Dean, who shot him a warning glance. "Pull yourself together. All your fans paid good money and they're gonna be plenty angry if things don't keep rolling."

Dean was right. Nick moved a hand up to straighten his tie, but a crinkling sound made him pause. He reached inside his suit jacket and encountered that folded page. What he'd written—before. Well, too late for that now. He sighed and tried to ignore the heaviness in his chest.

He didn't have time for anything but his performance and his audience. Thought he'd done the right thing. Be-

cause as that old adage went, only illness or death—his own—would stop the show. Nick checked his watch, about to step onstage again.

But Dean's hand on Nick's shoulder stopped him from moving forward. "Damn you and Miss Thompson." Dean hissed, his grip tightening. "For bringing out my sentimental side." His voice was sharp, accusing. "But I had a sweetheart once too, you know."

Nick looked over at Dean, and caught regret flitting across his face before brusqueness replaced it. "And for the record, this goes against everything I believe in so don't expect any favors in the future. But," Dean growled, his eyes narrowing. "I'll call her for you. See if she'll come back."

BELINDA SLIPPED HER KEY INTO the well-worn lock, the sound of her father's wracking cough meeting her at the door.

She rushed to his bedroom and placed a

cool hand on his forehead. "I came back, Father. I knew you needed me here and I- I came back."

But the ringing of the telephone interrupted any response he might have given. She tensed. Mr. Hart. It had to be. Offering her one more last chance?

But she turned her back to the phone. It was better this way, though she felt a catch in her throat even as another round of coughing came from her father. She started to pour a spoonful of medicine. But the phone shrilled again, startling her, and caused the thick liquid to drip onto the rag rug covering the scuffed linoleum.

She snatched a cotton cloth off the bedside table and stooped down to mop up the spill. The phone rang a third time. She scrubbed harder. It rang for the fourth time. Nothing was going to dissuade her. Nothing. She had made her sacrifice. Five rings now. Despite herself, she glanced over at the table where the phone sat and saw the corner of an album sticking out from a pile of newspapers. One of his albums. She bit her lip. The phone rang a sixth time. Her throat constricted and her eyes filled. It rang once more. But she let the last ring of the telephone die away. And with it, her dreams.

She stood, repoured the medicine, and hoped her father wouldn't see her anguish. But he did.

"Belinda, what's wrong?"

She didn't answer, just gave him the medicine. She must not have regrets. Could not.

He peered at her. "Sweetie?" He reached a thin hand across the bedspread to cover both of hers. "You have a life to live." He wheezed, fighting for breath. "Don't waste it all taking care of me. Go."

Instead, she stared down at him, unblinking. How could she leave him? She dropped to her knees. "But," she choked out, voice hoarse, "how can you say that? How can you sacrifice yourself"—she swallowed—"for me?"

His cracked lips formed a smile. "I've had more than enough time to think, lying here on this bed. And I've realized…" His breathing grew steadier as the medicine took temporary effect. "You're hiding."

She gasped and clutched the delicate metal of the spoon so tightly her knuckles turned white. "That's not true—"

"Let me finish." His grip stayed strong and steady on her. "You're hiding from yourself, my dear." His voice was gentle. "From what really matters here. And that is your singing."

Belinda looked down at the spoon. Imagined instead her hand around a microphone. Still she wavered, a frown on her face.

"I'll be fine for now. Besides, darling." He stroked her hair, and his eyes became moist. "It's never a sacrifice when it comes from love."

She took one breath, then another. And finally let go. The spoon clattered to the floor.

And suddenly, she could see it.

The lie she'd mistaken for truth. The false belief that caring for her father's life

was more important than her own. Her eyes were drawn back to the album cover.

And suddenly, she could hear it.

Yes. A whisper of melody gliding through her thoughts. And then she knew. For it was not her father's words that gave her absolution, though she understood now her father wanted nothing more than to see her happy and free; it was the notes themselves that called to her soul. She gradually straightened up, open-mouthed, as that faint syncopated rhythm became louder. More insistent. The notes falling one by one into her heart until they filled it to overflowing, until she swiped a hand across her face, kissed her father's cheek, and flew out the door, the song giving her the strength and surety to race through the foggy street, to climb up the final hill.

THE BABBLE OF A FULL house always gave Nick a buzz, and tonight was no different. But as he stepped back onstage, he saw a crew member take away the second microphone. The one Belinda would have used. Stage left, Nick saw the band rearranging their sheet music to skip over the duet. No, he realized, tonight was very different now that Dean had told him Belinda hadn't answered the phone.

And as the second spotlight faded out, the reality hit him. Performing with Belinda was as good as it got. The highest form of expression. He felt it as solidly as the floorboards beneath his feet.

For it was an act of love to sing together. And that was something he owed to himself. To her. And to the audience. Anything less would be a cheap charade.

He looked out into the crowd. "Folks, forgive me. I know this is going to be terribly bad manners. But there's something I need to do. If you've ever been sweet on someone, you might understand. See, a crooner needs his heart to put on his best show, and someone important to me needs to be up here beside me tonight—singing that duet I had planned. So if you'll excuse me just a moment again,

I'm going to get her back. What do you say?"

Applause erupted.

WOULD HE BE THERE? WOULD he forgive her? Belinda's blood pounding through her veins was her sole reply. But it didn't matter now, she realized. What mattered was she'd finally said yes—to herself. Out of breath, she came to a stop facing The Blue Mirror Club. And Nick.

She'd almost missed his silhouette by the lamppost. But his rapid steps in her direction sent her heart galloping again. It was well past show time, though. She frowned. Why wasn't he inside?

She watched him stride out of the thickening fog swirling around them and come toward her. Noiselessly. Almost as if he wasn't truly there. She blinked. But he was. She held her breath as he moved nearer. And nearer. Until she felt the scratchy wool of his suit jacket brush against her ungloved hand.

Would he forgive her?

"Belinda," he whispered, his voice caressing each syllable. She watched his gaze flick from her eyes down to her mouth. Felt her pulse quicken as he leaned in. Felt light-headed as he brought his lips to hers. Warm and soft. She tasted spearmint.

She brought her hand up to his face; the sandpaper sensation that rasped across her fingertips sent quivers into her stomach as his arms tightened around her waist.

"Nick," she murmured a few moments later, somehow finding the right words. "Please forgive me for running again. I thought I had to give up everything—my singing, a life of my own. You." A lock of hair came unpinned from her upswept style. "I thought it was all over."

Nick tucked the strand behind her ear.

"Of course I forgive you. I understand what it's like to be that close to losing something precious." He wiped away a trace of her tears with his thumb. "If anything, I should be the one asking your forgiveness. After all, I told you to leave. I'm sorry for my behavior earlier tonight. I didn't want to hurt you."

She saw trepidation in his gaze. She drew in a breath. She hadn't known it, didn't see it before but—she cocked her head—she'd sainted him, had given him that status. But right now, in his expression, she suddenly saw his humanity and his vulnerabilities.

Because, in truth, he was like the music itself. A composition containing every kind of note—whole, half, sharp, flat, major and minor. It was not a piece of perfection, though crafted by a greater

force than the human hands that had composed it.

She took a step back. A work's flaws could sometimes be its greatest assets when performed with integrity and finesse.

She smiled. He was simply a man. Flesh and blood just like her. She found herself looking at him—and seeing herself. Everything she could be, everything she was, and everything she wanted to be, do and have, right there in front of her.

Yes. There were no *wrong* notes—they simply became supporting chords designed to infuse the listener with a sense of appreciation and affection when taken as a whole.

"Apology accepted," she whispered. Then, because she could, she kissed him again. "But what are you doing out here?"

Nick's grin emerged. "Well, let's just say the audience and I have a little arrangement. They're expecting a duet. If you're still game, that is."

She nodded. With him, she could fly to the moon.

"Come on, then." He interlaced his fingers with hers. "Let's bring down the house!"

They ran for the entrance.

♫

HEADS TURNED AS SHE AND Nick burst through the doors of the club. They dashed onstage hand in hand, and she watched him draw out and unfold a familiar-looking sheet of handwritten music from his suit pocket.

"This one's for you." His breath whispered past her ear.

He moved to the microphone and addressed the audience. "Here she is!"

Everyone started clapping, Nick included. Then he turned and gave the ensemble the briefest of nods. "Ready, boys?"

Lively notes spilled from the trombones and saxophones as Nick moved a wingtip in time with the beat. Belinda leaned toward him and relaxed as she felt the music float through her.

She could do this. Now and always. She stood proudly. Looked straight into all those pairs of eyes. And smiled. She belonged here. With the bright horns and the eager listeners and those sweet, sweet melodies. And Nick.

She'd answered the call of her dreams— at last. Nick winked at her and slid an arm around her waist. They hit the final chord together.

Notes

1. "soul on hold" from verse 4, line 6 of "Operator, Please" written by Jukka Immonen/ Patrick Sarin/ Simon Wilcox/Matt Dusk Published by Air-Chrysalis Scandinavia/Universal Publishing/EMI April Music (Canada) Ltd./Hypnotizing Boogie Publishing/Matt Dusk Publishing. From Matt Dusk's *Good News* album getmusic.ca ℗ and © 2009 Royal Crown Records, Inc. Manufactured and distributed by Universal Music Canada, 2450 Victoria Park Ave., Toronto, Ontario M2J 5H3 All lyrics used with the express permission of artist/owner, Matt Dusk.

2. "I don't know why I'm calling" from verse 1, line 1 of "Operator, Please"

3. "I know you're not a doctor" from verse 1, line 3 of "Operator, Please"

4. "But you could do me some good" from verse 1, line 4 of "Operator, Please"

Disclaimer:
It is hereby stated that Matt Dusk and any music industry organizations, associations or companies or other persons associated with Matt Dusk and his music, do not endorse the material or content contained within this book in any manner. Furthermore, there is no affiliation with or endorsement by or from Matt Dusk and any music industry organizations, associations or companies or other persons associated with Matt Dusk and his music, in any way, shape or form regarding this material and this book.

Acknowledgments

I would like to thank everyone who has helped me bring my dream to life. I have witnessed amazing kindness, generosity and artistic support all throughout the creation of this story. I am so grateful to everyone. Thank you so much. Your help and support have meant so much.
—Jessica Eissfeldt

Story

Matt Dusk – jazz vocalist, who graciously allowed use of the lyrics from his song "Operator, Please" and who inspired the character of Nick Hart

Pat Steel – jazz vocalist, who kindly allowed use of her statement on the book cover

Danelle McCafferty – editor, who was great to work with and who loves jazz as much as I do

Suzi Arensberg Discou – copyeditor, who had a great eye for details

Caitlin Brezinski – who introduced me to Matt Dusk's music and who is a good friend

Marilyn Kurtz – who always believed in my writing

Maren Woodward – who was my creative consultant for both the photographs and the story, and who is a great, supportive, artistic friend

Tabitha Zimmer – who read early drafts and who is a great, supportive, artistic friend

SRW writing group – who helped me keep up my writer morale

Photos

Casting – Dawn Bird of B.E.Zee Productions, Regina, SK

Nick Hart – Actor Greg Ochitwa, Regina, SK

Belinda Thompson – Author Jessica Eissfeldt, Regina, SK

Suiting – Anthony's Fashion for Men, Saskatoon, SK; and Trino's Menswear, Regina, SK

Props – From Past Times Antiques, Regina, SK (telephone); Long & McQuade Music, Regina SK (microphone); Regina Little Theatre (Nick's fedora and Belinda's dress)

Locations – Regina Florist, The Diplomat Steakhouse, The Balfour Condominiums, The Artesian Theatre

Hairstyling and makeup – Deanna Nattrass and Adrienne Allen of Snax Salon, Regina, SK

Photography – Cydney Alexandra Toth Photography

Graphic design – Angela Waters Art, Inc.

Shattered
Melodies
A Novella
Jessica Eissfeldt

Shattered Melodies

A Novella

The Sweethearts & Jazz Nights Series of Sweet Historical Romance

Jessica Eissfeldt

Chapter One

CLAIRE DUPONT HAD JUST SETTLED in at her desk and put a fresh sheet into her Royal typewriter, prepared to transcribe the shorthand she'd scribbled, when a shadow fell across her page. She looked up.

Her editor shoved a fistful of letters at her. "Prove to me that it was a good idea to hire you, Miss DuPont, when there are probably ten men right now I could hire off the street who could do a better job reporting than this fluff. After all—" he ground out his cigarette "—this isn't *Good Housekeeping.*"

Claire raised a brow. "I don't report fluff. I cover the jazz scene in this city." *More's the pity.*

"Yeah?" Her editor spoke around the new cigarette he'd just lit. "Then what do

you call that last piece you did? Ten letters to the editor in twelve hours—all about how, and I quote, 'some dame who can't write worth a damn. And in fact, shouldn't even be employed by the *San Francisco Chronicle.*' Ten letters, I'm telling you."

Claire glanced around. But whether her colleagues smoked, drank coffee or actually wrote articles, everyone had some sort of task they were engaged in, unmindful of her.

Claire's editor shook out the match and looked almost amused. "It's certainly gotten our readership numbers up, my hiring you, devoting an entire half a page to your music musings. But I'm beginning to regret it; never mind that you're an authority on music because your father owns Golden Gate Records. If you don't get me something worthwhile by Friday— and that's being more than generous— you're gone. No more last chances, even if I did hire you as a favor to your father. Now, go over to The Blue Mirror Club.

Talk to Nick Hart. But more in-depth than that *Herald* piece that they ran on him yesterday. At least four inches. We need to really serve our readership."

"But Nick Hart—"

"Tick-tock, Miss DuPont."

Claire squared her shoulders. "Fine, sir. Fine."

She wound her way through the maze of desks toward the door, the ring of telephones and clatter of typewriters providing a soundtrack to her every motion. She wouldn't let him push her around.

She'd show him. She'd write the best damn story they'd ever seen.

A slow smile stole across her lips. Yes, she had a hunch that there was a great story out there. Her smile became a grin— she knew there was a reason she loved Mondays.

JOE LUCITANO TUGGED AT HIS collar and shifted in his seat as the bright melody

started. Clusters of laughing, chatting people surrounded him, but he stared into the bottom of his glass, at a table by himself.

He tried to shake the slight panic and claustrophobia that had set in. He'd come to The Blue Mirror tonight to try to enjoy the jazz, to overcome his fears, his past, but instead he'd drowned in them.

Since when had he become so fatalistic about life, so down and out, so distrustful? Perhaps since the war, he realized. Perhaps when he had everything he'd held dear hanging on a thread...

And he'd had to watch it snap.

God. He was depressing himself. He smiled wryly. He just needed a cigarette. And some fresh air. Then he'd feel better.

Joe headed into the foyer, the faint blue glow from the club's neon sign reflecting on the damp pavement outside, and the light fixture above his head washing the lobby in warm yellow.

He moved toward the doorway while fumbling in his suit pocket for his cigarette case. As he drew out the slim silver rectangle, he could see the silhouette of a woman on the street, about to approach the door.

The silhouette came nearer. His heart pounded. But this wasn't France. And the war was over.

He took a steadying breath and opened the door for her.

"Thank—"

She froze, halfway across the threshold. Her head whipped around toward him. Time seemed to melt in on itself, like a half-played melody only partially remembered.

When she looked up at him, he saw desperation in her eyes. Eyes he would've recognized anywhere. And now it was his turn to feel desperation. "Claire?"

"*Joe...*"

The breathy whisper of his name past her lips might have been his imagination, because she turned to him and put a hand on her hip. "Who else?"

The breeze blew in after her as the

door clicked shut, causing a curl to escape from her hat. He started to reach out, wanting to tuck the curl back in place for her. But then his hand stilled. This wasn't six years ago. He felt the cold drops of rainwater on his face, arms, hands. They reminded him of tears. Tears that Claire had obviously never shed for him.

His jaw tightened. "What the hell are you doing here?"

"I'm working a beat. But you're not carrying a tune, I see. Shouldn't a saxophonist like you be on stage?"

Joe remained tight-lipped, fighting the sweet memories that swirled through him at the scent of her powdery lilac perfume.

"Show's over."

"Then I'm just in time. I'm looking for Nick Hart."

"Why would you think I know where he is?"

"You're a jazz musician—"

He flinched.

Her eyes missed nothing. "—so why wouldn't you?"

"It's eleven o'clock at night, Claire. He's not here."

"So what am I supposed to do?"

Claire moved closer, water dripping off her trenchcoat and onto the polished floor. The janitor wouldn't be too happy about that.

"Just tell me where Nick Hart is."

His mouth tightened. It was *her* fault he hadn't—no. He wanted to blame her for his not setting foot inside a club again...but that wouldn't have been precisely true. Or fair to either of them.

What she didn't know, besides, was that he hadn't been in contact with Nick for ages. Just one more reminder of his failure as a musician.

"Nick Hart is my friend." Joe crossed his arms. "And I'm not going to invade his privacy for you. I can't help you."

"But a story's everybody's business, don't you think?" She surreptitiously adjusted a stocking.

"You *know* what I think. And it's not about your pretty little legs."

"Oh, no?"

He ignored the question.

"But you've always helped me before, Joe."

"That was the trouble. And then you tossed me aside like yesterday's news."

"You're funny. Yesterday's news. And look where we are."

"I'm very well aware of it. Now please leave me be. You've already worn out your welcome."

"You'll be seeing me again."

God, he hoped he wouldn't. He winced as the door slammed. Because he was still in love with her.

THE BLOOD POUNDING IN CLAIRE'S ears finally subsided as she walked out into the cool September night. She took a breath to steady herself but it didn't work.

Had it really been six years since they'd seen each other? After all that time, the guilt and sadness should have faded. They hadn't. Her heart squeezed. And to her annoyance, she couldn't stop the prickle of helplessness that had needled her as she'd seen him so close, yet so far out of reach. He'd looked even more handsome tonight than he had six years earlier; his strong jaw and warm hazel eyes had made her feel eighteen again. It hurt seeing Joe's cold expression. Not that she could blame him—she'd caused it, after all. She had only herself to blame for being all alone now.

She took another shaky breath and hoped that she hadn't given away her own feelings of fear in front of Joe. He'd un-nerved her more than she'd cared to admit.

But she realized she could use that to her advantage; because her hunch had been right—she knew exactly who and what to write about, now.

EARLY THE NEXT AFTERNOON, CLAIRE adjusted and readjusted the cuffs of her powder blue suit jacket, then laughed at

herself for being nervous. And afraid. He was only her father, she reminded herself. And she wasn't eighteen any more either. She was twenty-four.

She lifted her chin as she entered the offices of Golden Gate Records. There was no need to feel like he was going to bully her. He'd asked to see her, after all. She should be happy.

Except she wished she was anywhere but there, in that stiff, stuffy corridor that smelled like success and overconfidence, lined with framed records signed by all those artists her father had hand-picked for success. But never her. No, never her, because she wasn't one of his hallowed musicians.

Gregory DuPont picked more than a few greats, she thought with something akin to admiration. No denying he had an excellent ear, her father. Seeing the polished faces of fame did put a smile on her lips.

But more important than that was the face not among the framed photos on the wall—Joe's. She bit her lip.

And there was Nick Hart's photo, one of the newer acquisitions. Acquisitions and mergers, that's what her father liked to call it.

She and Nick had met, actually, thanks to Daddy. She frowned. Wondered how Nick had taken her leaving him.

He'd probably gone off to some smoky club somewhere, nursed his heartbreak with a glass of scotch and a handful of lyrics. But she shrugged. That was all over and done with now. That's the way she liked her relationships. No muss, no fuss...

But the sound of her father's voice raised in anger cut through her thoughts. "No. That's final. The current fiscal state of this business is—What? No. No. Of course not."

Claire paused at the closed door to her father's office.

"No, the board never approved of that move and—No, *I* am the board of directors' chairman. This company—" Claire's father's voice grew grave. "How much?

No, that can't be right. I just spoke with my accountant and the back taxes—"

She heard him let out a long, weary breath. She frowned again.

"All right, all right. Yes, yes. I will. Goodbye."

The click of the receiver gave Claire her cue. She pushed open the door.

"Hello, Daddy." She walked up to him and kissed him lightly on the cheek, for once not feigning her delight that he had actually taken the time to pay attention to her. The question was, why?

"Come in, darling. Have a seat." Her father gestured to the wingback across from his desk.

She settled onto the Moroccan leather. It was cold.

He poured himself a highball, then offered her a glass, but she held up a hand. She needed her every wit about her when dealing with the man.

"How have you been keeping?"

"Quite well. Now that rationing's ended, I went to Macy's and found this darling blue suit."

"Good, good." Her father took a sip of his drink. "That's what I want to talk to you about."

"My shopping habits?"

"No. And yes." Her father shoved aside the morning *Herald* with his elbow to lean toward her. Trust her father to subscribe to the paper that was in direct competition with the one she worked for.

Her father sighed as he shook his head, and the silver at his temples glinted in the sun.

Had he always looked so old? Old and...sad?

She felt a ping of regret. But before she could examine that feeling further, her father spoke again.

"Money."

"Money?"

"Yes, money. I need more of it. This record company is..." He made an impatient gesture. Took another swig of his drink. "Going under."

Her stomach flip-flopped. "What do

you mean?" She cleared her throat, wishing her voice didn't sound higher than normal. There was nothing to panic about. Something good would come of it all, she was sure. She frowned. Now where had that thought come from?

"Bankruptcy. They're going to foreclose in sixty days and I need to do something—fast. Normally I wouldn't dream of burdening you with such boardroom talk, my dear, but I have a plan in mind that involves you." He put down his glass.

She laughed. "Surely you're joking, Daddy. I know less than nothing about managing money or about running a record company." She worried the inside of her bottom lip with her teeth. "That's a domain best left to the men."

"Yes. But marriage is a woman's domain."

"Marriage?"

"Yes. That fellow you've been seeing—Henry. I want you to marry him. In fact, I've been talking with him and he's agreed to it."

Yes, she'd discovered the why of her visit. Claire narrowed her eyes. "You want me to marry him for his money and industry connections." Her lip curled. Trust her father to only have his company's best interests at heart.

She cocked her head, leveled her gaze. "This is strictly *business*, isn't it?" She pushed out that tiny voice inside of her that cried out for love.

Her father crossed his arms. "I'm proud of you, Claire. You are your father's daughter." A gleam of admiration came into his eyes.

To her shame, she felt her heart swell at this rare acknowledgment. And she supposed Henry was a decent enough fellow.

But she didn't *want* to marry Henry. She wanted—No. Her gloved hands tightened and she forced her mind back to the present.

She and Henry had seen each other off and on for the past month, but it meant nothing to her.

Suddenly angry, she stood up. "This is *just* a business arrangement to you, isn't it? You've never, ever cared about me." Hot tears came to her eyes.

"That's not true, Claire." Gregory DuPont started to pick up the whiskey glass again but then slammed it down on the desktop instead, making Claire flinch.

"This is 1946. I'll marry who I want to. Who I—"

"Hear me out, Claire. You've already moved out of that penthouse suite at the Hotel Whitcomb, and I can't afford your expensive shopping habits any more, not with the record company going bankrupt too. Now Henry, he's a good employee, and he's offered to help Golden Gate Records out financially; of course, that promotion I gave him helped him make up his mind, I'm sure. Henry's money won't be a miracle cure, but his cash contribution will help us back to our feet so we can at least take the next step. But more to the point, it seems he's sweet on you and he has more than enough money to support you. This company—" he took a breath "—is everything to me." He raked a hand through his hair. "I'm not getting any younger, and I'd like to see you settled down. Can't you see that? Can't you see that I've tried to build Golden Gate Records up, maintain it, grow it, for y-you?" He swallowed.

"Well, you have a funny way of showing it. Ignoring your own daughter all those years in favor of a bunch of jazz musicians." She folded her arms across her chest, as if that would keep her heart from breaking. "So why can't you just call up one of your friends on Montgomery Street and ask them for a loan?"

"None of the banks in the whole Bay Area would look at this company now. We're in trouble, Claire."

The rawness of his voice took her breath away. She'd never seen this side of him.

"Please," he repeated. "For me? For every one of those artists? I built this company for the way music makes me feel. To give that feeling to everyone I possibly can..."

Was her father begging?

"All right, Daddy."

She saw his eyes light up and sadness flashed through her. She bit her lip. Is this what it took to get his approval? His attention?

"But if I do this, Daddy, you'll let Joe have a record deal."

"Why should I agree to that?"

She looked at the carpet. "As a favor to an—" she cleared her throat "—old friend."

"Joe Lucitano." Her father frowned. "He hasn't played in years."

She raised her chin. "I know that. So if you offer him a record deal, or a demo session. Or at the very least, an apology, then—"

"Then your conscience would be clear." Her father banged a desk drawer shut. "It's your own fault, you know that, Claire."

"Not *all* my fault, though, Daddy. You

were there too. And I want you to apologize to Joe too. In public. Give him back his dignity."

"I never took it from him. He did that to himself."

"No, Daddy. It was *my* idea for Golden Gate Records to provide the band at prom. But *you* were the one who called him white trash not fit to represent Golden Gate and threw him out of this place. And what's worse, I've never forgiven myself for backing you up, for agreeing with you—in front of him." Her voice lowered to a whisper. "I-I should have stood by him because I *loved* him, Daddy. I loved him." Her knuckles whitened on the arms of the chair. "I *loved* him. And he's never forgiven me for it." She shook her head. "But he wouldn't have felt that way if you'd—"

"Golden Gate was just starting out then. I had a reputation to build. I couldn't sign someone from the wrong side of the tracks." He held up a hand.

"Cut to the chase. Yes or no."

"You drive a hard bargain." Claire's father studied her, sunlight gleaming off the silver strands in his hair. "All right. I'll agree to your terms."

She should have felt victorious. Instead she felt helpless. Hopeless.

Her father put his hands on his hips, but a smile twitched at the corner of his mouth. "This is cause for celebration." He stood up, the motion making the newspaper fall to the floor.

As he strode over to the drinks cabinet, she stared at her hands in her lap, forcing herself not to dwell on what she'd just agreed to. Her eyes strayed to the carpet and the lettering of a headline at the bottom of the front page caught her attention: *Crooner Nick Hart Announces Engagement.*

She nudged the paper with her peep-toe pump so that the picture accompanying the headline was in full view.

Her throat constricted. They looked so happy together. Even from this distance, she could see the photo had captured that quality she'd seen in so many head-over-heels couples; that light in Nick's eyes, the answering sparkle in his fiancée's.

She felt sick.

No one had looked at her like that in ages. And now, no one probably ever would again, thanks to her brash agreement to her father's plan. She got up so quickly she felt dizzy; but before her father could turn around, she was already gone.

Chapter Two

AS THE TROLLEY CLANGED TO a stop along Fillmore Street, yellow light spilled from the windows and doorway of The Blue Mirror Club. Exactly where she needed to be. And exactly where she didn't want to be.

But an assignment was an assignment; the less Joe knew about the real subject of her story, the better. After all, he was the subject of it, not Nick Hart. She pulled the stop, stood and waited impatiently as the trolley's doors rattled open.

She walked up the street, waved her press pass at the doorman and entered the club.

The wail of a saxophone seemed to understand her; the rich, mellow tones of the solo continued, and despite her best intentions to stick to cold, hard facts, she found herself winding her way between chairs and tables until she was at the very front, hoping to catch a glimpse of the player, hoping it was Joe.

But her view was obscured and so she had to content herself with the tug of beautiful heartbreak that spilled through the room, from the player's lips.

All too soon, the whole ensemble joined in again for an upbeat number, and her foot started twitching; itching to get up and dance.

She almost laughed aloud. Dance. She hadn't danced in years. Not since—She shook her head. No. Bit down on the inside of her cheek. She wasn't going to indulge in that fantasy. Not again.

Not like so many times before when that was the only thing that had kept her sane. All through the war. Tears filled her eyes. Joe had completely misjudged her. Or had he been right all along?

She hadn't forgotten—not about the war that had ended a mere year ago, nor about the one that still raged in her own heart.

She'd remembered it—all too well. But this wasn't the time or place. She'd come here to write an article for the *Chronicle*. Not to remember Joe or how much she hated jazz.

So she ordered a sidecar and sipped it slowly; the perfect excuse to deny herself the pleasure of actually dancing. Yet her toes—much to her annoyance—tapped away anyway, lost in their own sort of reverie, even as she scribbled notes.

The saxophonist came back again, this time more powerful, more potent than she'd ever heard before, as if his soul had somehow been wrenched into the body of the horn.

Now Claire could see that it wasn't Joe playing up there at all. She wished she'd taken time to eat something before the alcohol went straight to her head because this time, she couldn't save herself. She got up and danced.

Head flung back, eyes closed, she lost herself in the music. Time had no meaning; nothing, anymore, held any meaning for her except the call of the notes and her body's response. Twisting. Turning. Swaying.

Each note, each beat, providing her with the faith and the means necessary to unthaw—at least in these fleeting moments—from the icy shell she'd created for herself.

A single tear slid down her face.

Her lashes fluttered and her eyelids closed and she had no cognition of the ring of people who had suddenly formed around her; she knew nothing except the call of that melody and her fervent need to reply.

To somehow ease the player's heartbreak, or perhaps to simply find an outlet for her own. Because she'd shattered Joe's dreams and this, being around that which reminded her every day of the pain she'd caused him, was her own self-inflicted sentence.

Her eyes snapped open, though, at the sound of a single person clapping. She froze. How had she gone so far as to shame herself like this in public?

She hurried back to her table, the faces all around her a blur as she snatched up her drink and downed the rest of it in one gulp. Then ordered another. Because the person clapping—had been Joe. Or had it been just her own wishful thinking?

IT WAS A PERFECT AUTUMN morning, Claire mused: the kind that cleared her head after the closeness of last night's crowded club. The wind buffeted her hair, her skirt, the clouds heavy in the sky. But she smiled as she did up the neat row of jet buttons then snugged the belt of her yellow plaid coat more tightly around her narrow waist and admired how her yellow rayon dress matched so perfectly with the jacket.

One of the few things that brought her joy: a well-tailored outfit. That, and a well-phrased sentence. And, if she was honest with herself, or in a weak moment, a well-played jazz number.

As if to mock her, a few strands of re-membered melody seemed to blow in with the salty sea breeze as she walked along the pier, dodging sailors and sight-seers; but she shook her curls and the notes mercifully vanished from her head. A gull screamed. And the guilt remained.

As if she could physically move the guilt, she pushed open the door of the newsroom at the *San Francisco Chronicle* and smiled. One other thing she loved: the clack of typewriters and the scent of ink. Make that two.

She carefully placed her purse in a drawer of her metal desk and sat down to type. She supposed she could've, and perhaps should've, phoned in her facts to a rewrite man, but she wanted to write this piece herself.

But even the clack of the typewriter keys couldn't drown out the jazz number that crept again through her thoughts, that melody playing over and over and over, the last song Joe had played for her that long-ago evening when she had ruined everything between them.

It seemed to mock her, to come between her and the words her fingers yearned to form, growing louder and louder still until with a cry of frustration that echoed in the empty, half-dark newsroom, she wrenched the page from the typewriter and crumpled it up, tossing it into the trash.

She fed a crisp new sheet into the machine and settled her fingers onto the keys with a sigh of satisfaction. But sudden realization shot through her and she nearly knocked over the wastebasket in her haste to snatch the forlorn page from its metal prison.

She had to be fair to the artist—in this case, Joe. Which meant she could *use* all this in her article. Joe's actions, feelings, words. Her own, as well. She could create an article that would show exactly what had happened, the triumph to tragedy, the whole truth... Yes.

A sly grin crept across her face, followed by a burst of joy.

It would be the perfect way to honor him and perhaps, just perhaps, make amends with the past and what had happened between them, to uncover why he'd stopped playing, and to showcase him as the talented musician she knew he was.

And in a way, she realized, with a twist of her lips, to bring peace to her own conscience.

She would be fair and truthful. After all, she had a responsibility to hold her readers' confidence.

And if she lost her job, so what? She knew it might be a conflict of interest to write about someone she had been seeing, yes. But she was already about to lose her job, so what was a little more risk? She *had* to write it, had to tell the truth.

She was the one most qualified, since she'd been involved from the beginning.

Hell, if she could do that, write this, then who knew? Joe might even forgive her.

THE NEXT AFTERNOON, WEDNESDAY, JOE opened the door of his street-level apartment at the sound of a sharp knock.

"Hello, Joe."

He raised an eyebrow at Claire but waited for her to continue.

"Mind if I come in?"

"I don't think I could stop you even if I did. What are you doing here?"

"I told you I'd be back." She pulled out her steno pad and a freshly sharpened pencil. "Covering a story."

"Sure you're not covering a funeral, dressed in all that black?"

"This, *Mr. Lucitano*, is my professional attire."

"And what's that, black widow?"

Her fists clenched. "I'm not going to dignify—"

But he could see that she'd caught the brief twitch of his lips in a smile, and she snapped her mouth shut, then laughed aloud. "I'm glad to see you haven't lost your sense of humor," she said so softly he had to move closer to hear her. She leaned in, practically purring. "So tell me, Joe..." She took off her black gloves, one finger at a time, as she moved into the entryway. "What's a talented saxophonist like you doing with a horn that hasn't been played in how many years?"

She didn't see his grip tighten on the scuffed doorframe. "Careful. If I think about it too hard, I might come up with more than one meaning to your sentence."

She had the grace to blush.

He pulled the door shut behind her. "Why are you so interested in dredging up the past, anyway? You know perfectly well—"

"Oh, I don't know. Perhaps because of a little something called curiosity." She swallowed heavily. "Why can't we just pick who we fall in love with?" She said it so softly he could have sworn he imagined the words, as she looked, in that instant, like a china doll instead of a woman.

He would have almost thought it an act, were it not for that unmistakable dark-cloud moodiness that settled over her azure eyes. But she tossed her head and the moment vanished.

"Dunno, Claire. Dunno. You're asking the wrong Joe here. Now I suggest you get out of my apartment before I ask you to leave. Unless, of course, you want to fix a fella a cup of coffee?"

"Oh you—!" She stormed a few paces away from him, further into the apartment, her blonde curls bouncing with indignation. "Just talk to me, Joe."

"Can't do that, sweetheart, because you and I both know I don't trust you." He held up a hand. "And don't even think about using those vixen charms on me. It's not going to work." He crossed his arms across his chest, then gripped his suspenders and exhaled a stream of smoke from his clove cigarette.

"Oh, really?" She hitched a hip onto his desk, ran a manicured finger along the shiny black keys of his typewriter.

He gave her a hard stare. "Yes. Really."

A beat of silence before Joe spoke again. "You come marching in here after six years and pick up like we never left off."

"What can I say? There was a war on."

He snorted. "A war. Yeah. One you conveniently forgot."

She stood and moved closer. "Oh, be quiet and kiss me."

He turned away in disgust. "No. I'm not going to be your whipping boy."

"Why not?"

"You know very well why not. Six years' worth of why not."

"I don't see how—"

"Yes, I think you see very clearly. You always saw very clearly. It was me who couldn't. I swallowed all your pretty lies about my talent and your father's record label. And now you come sashaying in here and expect me to throw myself at your feet. Again. I'm through. Done with all that. Go write up your pulp fiction about someone else."

"No."

He studied her for a long, silent minute. Then two. And when three minutes passed, she started to squirm uncomfortably under his silent scrutiny.

But when she could stand it no longer, he finally nodded once, curtly, to her, as if making up his mind about something he'd long wondered about.

"So let me guess. Your next question will be something about what I've been doing with my time since I'm not playing any more."

"You read my mind."

"Don't believe everything you read," he muttered under his breath.

Claire cleared her throat and shook back her hair, then crossed her legs and sank, uninvited, onto his couch.

Joe crossed his arms and remained standing. "Go on then." His jaw clenched. "Quell your curiosity."

"Oh, it's not for me, exactly. It's for the readers, you see." She moistened the pencil lead with the tip of her tongue.

His gaze darkened into anger. "You expect me to bare my soul for the amusement of your readership?"

"No." But she'd waited a beat too long with her answer.

He stepped closer, his height towering over her. She didn't move a muscle.

"Claire," he whispered fiercely, his fingers inches away from burying themselves in her silky curls. But somehow he restrained himself. He realized, with a sudden jolt that made him step back, that he wanted to hurt her.

Hurt her as much—no, more—than she had him. To make her *feel*, goddamn it. To crack that icy exterior and make her feel something she should have never stopped feeling all those years ago and he—He had no right. He hung his head and abruptly turned away from her and set his jaw. "Just go."

"Joe."

She reached up and placed a hand on his arm; he shook it off. "You know exactly what you're doing to me. So just go.

Go." His voice lowered, dangerously soft. "Go. Because if you don't, I just might discover how very weak I am. Go before I give you exactly what you want."

"I wouldn't be a good reporter if I left now."

He sighed, then smiled wryly.

And suddenly, the smile became a grin, and the grin became a chuckle, and the chuckle became a laugh.

Claire looked at him quizzically, but not before his deep laugh caught her up in it too, and then it was too late; they were both laughing in earnest now, gasping for breath, unable to do anything but stare at each other helplessly as deep emotion swirled around both of them. Joe couldn't help himself, he felt transfixed as he saw a tear sparkle in Claire's eyes, felt a tug of hope as he saw Claire wipe that tear from her eye. A tear of laughter, Joe realized, and his heart quickened at the expression in her blue eyes. They actually shone with joy. He sucked in a breath.

"I haven't laughed like that since—" But

she cut herself off.

"The junior class picnic at Golden Gate Park," he finished for her.

"I swear I didn't know about the ants." Claire lifted her hands in surrender.

He chuckled. "I'm sure. You *and* half the class." He sank down on the couch beside her. "Does that mean you're still ticklish?"

Claire gave a little shriek and jumped away from him. "Don't you dare, Joe Lucitano!"

"Why not?" His voice lowered and he raised a hand, his fingertips feather-light against her ribcage.

The notebook and pencil slipped from her grasp.

He could feel her holding her breath. His own sped up. "I remember—"

"I'm sure I don't recall anything," she snapped, and scrambled to retrieve the pen and paper as she stood up.

Had the Claire he'd loved actually been replaced by this older, colder version? This minx who sold her soul for a story?

He narrowed his eyes. "I'm not the naïve kid you humiliated at the senior prom."

"Can I quote you on that?" Claire's pencil was already moving.

But he plucked the pencil from between her fingers and then snapped it in half. She looked up at him, her mouth forming an O of surprise.

He ran a thumb along the tender pink of her bottom lip. She gasped.

"Yes, Claire," he whispered, "two can play at this game." A muscle in his jaw twitched. No, she wasn't the same girl at all. He'd been a fool to think otherwise.

"Now get out." He backed her toward the entryway, over the threshold, and then slammed the door in her face.

For a long moment, he just stared at the door. Why had he been so suspicious of her motives?

Because time hadn't healed anything. It had only made things worse, much worse, for his heart. He couldn't bear the thought of not being with her, yet he couldn't stand the thought of being with her, either.

If only she would be straight with him. Then he could see where she was coming from. Understand her, and maybe then be able to give her the benefit of the doubt.

He hung his head. He couldn't believe he'd just treated *Claire* like that. But the woman drove him crazy. No, he couldn't believe that was possible. And yet...and yet...why had she acted the way she did? What had changed her? He frowned. Why had he thought he could hold onto the Claire he had once known? She was obviously no longer that girl.

But the scent of her lilac perfume lingered.

CLAIRE HURLED THE PHONE ACROSS the room. It gave a satisfying crash as it hit the far wall, leaving a dent so large it would put Daddy into conniptions when he got the month's rent bill. Good. Her lip curled. She hoped it would.

Joe had no right to treat her like a mere child. No right at all.

And she shouldn't act like a child, either. Remorseful, she retrieved the phone, and straightened her peplum jacket and her shoulders, feeling better now that she'd gotten rid of that pent-up anger. If only Joe could see what talent he was wasting.

She knew that he would eventually thank her for what she was doing, even if he couldn't see it that way now. Because in bringing his wounds to the light of day, she was certain others could relate, as well.

After all, that was why feature articles were published.

Besides, she didn't have time now to write about someone else, what with just two days left until deadline. She *had* to do something with what she had.

Claire fingered a velvety leaf of one of her pink geraniums blooming in the west-facing windowsill, wishing it was Joe's face she was caressing, wishing she could have smoothed away that look of anger and distrust.

"It was my fault," she whispered to the plant, though she somehow drew comfort from the steady beauty of the pink blossoms, as if the truth, the forgiveness, existed just as surely as the plant flowered. "I shouldn't have stormed in there unannounced," she admitted, watering the geranium carefully. "But why did I? Did I expect him to give in so easily?"

The low moan of a foghorn echoed through the evening air.

"Of course I deserved to be pushed away, just like I pushed him away..."

She dismissed that thought as quickly as it came. She had her career at stake. She had to go back and try again.

After all, she was a professional. And that was all Joe was to her—a source. Nothing more.

Because if it came down to it, she'd have to sacrifice the source for the sake of the story and the truth.

She sighed and sat down on the chaise

lounge, then reached for the bottle of champagne she'd been saving for a special occasion. Well, it was the end of a pretty rotten day; might as well turn it into something to celebrate.

She carefully poured herself a flute.

After seeing Joe again, and then that damned engagement article of Nick's, she deserved a second glass, she thought, as she watched the bubbles rise; only now, in the safety of her suite, did she allow herself to feel the sting of shame and dismissal at her editor's words, at Joe's face, at Nick's article, and at her father's outrageous demands. Ugh. She needed to shake herself out of this foul mood.

Perhaps it was time for a bit of a walk.

HER FAVORITE SPOT IN THE city—Baker Beach. She walked along the shoreline, the sea breeze cooling her anger toward Joe as memories rolled in: the sparkle of a broken piece of sea glass they'd found together on this very beach after the junior class picnic; the taste of clove when he'd kissed her for the first time before band class...

She sighed, wishing for half a second she could still be that sweet innocent girl. Now, she was always doing things to prove her guilt. She grimaced. Toying with people and things. Gauging the strength of their reaction to her barbs. She winced.

She found herself walking in the direction of the Golden Gate Bridge when it started to rain, which was exactly when the story started to write itself in her head.

She took the stairs up from the beach and headed out onto the walkway along the bridge, purple twilight giving way to blue-black velvety dark, her mind drifting back to Nick and his fiancée. Their starry-eyed expressions.

She pulled her coat more tightly around her. She'd lost that long ago with Joe, and she'd never get it back. He hated her now; that much was obvious.

She moved to grip the cold slick surface of the bridge railing, not seeing the choppy dark waves of the ocean but rather the mahogany and leather of her father's office from Monday's conversation. It was true—she *had* loved Joe, even on the day she'd broken his heart.

She felt tears prickle. They'd argued on the sidewalk. She'd flung the locket he'd given her back in his face, told him she never wanted to see him again, told him she'd never really loved him in the first place.

She sighed again. Joe wasn't hers now. He wasn't, he wasn't. And, he had been. He was, and she thought she'd had it all.

Instead, the war broke out and all hell broke loose because she was the one who planted that seed of doubt in Joe's mind, back in band class. She told him he was terrible; and then with the trauma he suffered after the war, well, perhaps if she hadn't sowed that initial seed back in high school, then he wouldn't have quit playing.

It was all jumbled up together: guilt,

anger, sadness...and fear—of having thrown away the last good thing she'd ever have.

She tilted her head back, welcoming the cold raindrops on her flushed face. And on that long-ago night she'd begun wearing this icy façade like a mink stole. Because what hurt most was that she'd found the locket on the street later that night; Joe hadn't even bothered to pick it up.

THE WINDSHIELD WIPERS SWISHED BACK and forth, back and forth, against the torrent of rain. Joe cursed under his breath. Crossing the Golden Gate tonight, heading back into town after visiting friends outside the city, probably wasn't the best idea, logically. Safely. But then again, when had safety ever been a consideration of his? He'd lived through the war, after all.

Anything else was practically inconsequential.

Well, maybe not. He thought again of Claire's blue eyes, and warmth spread through him. He swore again. He couldn't believe that one look at her after all this time would send him over the edge. But there it was.

The headlights cut through the dark and the fog that had started to roll in from the ocean as the Nash Ambassador rumbled across the bridge. Not another soul around.

But a flicker of white caught Joe's peripheral vision. He did a double-take. Jesus. Joe swerved to the side of the road. Someone was standing at the railing. In the pouring rain.

He guessed they weren't sightseeing.

Unmindful of anything but the other person's safety, he jammed the Nash into first gear and got out.

The person didn't even turn around. And, he saw as he squinted against the sluice of water on his face, it was a young woman. "Miss! Miss!"

She still didn't move. He took a step

closer. "Are you all right?"

No reply.

"Can you hear me?" The rain pounded louder, and thunder rumbled. "Let me help you." But the wind picked up and tore his words from him.

He closed the gap between them. Put a hand on her shoulder. "You're—Claire?"

"Let go of me!" Claire demanded. But his fingers only tightened on her shoulders.

"No. Not until you tell me what the hell you're doing out here."

"That's none of your business."

"Maybe not. But you *are* at the railing of a bridge in the middle of a rainstorm. Makes a fella jump to certain conclusions."

"Well, aren't you just full of puns tonight?" She jerked away from his grasp. "I bet you'd love it if I jumped."

"Lay off it, Claire. Just because you broke my heart in high school doesn't mean I want you dead. Let me talk to you, God damn it." He put his hand again on

her shoulder.

She lifted her hand to slap him, but he parried the expected blow.

"I'm warning you, I'll scream."

"Come on, Claire. See some sense."

"Let go of me. Let go. Let go. I don't want to talk to you."

"You need to tell me about what's really going on. Now."

She shook her head back and forth, and all at once, tears spilled out of those baby-blue eyes of hers and she started crying as if she never meant to stop.

"I-I-I—" Sobs shook her slender frame like a kitten in a hurricane.

He couldn't stop himself. He pulled her to him.

She started to push away.

"Talking is the only way you'll ever get over whatever it is," he murmured, his tone low and warm.

"What do you know about getting over anything?" She glared at him.

Joe clamped his teeth together, yet still he held her.

She struggled in his arms again, indignation flashing in her eyes. "Let go of me, oh, why don't you?" But her words had no teeth; she collapsed against him and wept into the soft cotton of his chambray shirt, the anguish of her tears soaking into his heart.

His grip relaxed, his arms slid around her, his hands now soft and gentle as he held her; he rested his chin on the crown of her head even as she continued to sob and shake.

"Shhhh, shhhh," he murmured, his hands on her shoulder blades, making a soothing circular motion as the last of her tears fell free.

"Come on," he whispered in her ear. "Let's get you home."

He half-carried, half-pushed Claire along beside him toward the passenger side of his car. He eased open the door, helped her in and then shut it firmly before walking around to the driver's side and getting in behind the wheel.

He put the car in gear and flipped on

the radio. "So where is it you're living now?"

"Take me home with you, Joe."

His heart leapt. "No, Claire." His voice was gentle. "You need to go to your own place. You've been drinking tonight and you're not talking sense."

"What's the matter? Worried about ruining my reputation?" She gave a low laugh. "As Mae West said, 'I used to be Snow White, but I drifted.'"

Joe didn't reply.

He glanced beside him. Claire's head lolled against the window as she finally spoke. "It's the women's residence on Geary Street."

Silent minutes passed. Finally, Joe spoke again, his voice soft. "What were you doing out there, Claire?"

"Why would you question what I did or didn't do?"

"Honey, I always question your motives." But he didn't want to. His throat tightened. He didn't want to play the bad guy, didn't want to believe Claire was anyone but that same girl who'd untangled the school loner's kite from a tree and scraped up her knees for her kindness.

"What do you think this is, some sort of detective picture?"

Despite himself, Joe laughed. But, he noticed, she hadn't answered his question.

He pulled up to the curb. "Here you go." He got out and opened her door for her.

Claire tried to get out but stumbled. Joe placed a steadying hand on her waist. "Where are your keys? It's past midnight and they won't let you in without them."

"In my—" She fished in her jacket pocket but came up empty. "Must be the other pocket." But that came up empty too. "The landlady's already given me two warnings. Said the third time, I'm out."

He held back a groan. "All right, then." A look of guilt flickered across her face. No, he must have imagined that. "You can stay in my apartment tonight."

HE FLICKED ON THE LIGHTS while she wobbled beside him. He shut the door behind them and locked it while she tried to wiggle out of her jacket.

He helped her out of it, then hung up his wet trenchcoat and hers, and took off his fedora. They went into the living room.

"Let me get you some pajamas. They'll be too big but they'll do."

But before he could move, she flung her arms around him. "You're very beautiful, *Joe. Joe. Joe.*" She wound her arms around his neck, chanting his name in a singsong voice.

He pried her hands off. "And you're very drunk."

She settled unsteadily onto his couch as he went into his bedroom and found a spare pair of pajamas after a minute or two of searching through his dresser.

He came back into the living room with the blue-and-white striped pajamas and a towel. "Here. The bathroom's just down the hall and to the left."

She let the bathroom door slam. He winced, then went to fix himself a nightcap. He had a feeling he was going to need it.

In the silence that followed her absence, he breathed a sigh of relief. He couldn't figure it out—why the hell was he being so nice to her?

Old habits died hard, or something like that, he guessed. His lips compressed into a line and he wondered how long she'd take to change clothes. Which led to thoughts of those long legs... He tossed back the liquor before his thoughts could get out of hand and strode over to the pile of dusty records next to his phonograph.

He thumbed through them thoughtfully. Jazz. There was nothing like it. In fact, it had saved his life—literally. For if he hadn't gone outside for some fresh air and a cigarette between sets that night over in Cannes, he would've been blasted sky-high like the rest of his company.

And he hadn't picked up his horn since. He was inept; a failure as a man because he wasn't playing, wasn't fulfilling his destiny as a musician.

His eyes wandered to the shine of brass, his saxophone on its stand in the corner beside the phonograph player. He made a move toward it. It'd been so long since he'd played anything...

His hand hovered over it as if it might break at his touch; the reed had to be replaced soon, he noticed.

"Play something for me, Joe."

He startled. Jesus. She could be as quiet as a cat when she wanted. But her words echoed in his ears, almost the same words uttered by a very different woman on that fatal night in France.

And, though he closed his eyes against the onslaught, he couldn't stop the scenes flashing through his mind.

Darkness and starlight, the cobblestone alley, the scent of spring mixed with cigarettes, the taste of freedom on his lips in that staccato melody he'd played for that nameless brunette in the alley. Oh, the war had felt so far away when she'd said 'Play me a tune?' in that voice, that voice, with those blue eyes that had *so* reminded him—he clenched his fists—of Claire.

How was he to know those words would be fatal? That she'd turn on him? He swallowed, but he was trapped again in the thick of the images, caught, just like he'd been caught in the force of the blast that threw him and his horn to the ground. When he'd opened his eyes once again, she was gone; the only thing he saw was that gleam of brass amongst all that rubble; the club destroyed, his band mates—everyone inside—dead. How was he to know she'd been working for the Germans? That *play me a tune* had been a code phrase?

His fists clenched as he recalled his vow on that April night, that he wouldn't touch his horn again as long as he lived.

"No." A bead of sweat trickled down his neck.

"That's your favorite word, isn't it?"

"Claire." His voice came out strangled. "Please."

But instead of the swift rebuttal or cloaked barb he'd expected, he heard the soft rustle of fabric and then felt her arms slide around him, felt his trembling ease as she put her head on his shoulder and simply held him, the concerned, searching look in her wide blue eyes too much.

He'd forgotten how she made him feel; it nearly knocked him to his knees. And right there, amid the sounds of muffled traffic and steady drips of the kitchen faucet, he felt a warm surge, a glow. He felt *hope* again, damn it.

Hope? He almost laughed aloud. So he set himself free, the story spilling from him.

He wrapped his arms around Claire; he could feel the span of her shoulder blades underneath the soft, striped blue-and-white cotton of his pajamas—so delicate, so fragile that it seemed her bones might snap at any moment. He let out a tentative breath, stirring the still-damp curls on her cheek.

After a few more moments and a few more deep breaths, he managed to disentangle himself from her embrace and crossed the room. Had that been a truce or a trick?

She sank onto the couch. He shook out the afghan that was neatly folded on the back of his easy chair, then drew the multicolored blanket up around her. She settled her head onto one of the crocheted pillows. Why was he helping her, after the way she'd treated him? Probably because he was a sucker. Being too nice had always been his problem. No wonder he was so screwed up from the war.

She patted the pillow his mother had made. "Mmmm," she murmured, half-asleep. "Feels like home."

He swallowed. "Goodnight, Claire." But she was already asleep.

CLAIRE YAWNED AND STRETCHED. PUT

fingers to her temple. Winced at the pounding headache. And her fuzzy memories of last night. Last night.

She sat bolt upright and flung back the afghan. She had to get out of Joe's apartment. But maybe she could make him some breakfast first? It was the least she could do to make up for her despicable behavior...

She snorted. Look at her, having thoughts of domestic bliss. Must be from the hangover.

She padded down the hall to the bathroom, took an aspirin and changed into her now-dry, albeit wrinkled, dress, then did her hair as best she could in the small mirror over the sink, the mint-green color of the tiny room doing nothing to calm her nerves.

What was she going to do with herself? Her hand trembled. She bit her lip, then wished for her lipstick.

She drew in a breath and straightened her shoulders. There was nothing for it. With a few quick movements, she folded up Joe's pajamas and placed them neatly on the edge of the bathtub before stepping out into the hallway.

And almost ran smack into Joe. She clenched her jaw. She'd hoped she could slip out without him noticing.

Too late for that now. He already had a worry line between his brows as soon as he saw her.

Well. In for a penny, and all that. "Can I use your typewriter?"

CLAIRE TOOK A SIP FROM the heavy porcelain coffee cup Joe handed her. It nearly burned her, so she put it down with a clatter onto its saucer and went back to typing.

"What exactly are you doing?"

"Wouldn't you like to know?"

"Yes, as a matter of fact, I would." Joe buttoned the cuffs on his crisp cotton shirt. "It's my typewriter. Besides, I'm sure there's more than enough typewriters down at the *Chronicle*."

She shifted on the oak office chair. Damn him for ferreting out exactly what she didn't want him to know. But she laughed; then for good measure, told him the truth, just to throw him off. "Just some notes for an article due in a day and a half. I'm not going to waste my boss's time with something like this."

"So you're going to waste mine." But Joe turned away before she could answer. "I'm going to shave."

She glanced over her shoulder. Good. She'd driven him away, and now was the perfect opportunity to type before the fleeting impressions left her. She closed her eyes and replayed their clash on the bridge...

It was almost worth her feeling the pain again just to be able to describe the look on Joe's face—a look she was sure readers would understand.

She didn't know why she didn't just wait until she'd gotten to the safety of the newsroom to write down these details. Perhaps it had something to do with the fact that it was exactly that—unsafe, or more accurately, unwise—that she did it. A small smile curved her lips as a zing of perverse delight shot through her.

But the silence weighed heavily on her even as she typed as fast as she could.

She'd only intended to use Joe's machine for a minute, just to get her words down on paper. But somehow, the silence seemed to stretch into eternity. She hated it. She couldn't type in silence. She had to have some sort of activity, some sound or movement going on.

She glanced around, then got up and switched on the phonograph, slotted the first record she came to into place, and lowered the needle.

Perfect. Nothing like a little white noise to block out the sound of her own fears.

But they jumped to the forefront anyway when she realized the mistake she'd made by choosing a record without looking. Because jazz poured into the room. She gritted her teeth.

Before she could do anything about it,

Joe had come back, a black expression on his face.

She tried not to flinch, but failed.

"What the hell are you doing?"

She took a breath. The scent of his Burma-Shave drifted toward her. She couldn't let him see how much she disliked what he thought was her choice...of music. She couldn't risk anyone finding out that she actually despised the very music she raved about in her reviews.

More importantly, she couldn't let him win. So she smiled through her pain. "Oh, it's just a little jazz. I am a music critic, after all."

"Don't I know it," he muttered under his breath.

"What was that?" She batted her lashes, pretending not to care about the hurt expression on his face, pretending that she hadn't been the one to wound him; yet still she stood, smiling, as if she didn't know exactly what he was referring to.

Who was she kidding? He'd never forgive her if he found out the article she was writing was supposed to *help* him. Because he'd never believe she was capable of goodness any more.

She snatched the paper from the typewriter, nearly ripping the page in half before she grabbed her coat from the hook and dashed out the door before he could see her tears.

Chapter Three

AFTER CLAIRE STORMED OUT, JOE wheeled around in the entryway. The gleam of brass caught his eye, and without thinking, he walked over to his saxophone.

He could feel his heart racing.

Why had he kept the instrument at all? But he wouldn't part with it, either. He kept it around as a reminder of what had almost been, as a reminder to himself never to get so caught up again in another person, in another woman.

And in some strange way, too, as a tribute to Claire, and to the love that they had had; to that melody, unfinished, that he had played for her back when war was the furthest thing from either of their minds....

As he reached out to touch the instrument, Claire's words, uttered on that long-ago day, came back to him.

"I never loved you anyhow. Daddy says you're no-talent white trash"—words she'd probably long forgotten and had, no doubt, relished. A wave of defeat washed through him.

But just as quickly, he pushed it down and snatched up the instrument, changed the reed, adjusted the neck strap, put the mouthpiece to his lips and blew.

He winced. A little out of tune. But at the familiar feel of the keys under his fingertips, he couldn't help but feel a glow. He'd actually picked it up again.

The glow became a flame. A flame that burned like fire. It spread through his veins, building and building until every note, every breath he took only reminded him of how much he had lost, suffered, hurt.

Yet still he played. He closed his eyes against the pain but that only made it worse. Only made him see the flames again, the anguish, the despair. They'd said he was lucky to be alive, after that fire bomb in Cannes. But then why couldn't he shake the guilt?

Maybe that was what he deserved.

He put the saxophone down none too gently, stuffed it into its case and slammed the lid. But it was too late. Jazz was back in his blood.

CLAIRE HELD HER BREATH AS she walked into the newsroom Thursday morning. But she needn't have worried. Her editor's door—firmly closed. She exhaled in relief, then glanced around.

She lowered her chin. She needed to get this article in tonight for tomorrow's morning edition, never mind that it was already noon. She grimaced, wishing for once that she hadn't taken the time to go home and change into a fresh dress and reapply her lipstick. Although on the other hand, a wrinkled dress might have garnered even more stares.

Never mind. She would figure something out. She always had. Her lips curled upward in a secret smile; resourcefulness, one of the few traits she could honestly say she was proud of having.

She settled in at her desk and put a fresh sheet into her typewriter, preparing to transcribe the shorthand she'd scribbled from her night at The Blue Mirror and the notes from Joe's. Had it all only been last night? It seemed ages ago.

Nonetheless.

She began typing, losing herself in the satisfaction of putting words on the page. Glee shot through her as she slid the carriage return hard to the right to begin a new paragraph.

As she studied the freshly typed pages an hour later, Claire chewed on the end of her pencil, then realized what she was doing and tucked it back into the spiral binding of her steno pad with a disgusted shudder. But the thinking had been worth the gnawed pencil, because she realized there were a few holes in her story. She reached for the phone.

JOE STARED INTO THE SHADOWS in his bedroom that night, Claire's face in his mind's eye; her questions in his head.

Why had he stopped? Did he miss it? He shook his head. Flipped on the radio.

What was he going to do with his talent now that it wasn't being used to play music? Did he want to rot away on some street corner or in some office job?

A slow jazz song came on. Joe turned off the radio with a click.

No, no and no. The answer was no. She kept bugging him, kept pestering him. In fact he wouldn't be surprised if the phone rang right now.

He glanced to his bedside table where the dark shape sat. Nothing but silence.

He rolled over but couldn't shut off her words, couldn't turn down the volume on his memories, couldn't bear to mute the melody he'd played somehow by heart just hours ago after Claire had left...

So he stared at the ceiling, wide awake,

almost seeing the notes suspended there, Claire's words swirling around them. He grabbed a cigarette, sat up in bed and fumbled for his lighter.

His gaze shifted to the window. The casing between the panes of glass seemed to form bars, reminding him of how trapped he'd felt since coming stateside again.

He lit another cigarette but couldn't shake the downward spiral his thoughts had taken. And it was because the music hadn't been there. He put the cigarette to his lips. He'd missed it. He grimaced. Missed it more than he cared to admit.

He smoked and thought. And thought and smoked. About all the ways he'd thought he'd forgotten that he'd felt when he had played...

Joe only came back to himself and the room when his cigarette burned him. He dropped it into the ashtray and mopped the sweat from his brow.

Why not, damn it. Why the hell not? His jaw tightened. He could play again. If only to prove Claire wrong. His lighter was unsteady in his hand. If only to show people that Joe Lucitano wasn't a quitter or a coward.

That he was the kind of man who could overcome his fears, not be cowed by them. He picked up the receiver and dialed Nick.

♫

GOD. IT WAS EXHAUSTING ACTING like she didn't care. She headed back to her type-writer and winced as she felt the beginning of a blister. Perhaps she shouldn't have worn her new shoes.

But what was a little more pinch, a little more pain? She laughed at herself. If only blisters could explain away all her bad behavior.

Never mind the fact that she hated it. Hated how she'd become, to quote Joe, this vindictive little minx. But it was far too late to give up the act. Wasn't it? No one would believe she could change, least of all her. She barely believed this newer, softer side of herself that had chosen to reveal itself in Joe's presence.

She swallowed and brought a hand to her lips.

Joe had been right. She didn't deserve any sort of love. Not even the broken kind. She was worse than worthless. There was nothing for her here. Or anywhere.

But she shoved those thoughts aside and sank into her chair. Better to roll up her sleeves than wring her hands. She kicked off her shoes and began transcribing her final draft.

As Claire hit the final key on the typewriter, she let out another sigh, a sigh that, it seemed to her, she had been holding for six long years, years in which she'd fought—fought so hard against herself. And now she was exhausted.

She got up. And suddenly tears welled. But it took her a moment to understand that these were tears of joy. Because, she realized, as she gently worked the page loose from the typewriter and studied the

black and white, this must be how Joe felt when he was playing. This fierce possessiveness, this pride, this hope and wonder and sense of utter completeness and rightness. It was, quite simply, love for her craft.

She stroked a finger across the page.

She could go to Joe now, and, she gasped, he *would* understand. Her lips curved into a genuine smile. He would forgive her now, because she had poured everything she had into the article, to honor him.

Chapter Four

FRIDAY MORNING, CLAIRE BOUGHT THE *Chronicle* from a paperboy on her way to the newspaper office.

She shuffled through the pages to the arts section, where, above the fold, the headline positively screamed: *Local Sax Virtuoso's Love of Music a Casualty of War.*

It was over and done with. She'd satisfied her boss and satisfied her own curiosity, so why did she feel so displeased, still?

Perhaps because, she mused, as she hopped onto a cable car headed downtown, she hadn't gotten what she had wanted: Joe.

She tossed her head. She didn't give two hoots about Joe. Yet the staccato beating of her heart told her that much was obviously not true.

She'd figure that out later, she told herself, as she walked into the newsroom.

This time, she didn't get to breathe a sigh of relief. Her editor's door not only stood open, but he was also making a beeline straight for her.

She calmly walked on to her desk, removed her hat and gloves, and proceeded to sit down.

"I wouldn't do that if I were you." Claire's editor approached her.

"What? Sit down?"

"Yes."

"Can I ask you why?"

"Have you seen the paper?"

"Yes. Why?"

"For a dame, you ask that a lot."

"Well," she smoothed her skirt, "I am a reporter."

"Not any more."

"What do you mean?"

"Again with the questions." Her editor narrowed his eyes. "Listen, Miss DuPont..." He lowered his voice. "I've gotten word of some misconduct, shall we say."

"Misconduct? I can't imagine what you're talking about."

He quirked a brow.

Her mouth went dry, but she raised her chin.

"Well, you damn well better hurry up and start imagining. Because you're fired."

"At least tell me why, for goodness sake."

"I don't think it had anything to do with goodness. But I'll tell you. Or rather, I think you need to tell me. Why didn't you let me know you were too close to your sources? Not only the former girlfriend of Nick Hart but also Joe Lucitano? I trusted your news judgment, and now we'll have to print some sort of statement about the article." He lit a cigarette, shook out the match, and stared at her levelly for a long moment.

"I trusted *my* news judgment too," she said quietly. "I was following my instincts, honoring my readership, and the sources, with the truth."

"Well, that's irrelevant now, because you're out of here. Conflict of interest is conflict of interest."

JOE COULDN'T QUITE BELIEVE HE'D decided to do this, that Gregory DuPont had contacted him. But it was too late to back out now. He wasn't going to let memories or pain or fear stop him. He had to accept things as they were.

And if it was a fool's errand, well, he knew that he'd never forgive himself if he didn't come. He had to put the past to rest and see if he had any sort of future with music again.

So that's why he was standing here, saxophone in hand, at the back entrance of Golden Gate Records after the rehearsal for the gig Nick had gotten him.

Yes, he'd been sharp with Claire. Tried to hurt her feelings. That didn't exactly make him a saint. But he didn't want her forgiveness. After all, they'd gone too far for that by now.

He raised his hand to knock. And maybe that made him selfish. Weak. But at least it was his own decision to make, not being pushed by her, or anyone else, for that matter, into something he might regret later.

So he knocked.

♪

CLAIRE'S HEELS MADE NO NOISE as she trod across the swirled green carpet that lined the hallway of Golden Gate Records.

She was only here to leave a note about her employment termination. She grimaced; she couldn't bear to see Daddy's reaction in person, which was why she'd come in after hours. But she also knew she wanted to try to make amends with him. Writing the article about Joe had shown her that, too.

She glanced left and right but, unsurprisingly, found no one here. And no wonder. It was nearly seven p.m.

She was looking forward to a long soak in her claw-footed bathtub, never mind

what Joe might like or dislike about the article.

As if on cue, the low, reedy sound of a saxophone began drifting toward her. She frowned. Someone had probably left the radio on. It was coming from the direction of her father's office.

Yes. The saxophone grew louder with each step she took. She reached Daddy's office at last and pushed open the heavy mahogany door. It swung soundlessly inward on its hinges.

The orange glow from the streetlight came pouring through the window, pooled across the paper-strewn desk, and spilled to the floor.

But the music wasn't from the radio at all.

Instead, she saw a familiar-looking silhouette of a man playing the saxophone.

Why was Joe in here? A surge of protectiveness toward her father shot through her and she was about to open her mouth to say something but somehow, as she continued to stare, she realized she wouldn't, because she'd made that mistake once already.

She raised a trembling hand to her lips instead.

He remained with his profile to her. His angular outline showed him to be sitting in the Moroccan leather wingback.

The breath caught in her throat. He hadn't seen her, after all; his mind somewhere else entirely, no doubt, from the way he played.

The notes felt so intimate, so close to the heart that a vague sense of guilt began creeping through her. She should leave. She had no right to be here...

She took a step back and collided with the solid wood doorframe.

He swiveled in the chair at the sound and her sudden movement.

She continued to simply stare at him, mesmerized by the way the light threw some planes of his face into shadow yet brought out other parts in stark relief.

It took her by surprise, the relief that flooded through her at the sight of him.

Her heart fluttered. It was *Joe. Her* Joe. Playing music. Her breath caught again.

And suddenly she wanted to give him everything, everything she'd so callously taken away from him with her sharp words and her hurtful actions. Suddenly she felt she couldn't do enough for him. And suddenly, she wanted to spend the rest of her life trying to do just that.

Oh God. She had been so wrong to hurt him, to try and crush that precious thing that they'd discovered all those years ago. But could it be revived?

She felt something sharp tug at her heart, and realized with a start that it was regret. Regret for having treated him so cruelly, for having been so unfair. With the article and with his heart back in high school. She never should have humiliated him in front of everyone that night at the senior prom.

"I'm sorry," she whispered, letting her eyes close, feeling as if she should be dropping to her knees in supplication, wondering if he would catch her if she did, wondering if he'd also catch her deeper shade of meaning.

He stood. Crossed the room to her. He took her cold hand and gently squeezed her fingers, the warmth transferring from him to her. "So am I." His voice came out husky. "See a picture with me tonight, Claire?"

She opened one eye, then both. She blinked. So much for deeper meaning. But still, she appreciated the gesture. "Yes, Joe," she whispered, her head still bowed.

Chapter Five

THEY WALKED ALONG CASTRO STREET, the bustle of evening moviegoers surrounding them.

"Do you know why I was at the office tonight, Claire? Your father apologized to me. So thank you."

"You're welcome."

But instead of pulling away from the comfortable silence that fell between them, Claire relaxed into it.

The Castro Theatre came into view. Its sand-colored façade, as usual, held her fascination. She tilted her head back to admire the elaborate mouldings; the marquee with its black lettering and the vertical sign with its flashing orange neon almost paled in comparison.

"Wait til you see the inside of this place," Joe murmured, coming to a stop close by.

She could feel his eyes on her, so she let him admire her as she continued to look at the theatre's façade, suddenly and girlishly glad she'd chosen to wear her favorite green dress with the sweetheart neckline. "Are you trying to impress me, Joe?" But she hid the pleased smile that came to her lips behind the upturned collar of her gabardine jacket.

He simply raised a brow in reply, then turned to the movie poster in front of them. "Looks like they're playing that new Ginger Rogers one."

"Good. I love Ginger Rogers."

"Funny, I had you pegged as more of a Veronica Lake kind of gal."

"Oh, I'm full of surprises."

After Joe paid the dollar and ten cents for their tickets, they made their way into the lobby. She couldn't help herself. She stared; she didn't know if it was the plush carpet or the potted ferns or the huge gilt mirrors on the sweeping staircases that lead to the balconies, but from the very first time she'd come here as little girl, she'd known that from this spot, you could go anywhere...the moment you sat down in that darkened theatre.

The Moorish, Italian and Spanish influences in the Art Deco décor filled her with a sense of joy she hadn't felt since she couldn't remember when. Or was that just because of her present company?

"This place has a great stage. They use it for live events, too, you know."

Oh, she knew. This place, after all, was where she and Henry were to have their engagement party tomorrow night.

Daddy loved the movies, so naturally, he thought holding the engagement party at the Castro would be great. A sort of publicity stunt. Good for business and all that.

She found herself reaching for Joe's arm, but her fingers encountered only empty air. She blinked. He'd gone to give their tickets to the usher.

She was glad for the low lighting as Joe returned and escorted her from the lobby into the dim theatre. Her heart pounded. She smelled popcorn and damp wool as they started walking down the aisle.

Joe's warm breath in her ear made her jump as he murmured, "Where do you want to sit?"

"Oh, I don't care."

"You still like to sit way too close to the screen?"

A wave of sadness washed through her. How did he remember something about her that she'd nearly forgotten? She nodded, not trusting her voice.

They settled onto the slightly worn green velvet chairs three rows from the front. Had the seats always been this close together? She leaned her arm on the polished wooden armrest and wished she hadn't agreed to this. Henry wouldn't like it.

But Henry, she reminded herself, was not here. Besides, it wasn't as if they were married yet, she and dear old Henry. Her lips thinned. No. They were simply engaged. Even less than that, just a few

promised words, because she had no ring on her finger. Yes, it was more like a business arrangement than anything else. Therefore, Joe didn't need to know. She and Joe were simply…two old friends, so she wasn't breaking any rules stepping out with him.

"Say, I almost forgot. Do you want popcorn? I can get something before the newsreel starts."

She opened her mouth, then closed it. He'd already paid for too much.

"What's this? Claire DuPont at a loss for words? I think this is breaking news." He gave her a nudge.

Despite her reservations, she laughed. "Oh, Joe. Stop flirting with me."

"Well, now, a fella can't refuse an open invitation like that." He draped an arm across the back of her seat.

She allowed herself a tiny moment of enjoyment in his arm around her before she crossed her arms and leaned away from him.

"Crossed the line, have I? Okay, okay.

No need to get uptight. I was only—I think I'm going to go get something. Be right back."

Had he read her article? But she couldn't bring herself to ask him, somehow, as he returned, a box of Cracker Jacks in hand. When he sat down beside her again, she caught the scent of his bergamot aftershave. Her heart twisted.

He opened the box just as the newsreel began and offered the box to her, eyebrows raised.

She shook her head, but her stomach growled.

He took her hand gently, turned it over and opened her fingers, tracing his thumb across her palm. But she couldn't resist his touch, couldn't find her usual cynical, biting comment to hold him at bay. Couldn't do anything but let herself be seduced by the tingles up and down her spine as his skin brushed along hers.

The caramel-covered kernels and peanuts fell into her palm and she, all too aware of Joe's eyes on her, ate them one

by one, savoring the salty sweetness.

She licked her lips.

Joe cleared his throat and shifted in his seat.

Good. She smiled. They were back on even ground now. Joe helped himself to another handful of the caramel-covered popcorn. Deliberately, so did she.

The lights dimmed, then faded to black. And for the next little while, she could forget. Forget this big mess she'd made for herself. Forget all her fears and insecurities as the story unfolded onscreen.

That is, until she felt Joe nudge her—offering her the last of the Cracker Jacks. She held out her cupped hand this time, annoyed with herself for her childlike enthusiasm for the sugary treat; but all that spilled from the cardboard container was the Cracker Jack prize.

"You can have it," Joe whispered.

She raised a cynical brow, her only protection against the double-beat of her heart. "A tin ring with a paste jewel?"

"Would you like it?"

"Why? Are you proposing?"

Had something like hope flickered in his eyes? No. It had simply been the changing light from the moving pictures onscreen.

But her heart fluttered anyway. Her traitorous heart. Desire and regret commingled inside of her, and she felt a sob bubble up, yet she held it back. God. She knew nothing *about* love, yet professed to be above it all with her barbs and her empty flirtations.

She had spent so long in the shadows of a life half-lived that she'd forgotten herself and what it felt like to be truly connected with others, with the man she loved.

The audience erupted into laughter around them. She burst into tears. "Take me home, Joe." She dug her fingers into the sleeve of his suit jacket. "Please."

He looked at her for a long moment. "All right," he said slowly, getting up. "All right."

THEY EXITED ONTO THE SIDEWALK lit by the glow of streetlamps. "Stop playing games," his voice lowered, "Cee-Cee."

"It's not a game. And don't you call me that!" she hissed.

"You know I've got you under my skin."

She gave a sharp jag of laughter as she took a drag on her cigarette, but he could see her fingers trembling. "That old song." She sniffed. "Children's nonsense. Don't remind me."

He started humming the melody anyway, leaning closer to her, sliding his arms around her waist. She tried to pull back but in that second, a small silver locket fell forward, suspended on its chain around her neck, and caught the light from the streetlamp on the corner of the intersection where they stood.

"If it's children's nonsense, Cee-Cee," he saw her stiffen but didn't relent, "then why are you still wearing this?"

He eyed the gleam of sterling around her neck and crooked a finger to lift the delicate silver chain; he could feel her pulse beating like the wings of a trapped hummingbird against the tissue-thin skin of her throat.

Her eyes darted around, but there was nowhere to run.

"After all these years?" His tone mixed disbelief with awe.

She reached a hand up to hastily stuff the necklace back inside her bodice, but the brush of his warm fingers against her skin must have frozen her in place because she could only watch, transfixed, as he held up the tiny silver heart, the metal still warm from her skin.

He chuckled softly. "Ever since I saw you wearing pink ice cream instead of lipstick that afternoon in the ninth grade." He smiled. "You were quite a looker, even back then."

She turned her face away but wasn't fast enough to prevent the tear from sliding down her cheek. She scrubbed it away.

"Don't hide from me." He caught her arm. "You're gorgeous as hell." Joe pulled her into his arms before she could change his mind.

"I'm too bad to be beautiful. I-I bring out the worst in everyone. Even you." But her fingers tightened on his shoulders and she leaned into him.

"Yes," Joe murmured. "But you do it so well."

"Damn it, Joe. Damn it. Don't you see what's going on here? Don't you get it? I'm *in love* with *you*!" Her voice came out a strangled whisper. "Happy now? Now just go away. Go away."

"And what if I don't? I can be just as stubborn as you, you know, Miss Claire DuPont."

Her eyes darted to and away from his face, and he saw her knees wobble. "Then I'll *make* you go away."

"See, that's the trouble. You think you can always make me do things. And it's true, you've made me do and feel many things. But the truth is, Claire, I'm in love with you too, and it's time to stop running, time to stop hiding, time to stop trying to make this into something it's not—a mistake. Because you think that you're no better than some piece of garbage in the gutter. But my telling you that won't make you believe it. Believe me, I've tried that already one too many times. But what I *can* tell you is how I've been feeling. And well, you drive me crazy. But I've come to accept that. That's just part of who you are. And I know you don't mean any disrespect toward me, because I've also come to realize that you're afraid of your own shadow."

She laughed. "That's exactly what Henry said. Well, mostly. I guess you men aren't quite as dense as I always thought." She put her hands on her hips.

He put out a hand, palm up. "Just listen."

She crossed her arms.

"You think you're not worthy of love. But Claire, what if no one is worthy of it? What if it simply *is*?"

She took a step backward.

"No," he said gently, "you don't get to run away again." He caught her wrist and she collapsed against him, a caged prisoner finally set free.

"I never thought I'd say this, Joe," she whispered, "but," she gave a shaky laugh, "you're right. I'm so tired of running away."

"Then stay here with me," he whispered into her hair, the light shimmering on her face, making it appear deceptively soft and innocent. And because he knew she wasn't that way at all, he stroked a finger along the curve of her cheek.

"But I can't."

He reached for a stray golden curl to smooth off her face. She jerked back, and that catty veil fell over her eyes so quickly that he would've missed the vulnerability if he hadn't known her so well.

"Now you listen here, Joe, and you listen good. It's over. We're over. In fact, we've never even begun."

"Well, that's the way you think it is, but

it doesn't have to be that way."

"Yes, Joe, yes it does." Tears sparkled in her eyes.

He reached out but she batted his hand away.

"*Yes* it does," she repeated, gritting her teeth and lowering her voice. "Because I'm engaged to be married. To Henry—"

"I mean it, Claire. No more games."

"Games? Is that what you think this is? Some sort of middle-school charade? Let me assure you, it is most definitely not."

She began walking away. "Do you think I enjoy being mean to you? H-hurting you? Just stay away from me, Joe. Stay away. We've both caused each other enough damage already."

"Oh, so it was my fault that you got yourself engaged to Henry?"

Claire's shoulders hunched and she stopped walking. "I've been a fool. And I'm not going to make myself one again. Although I suppose it's already too late for that."

"Claire..." He reached for her again.

"Please don't do this to yourself. Don't do it to us. We deserve this love. And you know it." His voice grew deep, husky. She shivered. "We deserve to be together."

"Joe, you don't need to be my protector. We're not eighteen any more."

"No," he agreed, and took a step away from her. "But you're still a woman."

"A woman in need of no one, least of all you."

"What if I need you?" His voice softened, lowered.

"I'd say you were a sap."

"Even saps have to be loved, Claire."

"Yes, but not by me."

"No, I think you're wrong there." But he turned and walked away. "At least *I* tried," he called over his shoulder, his voice echoing as the mist swirled around him then swallowed him whole.

As Joe returned to his apartment, he picked up the *Chronicle* on his doorstep and riffled through it to the arts section, as he always did.

He looked at the bold black headline. He wanted to rip it to shreds, to put his fist through a wall.

Instead, he made himself read the entire piece, then calmly flicked open his lighter and watched Claire's betrayal of him—and all her lies—go up in flames.

Local Jazz Saxophonist's Love of
Music a Casualty of War
By Claire DuPont

On a rainy cold Tuesday in April of '44, the city of Cannes in southern France sat silent, waiting for the smooth sounds of jazz to fill the air.

An explosion did, instead.

And a lone man in a battered U.S. Army uniform hunched his way across the street from the pile of rubble, a saxophone clutched in his hand...

Local jazz saxophonist Joe Lucitano never thought he'd stop playing his horn until one night

in the South of France when it all blew up in his face.

Lucitano, a veteran of the U.S. Army Band, recalls that spring night in Cannes. "I'd gone outside for a breath of air and a cigarette between sets when the club I'd just been in exploded behind me. As I threw myself to the ground, I spotted a woman out of the corner of my eye, walking away. The same woman I'd just been talking to. I wouldn't have thought anything unusual, except for the fact that she was now speaking with an SS officer. She'd been working for the Germans the whole time."

This horrific incident must have affected Lucitano more deeply than he might've wanted to admit, because, as The Blue Mirror Club frequenter and crooner Nick Hart confirmed, Lucitano hadn't played a note since he returned stateside.

"I haven't heard from Joe in

two years," Hart said. "We used to be very close—he played in my band several times before the war. It's a real shame because a fella like him has talent."

Talent, indeed. And yet, according to their files, Golden Gate Records, one of San Francisco's finest record labels, reportedly refused to sign Lucitano to a record deal before the U.S. joined the war. Gregory DuPont, Golden Gate Records' CEO, was unavailable for comment.

Upon paying a visit to Lucitano in his apartment, he said, "The irony is, my saxophone didn't have a scratch on it. And neither did I." But his voice shook as he spoke, and beads of sweat broke out on his forehead, though he tried to hide it by opening a window.

Obviously, he was suffering. But Lucitano himself didn't shed much more light on the matter, though the dusty pile of records

in the corner of his living room seemed to tell another tale. "Once I got out of the service, I spent some time in Napa Valley with my folks, but that didn't help. So I came up to the Bay Area again—I'd gone to high school here before the war—and decided I needed some peace and quiet. So I got a job pushing brooms at a local high school." Had he lowered his standards?

Lucitano paused at that. "No. But it did get me to thinking about just what had happened to me during my own high school career, how certain people affected my music career back then. And the more I got to thinking, the more my fingers itched for music even though I denied it at the time."

Because he was scared? Lucitano's throat worked, and he crushed the brim of his fedora between his fingers. "Before the war, music had always been there

for me," he recalled. "But after," his voice lowered and the
expression on his face seemed almost haunted, "it abandoned me."
When pressed, though, Lucitano
refused further comment.

The owner of The Blue Mirror
Club said that Lucitano had been
coming regularly to see the shows
for the past few months. Was this
an indication that the saxophonist truly wanted to play again?
Or was he simply enjoying the music?

"Music was my first love," he
said, and glanced at his horn,
propped up by the stack of unused
records, with what appeared to be
undisguised longing. "But Gregory
DuPont tried to tell me otherwise."

An obvious reference to the
fallen-through record deal. Perhaps some resentment had been
harbored all these years?

Whatever the reasons, perhaps
the greater truth is yet to be

All that time they'd spent together had meant nothing, *nothing* to her. He ground his teeth. He'd given her the facts but she'd embellished the truth. The little minx had double-crossed him again. Fool me twice. He gave a grim chuckle, holding onto his anger like a drowning man holds onto a ruined raft.

CLAIRE SAT AT HER DESK, staring at the first blush of dawn through the window as she packed up her things at the office.

Task done, she picked the receiver up with a heavy heart. Before she could dial, the newsroom door burst open.

"What the hell did you do? How could you do this, Claire? I trusted you." Joe's eyes narrowed as he shook the paper in her face. "How could you write this about me? You, of all people, had no right."

"No right? No right?" She snorted. "I'm the reporter."

"And a damn fine one too. Too good, that's your problem."

"My job was at stake."

He gripped the brim of his fedora so tightly his knuckles were white. But his voice was carefully calm. "And so you sold my soul for your job. You betrayed me, Claire."

"*You* betrayed *me*, Joe." She wiped a tear away from her eye.

"When will you stop with the theatrics?"

"They're—" her voice hitched "—not. You betrayed me," she repeated in a small voice.

"Of all the selfish, childish—"

Claire's voice rose in panic. "We *were* children, Joe."

"But we certainly aren't any longer." He jammed his hat onto his head. She put a hand on his arm, but the gesture was futile.

"Please, Joe... Try to...try to understand. I—I wrote it *for you*."

He laughed in her face. "Save it, Claire. You wrote it for yourself, no one else. You all but admitted that back at my place."

She shook her head, curls bouncing wildly, and hated herself for the desperation she now felt.

But even she knew when to quit. Still, she played her last, best card. "I wanted to show people how good you were, how good you can be again...I did it to honor you and your talent. Maybe, maybe at first I did it for me, but now that's nothing compared to losing you."

"Oh, I'm sure it kills you to say that." Joe reached for the doorknob. "Save your pretty lines for your writing, not for me."

"Joe, you have to believe me." It came out strangled. Desperate. "Joe...Joe, running the article was a mistake. We both know it. Please...please... I—" She stopped abruptly, took a breath. "Nothing I say to you is going to change your mind about the article, is it?"

"No." Joe shook his head, the single word coming out a faint whisper, yet almost choking Claire with its pain. "No, *Miss DuPont*, I'm done with believing you. And by the way," he jerked open the door, "desperation doesn't look good on you. Goodbye." The door slammed shut.

"Goodbye," she whispered into the darkness, wishing it wasn't so. Wishing she could change everything and make things back the way they had been when they had first met. When it was simple and easy and oh so divine.

Claire traced a finger along the edge of the desk, wishing she could erase that look of hurt and sadness that flickered just beneath the surface of those once-so-warm hazel eyes. Wished she could take it all back. But she couldn't. And she wouldn't. So there it was.

Leaving the newspaper building out the back door, Claire returned to the residence on Geary Street and let herself in to the sunlit suite; her legs suddenly had no

strength and she sank onto the footstool. This suite had seemed so bright and full of beauty mere hours ago. Now it seemed like a prison.

AS JOE STEPPED ONTO THE sidewalk outside the front entrance of the *Chronicle* building, the gleam of metal caught his eye, and he spotted what looked like a necklace at the edge of the busy sidewalk.

He bent forward to pick it up and discovered it had come open. He frowned, separated the two halves, and found a tiny sliver of paper wedged inside. He fished it out with a finger and carefully unfolded it.

Done in pencil, the small sketch showed a music note, embellished with 'Joe: the melody of my heart' written across it in a bold, familiar slanting script.

Claire's handwriting. All those years ago when he'd first given her the necklace and she'd never said anything. He touched a fingertip gently to the words. What good would they do him, now? Too little, too late.

But surely he had to return the necklace to her. Somehow, though, he couldn't bring himself to.

♪

SATURDAY EVENING, CLAIRE STUDIED HER reflection in the beveled mirror of her dressing table.

She fiddled with the edge of the emerald-cut diamond earring she had been trying to put on, but somehow it kept jumping out of her hand. How could something so valuable that Henry had given her have no value for her ever since Joe had given her the Cracker Jack ring?

She'd just gotten a firm grip on the earring for the third time when the jangle of the telephone jarred her.

The earring fell with a clatter into the crystal dish as she dashed for the phone, her red chiffon dressing gown fluttering around her. Would it be Joe?

But even as she caught the phone on the third ring, she knew that would never

happen.

"Hello darling."

"Henry." The weight of the handset felt as heavy as the heart in her chest. But she forced herself to paste a smile on her face.

"Listen, I'm running a bit late. I'll be there at half-past. You wouldn't go without me?" His teasing manner, usually what she considered his best trait, now only made her sad.

"Of course not. Wouldn't miss it for the world."

After she hung up, she turned to the record player and adjusted the volume so that the syncopated rhythm was loud enough to drown out the doubts that had popped into her head. She sat down again at the dressing table, expertly applying mascara across her top row of lashes. She batted them at her reflection for a second, glad for the added illusion of confidence they created.

The tempo increased and before she realized what was happening, her foot was tapping along with the beat and a frisson of excitement coursed through her. She could at least allow herself to enjoy the music tonight, if not the company.

A FITTING END, JOE THOUGHT without satisfaction. In fact, as he precisely balanced his cigarette at the edge of the ashtray on the dresser so he could tie his bowtie, the last glow of rage toward Claire, the article, and their conversation that morning in the newsroom, waned into something like...sadness.

But suddenly, he was grateful. At least he had a gig tonight. Yes, she could do this to him, but he would always have his art, his music, his jazz, to keep him company, even if she never would keep him company again.

He drew in a sharp breath. That was it. He reached for his horn.

All the frustration, all the confusion and all the betrayal of Claire's article, found its home in the aimless melody Joe played. He closed his eyes, let the melody

take the lead, let himself wander through octaves, the music taking hold of his heart and stealing his breath, if only to serve as more inspiration for the next breath, the next note, the next piece of tune that had somehow snuck into his soul and caught him unaware.

Let himself get lost in it, get pulled under; seduced. There was no stopping it, he realized, no beginning and no real end, either. Claire's face flashed before his closed eyes. Best to give in to the undertow.

And so he let himself drown.

But that's when he could breathe at last. Because it was Claire who had actually, in her stubborn, sharp way, given him something more beautiful, more profound, than either of them could have realized in the moment she had first betrayed him, all those years ago.

Because inadvertently, with her barbed words, her barrage of questions and her barging into his apartment, he'd received the gift of healing. She had given him that thirst again, the thirst for music.

She hadn't meant the article as a lie, or deception. She'd been writing the truth—his, and hers.

HENRY'S IMPORTED MERCURY MONARCH GLIDED up to the curb just as Claire had begun to shiver in her too-thin satin wrap. He hopped out.

She watched as he strode around the shiny hood of the maroon coupe and opened the passenger door for her. But his boyish good looks with that wavy blond hair and those aquamarine eyes were no longer a source of delightful distraction and affianced pride.

She got into the car and shook her head; she and Henry were *not* engaged. She swallowed. At least not for another hour.

THE MURMUR OF SO MANY voices and the crush of the crowd put Claire's bad mood

in check as she and Henry walked through the doors of the theatre, the shirred hemline of her dress cascading in ripples of midnight-blue sequins and satin as she moved.

This was their engagement party, after all. She needed to be ecstatic. For the sake of the record company, if not for herself.

But the only thing she could get really excited about was the music. She closed her eyes and indulged. What was it about this kind of music that had that kind of effect on her?

She felt herself begin to sway. The crush of bodies, the murmur of voices, all fell away as she allowed herself to get caught up in the moment, the melody, the meter.

The jostle of people coming in behind her had her eyes fluttering open again. She saw that Henry had disappeared. Hastily, she made her way into the crowded room, her eyes adjusting to the mellow lighting, the lamps on each of the white cloth-covered tables throwing out pools of yellow on the seated couples.

Resolute, she kept walking. Through the haze of cigarette smoke, she finally made out Henry's silhouette on the far side of the room. He was leaning up against the bar, his white suit jacket immaculate, two drinks in hand.

When she reached him, she touched him lightly on the arm.

"There you are. Here." He handed her the martini. "Dry, just like you like it."

She hated her martinis dry, but took the drink without a word to him about it, this time.

"Come on, Claire." Henry's hand moved to the bare skin of her low-backed evening gown. She wished it was Joe's touch. "Let's go find our table."

Henry steered her to a table much too far away. Claire strained to see the musicians onstage.

She tapped a slim manicured finger in time with the beat, a small smile playing at her lips.

"Glad you're enjoying yourself." Henry

reached out to take her hand across the table.

But Claire pulled away.

The music changed tempo to a slow number. Anxious Henry might suspect something, Claire changed tactics. "Oh, let's dance, Henry."

"You don't need to ask me twice." Henry grinned as he led the way to the parquet dance floor.

She let him put his arms around her. In keeping with the façade, she laid her head on his shoulder. She could feel his warm breath on her cheek, but she had never felt colder inside when she saw it was Joe playing onstage.

At once, a memory rose unbidden to the surface of her mind. One she hadn't recalled in years. Six, to be precise. In fact, she had almost fooled herself into forgetting it had ever existed...

The scent of her gardenia corsage had mingled with the scent of his clove cigarette and had clung heavy and rich to the slippery silk of her dress and the rough folds of his wool suit jacket. He was so young. She was so naïve.

It had been their senior prom, hers and Joe's. Joe had asked her, and in her foolish heart, she had thought she'd loved him. Thought she had *understood* that word and all its nuances.

But she hadn't. And she didn't. Not even now. Her lips twisted into a wry smile, yet she went right on pretending she was in his arms. Even now. No, she corrected herself—*especially* now.

But the music didn't let her stay sorry for herself long because it changed tempo again, into a fast, snappy swing tune.

"I'm sure you remember this one." Henry spun her out and dipped her back, and she remembered the reason why she'd let herself think she could be happy with him, flimsy though the reason was— the man danced like a dream.

Despite herself, she felt a laugh bubble up within her. Henry needed no more encouragement. He lifted her up into the air only to swoop her down again as they moved in perfect time to the song.

Chapter Six

JOE ADJUSTED HIS BOWTIE AND immediately wished he hadn't worn it onstage tonight. It always interfered with his playing. But it was far too late for regrets now—this gig required a tux.

He settled onto the chair in amongst the other band members as they arranged themselves just before curtain.

And then the curtain rose and the show began.

As Joe's eyes adjusted to the stage lights, and the music spilled from his horn, he felt himself begin to relax.

He hadn't thought he could do this again. Yet despite everything, here he was. He looked out into the crowd; couples everywhere—at tables, and on the dance floor—were smiling, laughing, having a good time.

And it was partly due to him. He felt a chink of his soul fall back into place. He'd missed this; oh, he really had. If it hadn't been for Claire coming into The Blue Mirror on Monday evening, and if she hadn't played that record in his apartment on Wednesday morning, then he might not have ended up on this stage tonight. And if he ever saw her again—his heart twisted at the thought—he would thank her.

A swirl of skirts caught his attention. He squinted, darting his eyes away from the music and trying to make out the outline of the woman.

He missed his cue as he realized who he was looking at. Claire. In the arms of Henry, no doubt.

Why had no one told him that this was *her* engagement party? He shook his head. Realizing his mistake too late, Joe tried to get back on rhythm, but as the instrumental soloist for the interlude, it became all too obvious his timing was off.

So he deliberately paused, the silence so much louder than the melody.

Just as one of his band mates raised his instrument to cover for Joe's mistake, Joe started playing again. Shame washed through him. What had he been thinking, letting himself get distracted by her?

Anger made his jaw tighten and his tone off. But he kept playing.

He watched the pair as he played. Anger softened to admiration. They certainly danced well together.

He swallowed, pulled his eyes back to the page and increased the tempo. Did she even know who was playing?

But that didn't matter now. What mattered was that he was right there in that bright, raucous melody, right smack in the middle of the notes.

Because in that moment, he belonged to himself once more, to the music, to his own heart and soul.

BUT WHEN JOE GOT HOME a little after one a.m., he was far from happy.

The silence and darkness seemed to

hide Claire's silhouette. Her perfume seemed to cling to every air particle, though he made sure he'd opened a window.

He tossed his fedora at the coat rack. It missed and fell onto the floor. He muttered an oath and went to pick it up. Brushed it off.

Then he tugged at his bowtie until it finally came loose. He gasped his relief.

Why hadn't he gone after her? Accosted her and Henry—no. Of course it wasn't his right to do anything like that. Perhaps the more important question was, why did he think it was?

He scrubbed a hand across his chin, blinked and grabbed a glass of water from the kitchen. He grimaced. He needed a drink. No he didn't. He wasn't going to drown this particular sorrow in anything less than pure honesty.

Was he going to let himself get caught again? He stared out into the night. And for what? For nothing, that's what.

He tightened his fingers around the window ledge. He just had to let her go.

Chapter Seven

CLAIRE GNAWED ON THE INSIDE of her bottom lip as guilt gnawed at her. Henry helped her on with her wrap in the foyer of the theatre, then kissed her neck.

"Do you have to be so perfect all the time?" Claire snapped.

"Gee whiz, someone's in a bad mood tonight." Henry continued kissing her neck. "But I know something that'll make you feel better." He slid his hands around her waist.

"Lay off it, Henry." She shrugged free of him and stepped out onto the sidewalk.

"All right, all right. I'll go get the car."

He gave her a sideways look as she got in and he put the Monarch into gear. "I'm not perfect, you know."

"I'm sorry I snapped at you." She sighed. "Oh, let's drive around for a little while.”

They pulled away from the now-darkened theatre, the silence stretching between them.

“Why are you doing this, Henry?”

Henry put an arm around her and steered the car with the other. “How do you mean?”

“You know what’s going on with the record company. You know everything that’s happened, but—”

“But business is business. It’s a promise I made to your father.”

“Well, easy for you to say. He loves you and hates me.”

“I wouldn’t say he hates you, Claire. Say, why are we talking about such an unhappy topic when we should be the toast of the town?”

Claire wriggled the rock on her finger. “I don’t know if I can make a toast with my hand so weighed down.” Somehow, though, it didn’t sound like a joke when she said it out loud.

Sure enough, Henry frowned. As the

car cruised along, Claire caught a glimpse of the ocean. Though Claire stared at the water, she couldn't help but see the expression on Joe's face when she'd seen him on the bridge.

She twisted the ring round and round on her finger, as if it was somehow choking the life out of her. Well, maybe it was.

And suddenly, she'd had enough.

More than enough, in fact. Enough of the pain that she'd caused not only herself but also everyone around her. Enough to last a lifetime. She couldn't keep doing this, couldn't keep holding herself back and hoping it was the right thing to do when she'd known all along it was beyond wrong.

She couldn't lie to herself any longer. Not when Joe's face flashed through her mind again, or when the feel of his arm around her at the movie theatre had felt so right, while the weight of Henry's arm around her made her feel so off-balance, like she was drowning instead of flying.

And oh, how Joe made her heart soar.

And sore. She frowned, seeing him on stage, over and over again. Imagining his expression, and his point of view, as he read her article.

She'd ruined everything for him, for them, with that article and with her actions. And she had to make it up to him. For him. Because she saw now that everything had been her fault—entirely.

"Stop the car, Henry."

Henry looked at her.

"Just stop the car. Please."

"Sure, sure." Henry pulled up along Baker Beach. Claire could hear the pounding of the waves as they crashed against the shoreline. She got out before she could change her mind.

"Where are you going, Claire? It's past midnight."

"I know." She slammed the door behind her.

"Claire, wait." Henry put the coupe into first, switched off the engine, got out and followed her across the sandy expanse. The lights of the cityscape danced on the

water like so many pinwheels at the fair.

Claire kept walking. "No, I've done enough waiting to last a lifetime." She slid the ring off her finger and grasped it in her fist, the weightiness of the decision not lost on her. To say no and lose Daddy's approval forever, or to say yes and stay trapped forever?

Well, perhaps that was a bit dramatic, but dramatic was how she felt. She tossed her head and inhaled the briny air, welcoming the cool sting of the Pacific as she walked farther down the beach, away from Henry, wondering if it'd be easiest to simply throw the ring into the ocean.

She glanced over her shoulder and saw Henry trailing behind, the wind and the sand doing their best to obscure his efforts to come toward her.

"Henry." Her voice came out a whisper as he approached her. She extended her hand, the ring glittering in the moonlight as it lay on her palm. "I can't marry you."

He met her gaze. "I know. Known it all along."

Claire frowned.

"You're not as coy and secretive as you convince yourself you are, you know." Henry shoved his hands in his trouser pockets.

Claire felt her shoulders tense, then relax. "So you were prepared—"

"—To go through with it, yes."

"You're far too gallant for your own good, you know that?"

"So I've been told." He took the ring from her.

"But Golden Gate Records...?"

"I'm sure with my new position there, and with the extra capital, things will be looking up soon. But don't worry about that; now you're free," he said softly.

She exhaled. "Yes. I guess I value my freedom."

"Somehow I don't think that's quite all you value."

She shot him a sideways look. "Were you always this smart?"

"Ouch." He chuckled good-naturedly. "I did go to Harvard, you know."

"Touché. Well, then, I guess this is goodbye."

"Guess so." His lips lifted in a sad half-smile.

There was a beat of silence.

They looked at each other, there on the beach, in the moonlight, and she realized, with all the force of the waves beating on the shoreline, that he'd shown her the best thing that he possibly could. He had cared about her, in his own bumbling way. He had. Her eyes brimmed for a second.

Her hand, of its own volition, crept up to the tiny heart locket she wore around her neck and her fingers fumbled for the familiar shape.

But it wasn't there. Panic, illogical and intrusive, set in. How could she have lost it? She patted her neck. No, it wasn't tangled up in anything. She scanned the ground; felt around in her purse. Nothing.

"Lose something?"

For some reason, she blushed. Tried to shrug it off. "Nothing of importance." But her heart beat faster. If she'd lost it, she'd never forgive herself.

"You, uh, need a ride? Because walking all the way back to your place with sand in your shoes doesn't sound too comfortable."

She leaned in and kissed him on the cheek. "Thank you, Henry."

"Well, it's only what any fellow with half a brain would do." He shrugged as he tugged open the passenger door for her.

"No, not that. Although I do appreciate the lift. Thank you—" her voice broke "—for showing me I *am* lovable."

Chapter Eight

DESPITE THE WARM GLOW OF the street-lights, Claire shivered as she stood on the wet sidewalk outside The Blue Mirror Club the next evening, her ungloved palm pressed against the cold surface of the windowpane.

But the jazz that crept through the mist, like the raindrops that had begun to fall, brought her a measure or two of peace; she sighed as she watched him. Joe certainly knew how to play. But she'd played him. Played him good.

She looked through the window of the club again, the figures haloed against the bright stage lights, their images blurring and running from the rain on the windowpane.

Or was it from her tears?

She blinked and looked away, yet her

ears strained to catch the tiniest trail of melody, her blood humming with unsung desire as she watched Joe put the horn to his lips, wishing it was her.

She'd been such a fool. She knew she couldn't lie to herself any longer. That was why she'd come back here, to look in the window as they rehearsed, searching for something she hadn't realized she'd already lost—until now.

Her heart.

She'd only been under an illusion that she had any control or say in the matter. She couldn't choose who she gave her heart to; her heart had chosen for her all those years ago.

She stared unblinking at her reflection and realized exactly what she needed to do. She checked her purse. Yes, she had enough paper to write Joe a letter; maybe if he knew she'd gotten fired for writing the article...

She turned on her heel and descended the steps, headed toward the café a few doors down, that saxophone melody still

playing in her head.

NICK HAD JUST DISMISSED THE ensemble for a break. Joe put his sax back into its case and clamped his jaw together so hard the cigarette nearly snapped in half as he caught a glimpse of a retreating yet familiar form framed by the window.

No. He threw down the cigarette and crushed the broken end. He wasn't going to let himself get away with being a coward or a fool any longer. But he certainly wasn't going to let Miss Claire DuPont get the best of him. He'd already given her his worst.

So he left the club and followed her down the sidewalk, watching her hips sway side to side.

"Damn it." The woman was breathtaking. That was the problem. No more oxygen to the brain. He smiled wryly. He couldn't afford to let himself get distracted by her, especially not tonight. He couldn't goof his return to the jazz scene—not with Nick's good name, or his own reputation, hanging in the balance.

Yet he called after her. But his voice was drowned out by the roar of a bus speeding by. Or at least that's what he thought. Maybe she had simply chosen to ignore him. That was the more likely reason.

Damn the rehearsal. It could wait a minute. His love life couldn't wait one moment more.

♫

THE FINE MIST THAT CLUNG to Claire's skin as her heels clicked against the concrete did nothing to cool the glowing embers of her desire as her thoughts again turned to Joe.

The way he moved. The way he smelled. That laugh. Those eyes. That smile.

Joe was utterly and exactly who she'd been looking for her whole life. Just exactly that. In every detail. And in every way.

Footsteps behind her made her quicken her pace and hunch her shoulders against the slow increase in precipitation.

"Need an umbrella?" Joe's rich timbre shot through her like a stiff drink. Straight to the marrow—into every cell of her being.

She whipped her head around, her damp curls clinging to her cheek even as he came up beside her. Her heart almost leapt out of her chest.

He smiled, and even in the dark broken only by the amber glow of streetlamps against darker pavement, she knew every crease and angle and slant that his lips would be making in order to form that smile. That little upturn of the corners of his mouth that made everything all right again. Made her forgive him for every-thing. Forever.

Claire simply nodded. Their shoulders bumped briefly as he switched the um-brella to his right hand and offered her his arm.

He'd used that bergamot aftershave

again. Oh God. Claire wished for a hand-kerchief but hers lay crumpled at the bottom of her handbag. So she squeezed her eyes shut for a second instead. Opening them once more, she discovered his hazel gaze looking into her own.

Oh no. No. No. No. Not this again. She couldn't stand it. Oh, how she longed to throw herself into that sweet abyss. Drown in all these deep longings and pools of desire. She blinked, trying to break his gaze. But she couldn't. Just like she couldn't that first time she'd met him all those years ago. It was as if they'd never been apart. As if the passage of time had never happened, but instead hung, suspended, from the very fibers of their souls.

Oh, why couldn't this have been in another place, another time? Was he supposed to think they could just—oh, damn her fears and insecurities all to hell.

In one swift movement, she stepped in close, inhaling the familiar intoxication of his scent and her desire. And she dove in.

Straight down to the bottom. Crushed her lips against his. That electric buzz jolted through her system, pouring through every crack and crevice and hidden pathway of her body, her heart, her soul.

She felt his solidness, his strength, as he brought a hand up to her face, pressed it against her damp hair and the back of her head, drawing her even nearer. The bitter acidity of his last cigarette tasted as sweet as honey; the tang of his peppermint breath-mint more delicious than chocolate mousse. Oh God. She felt a moan escape her lips even as she pressed closer, and closer still, against him.

It had been too long. Much, much too long. Claire felt his tongue slide out, a question mark to her declarative sentence, and opened her mouth in answer.

Reaching up, she felt the scrape of his stubble against her fingertips before her fingers moved on and wove themselves of their own accord into his thick brown hair, slightly stiff from the Brylcreem he'd applied earlier this evening.

Her fingers, undeterred, burrowed in anyway, and she felt his arms tighten around her in response. The umbrella fell with a clatter onto the sidewalk.

His tongue explored the ridges of her teeth and the dark interior of her mouth with the authority of one very familiar with the territory—the sweep of moist flesh against moist flesh an aphrodisiac all its own. She felt herself melting against him almost against her own will.

His hand slid down to stroke the curve of her neck, his thumb moving in that ached-for back and forth motion he knew she loved. She moaned again in surprised pleasure and felt tears spring to her eyes. How could *he* remember all about such a tiny detail when *she'd* forgotten all about his heart? Her eyelids trembled, then flew open.

Claire tore herself away from him, gasping. "I-I need to—" She choked back a sob. "—explain."

She took a deep breath, and rushed on before he could say or do anything. "I was jealous of the way you played that saxophone so well, *so* well, and everyone in band class had such admiration for you and I couldn't play clarinet to save my life. Yet Daddy was the head of Golden Gate Records, so I felt that I should be this wonderful musical talent of the family to, I don't know, carry on the family legacy or some such nonsense. But I didn't, I couldn't. I *loved* jazz so, but I couldn't play it at all. I found I was good with words and that made me ashamed and angry with myself because I thought I should be someone else—that I should be a musician instead, to get Daddy to finally *notice* me, because oh, he spent every last waking hour, it seemed, with those jazz musicians, wining and dining them and I, his own daughter," her fists tightened at her sides, "came in second place to that. Sometimes even third." Her laugh was brittle. "I was such a failure, I felt like I'd failed him. Because I couldn't be a musician. I could only be who I was and that...that *hurt*."

She stared down the hill, out to the bay. "And so I thought that if I brought you home to Daddy that night, I could at least accomplish that much by giving him another artist to produce, maybe make him proud of me. Or at least thank me. But that did not go as planned either." She moved her gaze back to him. "And you know what else? The truth is, I still really *do* love jazz—I just thought I had to punish myself by rejecting it because of what I'd done to you, to us."

"Oh, darling," Joe murmured. He held up the locket. She watched a raindrop wink off the shiny surface.

She hardly dared breathe as his cold fingers brushed her bare skin as he refastened the necklace around her neck.

He touched a fingertip to the locket, now nestled against her collarbone, then traced the outline of her chin. "You know what your name means, don't you, Claire?"

She didn't reply; simply looked at him, her eyes round.

His voice roughened, got deeper. "Clear. It means clear." He took a step closer to her. "And it's very clear to me..." He cupped her face with his long fingers. "That I love you. And I forgive you."

She uttered not a sound but reached up and splayed her perfectly manicured fingers against the rugged disarray of his wind-buffeted hair, smoothing it down.

"Claire, to be honest, after I started playing—and practicing—regularly again, it just washed away everything: the need to prove anything to you or anyone else, because what mattered was how I saw myself. The joy, the pure joy of playing again, cleared out all those other false notes of anger and jealousy and pettiness and brought me to life again. And that's when I got it. Because if you hadn't been badgering me about that damn article, then I never would've picked up my horn again. So I have you to thank for the whole thing."

"I got fired for writing the article." She paused. "But that doesn't matter right now—I can find another writing gig. Oh, Joe. I love you and I forgive you, too. And I'm so sorry. For...everything. All that hurt and pain I caused you, and myself."

She twisted her lace handkerchief.

"I know, Claire." He gave her arm a gentle squeeze. But his gaze was firm. Direct. She shivered.

He traced a finger up her forearm. "Let's not go back there again, hmmmm?" he murmured, his hand slipping down the sleek slope of her back. "Not tonight. There will be no ghosts of our pasts tonight. Tonight is for us. As we are. Right here, right now. Living. Breathing. Alive."

He began whistling, tuneless at first but a melody began to take shape after a moment, and before he could stop himself, he began to sing.

You know you want me
And I want you to see
How good we can be
Just you and me

Claire grinned, and started to hum along with his words.

Cuz it's something to be celebrated
Not carefully calculated
I think I'm infatuated—with life; with love
Oh! Ain't it a grand thing?
Just you and me

He pulled her into his arms and, wordless and breathless, she let him.

"I didn't know you could sing, Joe."

"I can't. But for you, well, I took the chance."

Claire smiled and sighed with happiness as they danced cheek-to-cheek there on that rainy sidewalk.

Acknowledgments

Heather Osborne – editor, who helped me smooth out the story

Shannon Page – copyeditor, who had a great eye for detail, especially about San Francisco

Angela Waters – graphic designer, who gave me a beautiful and classy cover for the story

Lori Saigeon – writer friend and beta reader, who graciously read over my manuscript with a fresh set of eyes

SRW writing group – who helped me keep up my writer morale

Fancy
Footwork
A Novella
Jessica Eissfeldt

Fancy Footwork

A Novella

The Sweethearts & Jazz Nights Series of Sweet Historical Romance

Jessica Eissfeldt

Chapter One

AFTER VIOLET SWANSON GLANCED OVER her shoulder just to make sure no one was looking, she gave a little skip. She grinned to herself, her belted green cotton dress swishing around her legs. She was here at last in the City by the Bay. She'd done it—escaped Hollywood and bought the dance studio of her dreams. Never mind that it was in need of more than a little fixing up. How hard could that be?

She rounded the corner of Fillmore Street and saw the faint blue neon glow of a sign in the distance: The Blue Mirror Club. Just where her roommate Molly said it'd be.

She quickened her pace as the drizzle increased. She'd meant to buy an umbrella. She shrugged. A little water never hurt anyone.

The doorman eyed her as the strains of a big band song began to play. "In or out, miss?"

Violet stopped all at once. Could she show her face in a jazz club? But no one would recognize her here. This wasn't L.A. She held her breath, then let it out slowly.

Violet bit her lip. "...In." She made a move toward the door, but the doorman moved an arm across the entrance. "That'll be a nickel."

A laughing couple brushed past her spot on the sidewalk, caught up in a swirl of rustling silk and Chanel.

Violet reached for her rather rumpled coin purse and undid the clasp. But stray cookie crumbs and a slightly crushed package of Juicy Fruit were probably not something this fellow would accept in place of change—nor was her dog-eared Dashiell Hammett novel.

Rats! She'd forgotten her money on top of the breadbox *again*. And Molly was already inside waiting for her.

"Keep the change, Eddie."

Violet glanced behind her to see an immaculately dressed young woman toss a quarter at the doorman, who caught the coin with practiced ease. "That's for both me and the gal in front of me."

The young woman linked her arm with Violet's, and pulled her along into the crowded foyer.

Violet's eyes widened. "Listen, I don't mean to sound ungrateful or anything, but what did you do that for?"

"'Cuz you looked a little friendless," the young woman with the direct blue gaze said. "You reminded me a bit of myself, once upon a time," she continued, her blonde curled coif completely frizz-free. Violet attempted to flatten her Bettie Page bangs more smoothly to her forehead.

"And this place, well..." The woman shrugged a slim shoulder clad in a tailored royal blue peplum jacket. "...you'll see for yourself. Now, I'm off to find my sax player."

And before Violet could reply, the woman had gone, leaving only the lingering scent of her powdery lilac perfume behind.

Violet took a deep breath and surveyed the crush of happy, laughing people.

She waved as she spotted Molly and made a beeline for her table across the dance floor.

The strains of *It Might As Well Be Spring* pulled her across the floor, but the bright red of one woman's dress brought to mind a very different place...

The tang of ripe cherries, the flutter of summer-green leaves high above in the old cottonwood tree, her hands sticky with melting ice cream, and the gilded sound of her own laughter as she'd danced for the very first time with Gran teaching her every step—

"Oh!" Violet hadn't known her eyes had closed until they flew back open as someone bumped into her and she nearly tripped. She quickly made her way to the edge of the dance floor and Molly's table.

"Glad you found the place." Molly smiled. "All the hills make this city a bit tricky to navigate, especially in your first week here."

Violet nodded and sank into a chair.

"Say," Molly dug through her purse, "do you have a cigarette? I'm fresh out."

"'Fraid not. Piece of Juicy Fruit?" Violet offered the gum in Molly's direction.

Her eyes brightened. "I didn't know they'd started making that again."

"A few months ago, now that rationing's ended. Don't you love the new yellow packaging? I went out and bought six packs—it's my favorite gum."

Molly popped a piece into her mouth, then touched up her lipstick. "Thanks! You're a star."

Not anymore. But she'd almost been, once. Violet started to gnaw on her bottom lip, then caught herself. She'd smear her favorite lipstick if she did that.

Molly leaned forward. "So, did you go by the studio today?"

"It was the first thing I did this morning. Oh, Molly, I didn't expect it to be in such bad shape. The plaster's cracking and some floorboards are rotting. I think the roof's leaking, too. Gran polished that floor every night after her classes." Violet studied her nails. "I remember the first summer I came out to San Francisco to visit Gran and took the train all by myself. We had the best time. I stayed up 'til midnight. We fed the seagulls. And she taught me so many dance steps." Violet sighed. "There was so much music, so much laughter, every night at the studio...I felt like I could do anything, be anyone. I can't just let it go to pieces—but it's mine now, and I'm going to do whatever it takes to get it up and running again."

"Well, you certainly got a great deal on it," Molly said.

"I bought it when I was still in L.A. I was so lucky, too, because I heard that some big fancy corporation—Golden Gate Records—wanted to buy the property. But I beat them to it! Can you imagine that?"

♬

HENRY PARKER TOOK A SIP of his martini at the bar of The Blue Mirror Club, and nearly choked on it as he noticed a young woman in a green dress almost fall by the edge of the dance floor. But before he could make his way over to help her, she had caught her balance and crossed the dance floor.

Henry took another sip of his drink as his eyes lingered on her for a moment longer.

As the jazz melody washed over him, he loosened his tie a bit further and his shoulders relaxed. He'd come here to escape from the office downtown. Though he hated to admit it, things at Golden Gate Records had begun to wear on him, despite his new promotion.

Truth was, he'd rather be dancing than be behind his desk. At least his engagement to Claire, the CEO's daughter, was ancient history now. Henry'd even managed a civil hello to Claire, whom he'd

seen earlier in the evening, dancing with her now-fiancé, saxophonist Joe Lucitano.

He wished them all the best, he really did. Funny how this city seemed more like a small town sometimes.

Henry drained his martini glass and sighed. He supposed he should get an early morning in at work so he could finalize the paperwork for the buyout of that run-down property next door to Golden Gate Records. But what he really wanted was to spend his time working on his idea for a talent show.

But, then again, doing up the paperwork and seeing through the property buyout would give him enough reason and time to pitch his talent show idea to DuPont at that big meeting. He might want to leave his job, but he wasn't about to do something as irresponsible as walking away from it.

His fingers danced along the stem of the empty martini glass in time to the melody. He threw another look at the woman in the green dress, who watched her friend get led out onto the floor. The woman in the green dress now sat alone at her table. Henry got up from the bar. He knew he'd like to dance. And maybe she would, too.

He approached her table and cleared his throat. "Excuse me."

The young woman twisted in her seat and looked up at him. Henry blinked, and felt himself take an involuntary step backward. Had he seen her somewhere before? Was she from around here?

The young lady looked like spring—with her emerald green dress, her glossy black hair, her pink lipstick, and her expressive green eyes.

No, he reminded himself, he was just looking to dance, not for romance. He didn't have the time.

"Care to dance?"

"Dance?" The young woman's eyes widened and darted away from Henry with what looked like fear.

She opened, then closed her mouth.

Henry felt his gut tighten. "Say, I didn't mean—"

She jumped up and darted past Henry.

"—to upset you?" He watched as she nearly ran to the powder room.

"...I'll just go, then..." Henry said to her retreating back. Her posture, Henry noticed as he watched her go, was perfect.

HENRY STRODE ALONG UNION SQUARE on Monday morning, his suit jacket tossed over one shoulder. The early March sunshine was pleasant enough that he'd taken off his fedora and tucked it under his arm, and whistled tunelessly to himself.

But his tuneless whistling soon faded, and he winced. He hoped he hadn't upset that gal in the green dress too much Thursday night. He shook his head at himself. He tended to misread women— even mixing up their drink preferences. Ironic, considering he'd always been such a good rule-follower.

He crossed the street and headed toward Golden Gate Records. But the gleam of a freshly washed, cracked plate-glass storefront window caught his eye.

That dance studio window hadn't been clean like that last week...

He frowned. He hadn't thought this building had been occupied since before the war... Had someone just moved in?

On impulse, he stopped in the middle of the sidewalk, then turned and walked up to the studio door and pushed. It stuck slightly, but a small bell tinkled overhead as it opened at last.

But no one came to greet him. In fact, he could hear nothing but the ticking of a clock hanging on the wall above his head.

Henry was about to go when he heard the muffled sound of footsteps in the next room, which must, he surmised, be the studio proper. He poked his head through the half-open door and was about to speak, but snapped his mouth shut when he saw it was the woman from the other night. Crying.

He was about to ask her if she was all right, but the sudden blare of a Gershwin number drowned out the sound of his voice.

He watched, motionless, as the young woman stepped out onto the floor in her stocking feet, sunshine filtering in through the cracked window facing the street. But she wasn't dancing. She simply stood there, eyes closed, head thrown back, as a tear slipped down her face and the crash of cymbals and the blare of trumpets and saxophones filled the air around her.

Henry's chest tightened. He couldn't let a lovely young lady cry over jazz. He saw her eyelids tremble, and all at once, he wanted nothing more than to see her eyes alight, with laughter tumbling from her lips. He took a step forward and a floorboard creaked under his weight, jarring him out of himself.

What was he doing? Henry didn't know the woman and he had no business intruding. Besides, the young lady, it seemed, wanted to be left alone.

He turned and left, suddenly wishing he could forget that this property was the run-down place DuPont wanted him to buy out for record storage space.

Chapter Two

VIOLET, WEARING BLUE OVERALLS AND with her hair tied up in a red paisley kerchief, perched on a stepladder in the middle of the studio Tuesday afternoon.

She rubbed her nose with the hand not holding the paintbrush as she dipped the brush back into the paint can. This bright color had been Gran's favorite, and then Violet could use those extra cans she'd found lying around to finish up the hall-way.

She hummed an aimless tune to herself as she continued to paint the ceiling. Perhaps if she had time this evening, she'd go into The Blue Mirror to see if she could catch a glimpse of crooner Nick Hart. Not that she had anything but a schoolgirl crush on him.

She shook her head at herself. She

didn't quite know why she'd been silly and run away from that blond man on Thursday evening. He had been rather handsome, after all... But she hadn't thought anyone would recognize her in this town. Then again, maybe he hadn't. Maybe he'd just wanted to dance?

Her mind drifted back to *Dancing At Midnight*. She couldn't quite believe things had turned out this way. But she was making the best of it, wasn't she? She dipped the brush in the can again and leaned forward.

"You missed a spot."

Violet jumped, nearly knocking over the half-full paint can in the process. Then she almost lost her balance as she twisted around on the ladder and saw it was the blond fellow from The Blue Mirror Club.

"Where?" She frowned as he pointed at the tiny patch that she'd been struggling all afternoon to reach. But she didn't tell him that.

The man raised his hands. "I meant no offense. Only trying to help." He pointed again. "Just above the... Here." He stepped forward and rolled up his shirtsleeves. "May I?"

Violet gave him a long look before she surrendered the paintbrush and stepped off the ladder.

She watched him reach up and easily dab the tiny patch on the ceiling. Somehow, him coming into her studio like this, unannounced and trying to help made her feel like she couldn't do things on her own. Made her feel like she had to be rescued when she had a plan already, thank you very much. She could see it through herself. He stepped off the ladder and looked around as she resumed her perch.

"See?" Violet said. "It's amazing what a fresh coat of paint can—" A chunk of ceiling plaster landed on the floor between them. The man raised his eyebrows.

"I assume you're not the handyman I called to fix the roof leak."

He chuckled. "Oh, what gave it away?"

"The briefcase, for one. You're the fellow from the other night." Violet couldn't help but notice his broad shoulders as he neatly placed the brush on the paint tray.

"And you're the gal who didn't dance with me."

Violet straightened her posture, hoping for an air of authority despite her paint-spattered overalls and dusty kerchief. "That's right. What can I help you with?"

"I think you're going to be the one helping me out. Well, actually, Golden Gate Records."

Violet adjusted the knot on her kerchief. "How do you figure?"

He shoved his hands in his pockets. "Because we'd like to take this studio off your hands."

Violet laughed. "I bought this, fair and square. It was my grandma's and now it's mine. It might be a mess, but it's my mess."

"Well, I'm sorry." And for a second, he truly did look it. "You and your grandmother must have been close. But business is business. Golden Gate Records is expanding its warehouse space and needs the additional area for record storage. We're prepared to give you $5,000. Which is quite generous, considering the condition of the place."

Violet frowned. "I'm not going to take your fancy corporation money, Mr.—"

"Parker. It's Henry Parker. And you're Miss Violet Swanson."

Violet turned pale. "H-how do you know?"

"It says right here on the property title." He pulled out a piece of paper from his briefcase, then glanced up, studying her. "Say, the other night, I thought you looked familiar. Do I know you from somewhere besides The Blue Mirror?"

Violet bit her lip and wiped her sweaty palms on her overalls. "I-I'm sure you're mistaken about that, Mr. Parker. But don't think you can just change the subject." She crossed her arms and the ladder wobbled. "Because I'm not selling at any price."

♫

Bᴀᴄᴋ ɪɴ ᴛʜᴇ ᴏꜰꜰɪᴄᴇ ᴛʜᴀᴛ afternoon, Henry couldn't help but recall Miss Swanson's stubborn expression during their encounter earlier or her tearstained face from a few days ago.

He set his mug of coffee down on the ink blotter and rubbed the back of his neck. He picked up his pen and stared down at the buyout paperwork. He'd read the same sentence at least five times. It didn't help that his eyes kept drifting to the phonograph in the corner as the last rays of late afternoon sunshine glinted off its polished surface. Or that his mind kept drifting to new dance steps he'd invented.

Well, at least he'd accomplished something today and sent off that ad he'd written to the *Chronicle* for some help with his office work. Then he'd have more time to work on writing up his pitch for the meeting and sorting out all this buyout paperwork. He needed this buyout to happen. Otherwise DuPont wouldn't look favourably upon his talent show idea.

He was just about to sign the page he held when Dean, Nick Hart's manager and head of distribution at Golden Gate Records, leaned around the doorframe.

"Henry, you got a minute?"

For Dean, you'd better always have a minute. "Sure, Dean. What'd'ya need?"

"Those crates of records that just came back from the radio station—I need you to take care of them after work."

Henry held back a sigh. "Of course. I'll do it right after I finish up here."

"Good." Dean eyed him. "You *know* how I feel about all those jukeboxes everywhere." He flicked ash off his cigarette. "No one appreciates live musicians any more." He gave Henry a curt nod as he left.

♫

HAVING FINISHED HER PAINTING FOR the day, Violet locked the door of the studio behind her as the early evening shadows began lengthening.

Yes, she thought as she glanced around at the fog beginning to gather, this would be a perfect night to start reading that new crime novel she'd bought...

She turned right, about to pass the alley between Golden Gate Records and her studio, when a slight movement in the shadows caught her eye. What was that?

She gave a little shriek as she felt something butt up against her leg, almost sending her sprawling headlong onto the sidewalk. She caught herself just in time by clutching a lamppost.

Only then did she look down to see a lanky Siamese cat blinking up at her from amid the puddles.

"Cat," Violet put her hands on her hips but a smile tugged at her lips, "are you sure you're not in league with Mr. Parker, tripping me up like that?"

The cat rubbed against her leg and she could feel it purring. Violet broke into a grin and bent down to pet it, but before she could, it slunk around the corner and into the alley.

Violet moved to follow, the click of her heels loud on the pavement as her eyes darted into the twilight.

She gasped. There in the alley, blending in with the fading daylight, stood a shadowy figure. When she peered around the corner of the building to make sure, her heart beat a little faster. She pressed her back up against the brick wall, a small frisson of excitement coursing through her. This was straight out of a Dashiell Hammett novel! She reached up to tug the brim of her fedora lower before she remembered she wasn't wearing one.

She held her breath as she crept closer, and watched a tall—quite handsome, she noticed—man pop open the tailgate of a truck. Wait. That was Mr. Parker!

Was he...stealing something? No. That couldn't be. She shook her head. That was the product of reading too much pulp fiction.

But as she watched him unload crates with the words Golden Gate Records stencilled onto them, she became sure of one thing—that he was up to something.

And there was no room for doubt when Mr. Parker plucked up the first few records on the pile, slipped them out of their cases, and broke them in half.

"STOP! I'LL CALL THE POLICE!" A woman's voice echoed down the alley toward Henry.

Henry swore under his breath. From under the brim of his fedora, he watched the figure of a woman emerge out of the shadows.

Miss Swanson? He watched her as she bit her lip, then brushed some dust off her overalls and strode up to him. "Do you make it a habit of hanging around back alleys, Mr. Parker?"

Henry eyed her. "I could ask you the same thing."

"Yes, well, you could."

"All right, I will."

"You will what?" Miss Swanson lifted her chin.

"Ask you what you're doing here."

"I was following a cat."

"And I was following orders."

"Illegal orders."

"What I'm doing isn't illegal, Miss Swanson."

She planted her hands on her hips. "Prove it."

"I don't have to prove anything." He held up his hands.

"Oh no?" Miss Swanson gave him a long look before she picked up the cat, spun on her heel and walked away.

VIOLET'S MIND WAS STILL WHIRLING when she woke up the next morning. She felt slightly nauseous as a wave of helplessness surged through her: the buyout. What if Mr. Parker took the studio away from her even though she'd already refused?

What could she do to make sure that didn't happen? She wasn't going to do nothing, that was certain. She'd put al-

most every penny she had saved into buying that studio and now needed to use the rest for repairs. Violet grabbed her flowered dressing gown off its hook in the closet and tightened its belt around her trim waist as she yawned and then headed into the kitchen.

"Morning, Violet."

"You're entirely too perky in the mornings, you know, Molly," Violet grumbled, then immediately regretted it. This Henry Parker fellow was already bringing out the worst in her. She worried her bottom lip with her teeth.

Fortunately, Molly just laughed and went back to the crossword she was working on in between bites of toast. "It's nearly noon."

"Says the gal with her hair in rollers and cold cream still on."

Molly shrugged. "My getting up so late might have something to do with the fact that the alley cat you decided to rescue kept me up half the night with his prowling around the kitchen." Molly fanned herself absently. "It's been so warm I've had to keep that window open. He probably thought he could escape out it."

Just then, the cat in question hopped up onto the table and plopped down in the center of it.

Violet grabbed up her favorite blue Fire King mug just before Mr. Mischievous could knock it to the floor, and made herself some tea.

"Jeepers! Did you hear about this?" Molly held up the *San Francisco Chronicle* and began reading. "Mr. Frank Wallace, who directed the smash hit *Dancing At Midnight*, has a court hearing for charges related to fraud..."

Violet put down her mug with a heavy thunk.

"Guess that's Hollywood for you." Molly shrugged and tossed the paper down. "I have to get ready and go. 'Bye!"

Violet nodded, only half-listening. She'd been right all along to suspect Mr. Wallace had been up to something when she was on the set of *Dancing At Midnight*.

So. She drummed her fingers on the white enameled tabletop. Because she'd been right about Mr. Wallace, that meant she was right to suspect Golden Gate Records—and Mr. Henry Parker—of being up to something, too. Violet lifted her chin. And since the record company was up to no good, Mr. Parker would certainly have no qualms about taking away her studio even though she'd already told him no. She was positive of that now.

Violet got up from the table and moved to clear away the dirty dishes Molly left behind. But in doing so, she reached a little too far and spilled the half-filled teapot, splashing tea across the stray pages of the *San Francisco Chronicle* and down the magnolia flower pattern that decorated her dressing gown, turning the flowers from pink to a muddy brown.

She reached for a striped dishtowel and began mopping up the mess. As she picked up the dripping paper, the classifieds section fell out. She was about to toss it out when a want ad caught her eye.

She paused and a grin spread across her face as she sat back down on the yellow kitchen chair:

Golden Gate Records
Office girl needed, flexible hours
Contact Mr. Henry Parker
Phone Bayview 221

Perfect. She'd beat Mr. Parker at his own game. She circled the ad in red.

♪

"GOLDEN GATE RECORDS. HOLD PLEASE." The receptionist looked up at Violet with a rather dour look. Violet smiled at her anyway.

"I'm Violet Swanson and I'm here to apply for the office girl position."

The receptionist pressed a long, polished nail on a shiny black button and spoke into it in a low tone that Violet couldn't quite make out.

The receptionist gave her an application form to fill out. She waved Violet to a chair in a cluster of five arranged neatly in the green-carpeted lobby.

After Violet filled out the document, she tapped her brightly painted though slightly chipped nails on the arm of the chair and looked around. She tried not to feel intimidated by the large number of framed records on the walls or the general buzz of low-key excitement that hummed through the corridors.

Violet dropped her gaze to the glossy new Dashiell Hammett paperback she'd stealthily pulled out of her handbag. Maybe she could pick up a few hints about snooping—er, sleuthing, from it.

"Follow me." The receptionist loomed over her, making Violet jump.

"Y-yes." Violet cleared her throat and stuffed her novel back into her purse. She forced herself to collect her thoughts as she followed the receptionist. She had wanted to beat Henry Parker at his own game, after all...

"Mr. Parker will see you now."

Violet tightened her hold on her purse,

conscious of the fact that she'd forgotten her gloves at home. The receptionist knocked on Mr. Parker's office door. Violet's mouth went dry. But she wasn't about to back out now. Gran's dance studio was too important, and Violet needed answers.

"Come in, miss—?" Mr. Parker sat at his desk, calculating a long string of numbers, and hadn't yet looked up.

"It's Miss Violet Swanson."

The second she sat down, Mr. Parker jumped up. "What are *you* doing here?"

He hastily neatened an already-neat pile of papers on his desk, then cleared his throat. His blue eyes met hers and she felt her cheeks flame.

"Why, applying for a job, Mr. Parker. Besides, we're already acquainted, so I'm the perfect candidate." Violet handed him her application form.

He slowly sat back down, then leaned back in the desk chair. Violet could almost see him lacing his hands behind his head and propping his feet up on his desk, the ceiling fan rotating above him, when suddenly the telephone on his desk would ring and the distressed but beautiful woman would burst through his door, clutching a handkerchief and sobbing about the betrayal of—

"...Miss Swanson?"

"Yes! N-no? Er, I mean, can you repeat the question?" Violet shook her head. She really *had* to stop reading so much pulp fiction.

Mr. Parker looked suspiciously like he was hiding a smile. "I was asking you how much office experience you've had, but I think you're right—we already know each other, so you are the perfect candidate. Because," he looked away, out the window, then back to her as he scribbled something on a piece of paper already filled with notes. He put the page into a folder and slipped that folder underneath the pile of paperwork on his desk, "to be honest, I'm too busy to interview anyone else. So, consider the job yours."

Violet felt a thrill trip up her spine.

Now she could start on some real sleuthing! Her heart pounded. He was certainly handsome enough to be up to some dastardly deeds. Not that being handsome had anything to do with that but—Wait. Wait. She couldn't let herself get distracted. "I accept your offer."

"Let me show you around, then."

FRIDAY AFTERNOON, HENRY RAKED A hand through his hair as soon as he heard the receptionist leave for the day. He glanced at his watch. Just after 5:15. He'd give it a few minutes more...

Sure enough, the babble of voices slowly faded as the clock ticked its way to 5:30 p.m. Henry remained at his desk while the lights blinked off one by one and his colleagues left their desks. With any luck, they'd all simply think he was working late. Which, in a manner of speaking, was true.

The last footfalls faded and quiet settled around him. Henry reached up and

pulled the gold chain of his green-shaded desk lamp on. Then he got up and left his office after shutting the door firmly but quietly behind him. He stole a glance over his shoulder as he took a left instead of his usual right. No one around. He continued down the hall to the recording space.

He breathed a sigh of relief as he fitted a record onto the turntable and the toe-tapping tune started. He let the notes wash over him, soothing his uncertainties.

At first, it'd been enough, simply working for Golden Gate Records, simply being near jazz and artists. But now, it wasn't.

Henry executed a perfect spin. Especially after his conversation with DuPont today. He couldn't believe what his boss had said. That movie studio executives from RKO would be coming to that board meeting in two weeks.

It was the perfect opportunity. If what DuPont said was true and Golden Gate Records did have an opportunity to work with one of the best film studios in Hollywood to produce new soundtracks, well, then, if Henry's talent show pitch went well, maybe he'd finally get his chance to make some Hollywood contacts of his own who just might let him swing dance in a commercial or two... Or maybe even a movie?

He grinned and tried to pay attention to the melody.

As he executed the series of steps he'd invented, his mind turned to thoughts of growing up, and how it had been to have family money. Yes, he didn't have to work. Yes, he didn't want for anything.

But there was no challenge in that at all. That was why he'd signed up for the Navy when the war broke out. And why he'd taken up swing dancing the first moment he'd seen it performed even though everyone said he had two left feet. He grinned. He'd proven them all wrong, thanks in part to all those Fred Astaire pictures he'd watched.

But after the war ended, so did Henry's sense of freedom and he began to feel restless again.

So when Gregory DuPont said he was looking for a record man, well, he decided to accept that challenge. He loved music, after all.

Right away he could tell that DuPont wanted to use his family's money. Not that that upset Henry. He'd felt pleased about it because he'd buck family tradition and could hand someone else something, for a change.

He shook his head, dislodging the stray thoughts and took a breath, listening for the next downbeat.

♫

FRIDAY AFTERNOON AT FIVE O'CLOCK, Violet, perched on the edge of her desk around the corner from Mr. Parker's office, wound a strand of hair tighter and tighter around her finger as she read. She'd just finish this chapter—then she'd go.

But the cookie she'd taken a bite of turned to dust in her mouth. She bit her lip, her eyes widening as she started to turn the page of her latest crime novel.

"Good night."

Violet gave a little gasp. But it was only one of her co-workers leaving for the evening.

"Good night," Violet called, then chuckled to herself at her own vivid imagination. Who had she expected? A gunman?

She returned her attention to her book. Just one more page...

Only when Violet's stomach rumbled as she finished the final chapter did she glance at the clock. It was well after five o'clock now.

She jumped up and straightened the last of the files next to the typewriter, stood and stifled a yawn. She reached for a third cookie. Wait a minute. This was a perfect opportunity for a little snooping—er, sleuthing—she corrected herself. Mr. Parker—and everyone else—was gone by now...

Brushing the crumbs off her pleated hound's-tooth print skirt, she stood up, on

the pretext of leaving, with her purse over one arm and her coat over the other. But she headed around the corner and down the hall instead of down the stairs and out the door.

Violet peered through the keyhole of Mr. Parker's office but saw only snatches of objects. She tilted her head but that didn't help. In fact, it gave her a crick in her neck.

She straightened.

She put her hand on the shiny brass doorknob, then hesitated. Oh, why not? She was tired of being cautious. She deftly plucked out a bobby pin from her victory roll and started to ply it in the keyhole. Nothing happened.

She pursed her lips, then grabbed the knob again and twisted it slightly, thinking it might jiggle the lock mechanism, but the knob easily turned all the way.

Oh. She flushed as she slid the bobby pin back into place in her hair and stepped into Mr. Parker's office.

She glanced around, and saw that the

only source of light came from the small green-shaded lamp on his desk.

Violet made her way over to it, her pulse quickening. Then she wondered why. She was most likely being ridiculous, so why was she letting herself get so caught up? Probably because it was fun.

Violet sighed. And, she had to admit, she wanted to prove Mr. Parker wrong so she could prove to herself that she could do something on her own, that she could make things all turn out all right for once...

Violet was a long way from Hollywood. And even farther from her home in rural Washington State. Though she'd gained a few friends like Molly, somehow she'd found herself only slowly adjusting to life in a big city instead of the small town she'd grown up in. There, she'd known everyone—and everyone's business—and no one would pass by her on the street without saying hello.

Oh, how she'd wanted and hoped for that in L.A. But after her contract with

MGM had fallen through even after *Dancing At Midnight* had done well, she didn't have any choice but to leave.

She raised her chin. Now was not the time for feeling sorry for herself. Violet had an obligation—to her grandmother—to stop the buyout from going through.

She felt her skin prickle as she took in the very neatly organized desk. A paperweight sat in the far right corner, and there was a dish full of paper clips on the far left. Hmmm, she could learn something from Mr. Parker. His desk was neater than her and Molly's whole apartment.

But never mind.

Back to her mission. Violet moved around the desk to get a better view of the neatly typed pages stacked on the ink blotter.

With a clenched jaw, Violet reached out a hand to riffle through the pages until she found the one she recalled him hastily stuffing under the pile during their interview.

She tugged it out of its place on the bottom of the stack. Why else would he hide this under the pile of papers unless it was illegal? There it was—she narrowed her eyes—the evidence of his illegal buyout activities staring her right in the face. She squinted to make out the words Mr. Parker had hastily scribbled:

'...zoning committee...adjacent property seizure—condemn building?—over $10,000? talk to Dean to set up; 1 p.m.? negotiations completed outside parameters? Worth the risks?... Along with the show planning'

She grabbed up the piece of paper and gasped. He was giving $10,000 bribes to the city zoning committee? But why? Unless...

She scanned the page again, her convictions growing. Of course. Golden Gate Records planned to bribe the zoning committee to condemn her studio—Violet had to admit it was in rough shape—so Mr. Parker could swoop in and seize it from her! With his big money and big corporation. And who knew what he would do with it then.

She shoved the piece of paper into her purse. This was just the leverage she'd guessed they might have.

Her hands clenched into fists. This meant he didn't care about anything except the money. Once she'd proven it, she'd—

She'd—what? Her anger faltered. What did she expect to get out of this, really? Did she expect the police or lawyers to make him confess? To have him hand her back the property? She sighed. He hadn't even taken it from her. Yet.

Life wasn't some piece of pulp fiction. But she wanted it to be, she realized. Because it was easier than reality. Her lips trembled. She would not cry. She would not.

She sniffed instead and slowly backed away from the desk. The sudden, distant sound of a bright swing tune made her cock her head. She held her breath, as if that would help her locate the source of the sound.

And just like that, all her fear and sadness vanished as she listened to the music. She stepped over the threshold of the office, softly closing the door behind her.

Right or left?

Well, the sound seemed louder from the left, so she'd head in that direction.

She was congratulating herself on the fact that she was making no noise when she remembered the hallway was carpeted.

The music got louder with every step she took. Violet finally reached the end of the hallway and realized she'd reached what was most likely the recording space. Though she couldn't say for sure, since she'd actually never been down this way before.

Violet paused. The door was open a crack, and light spilled out into the dark hallway; the notes seemed to dance out the door as well.

Dance?

A raucous melody surrounded her as she inched the door open, the notes loud and reckless, but Mr. Parker...she felt her knees go weak. He could really dance. Her eyes widened. Violet held her breath as she watched him, haloed by a large triangle of golden light spilling out into the dark hallway. The room's windows were flung open and the curtains were fluttering, letting the loud, reckless notes spill out into the night.

"Ha!" Violet flung the door wide. "I've caught you red-footed."

Mr. Parker froze, one arm still outstretched as if twirling an imaginary partner, his weight balanced on his back leg. "But my shoes are black." His eyes met hers.

Violet wanted to put her hands on her hips, say something snappy back, to accuse him right then and there, say something to match the anger she'd felt in his office. But she was helpless to the familiar disordered world of the music washing over her.

Mr. Parker, without breaking eye contact with Violet, crossed the room to where she stood.

Still wordless, he took her hand in his. Henry slid an arm around Violet's waist, and before her mind had time to fully process what had just happened, her feet had already begun moving and she was dancing—dancing!

The slightest pressure of his hand on the curve of her back as they spun round and round each other served as her only anchor; that, and the beats of the song.

As she followed his lead, she felt herself expand and let go. Violet closed her eyes and allowed her feet and her body to sync with his, the softness of his cotton shirt under her palm, their breathing in unison as the rhythm sped up, and up, until she let out a peal of laughter. She could taste again those sweet, ripe red cherries and the cool vanilla ice cream, could feel the warm earth soft beneath her feet, could find her footing once again.

The music changed tempo. Out of breath, Violet opened her eyes and found Henry looking back at her. Now both of his hands rested on her waist as they stepped closer together, so close that she could feel his breath on her forehead, smell the cool, lemony scent of his cologne, and see his blue eyes studying her. Yet he still hadn't said a word.

But he didn't need to, because his hands and his eyes told her everything she needed to know in that moment, and that was enough.

Her pulse quickened.

She felt him lift his arm and she whirled around twice, her skirt flaring around her legs, the soft fabric falling into place again, brushing against her thighs and hips. Henry's fingertips still held onto hers.

She saw Henry's chest rising and falling. His blond hair had darkened slightly at the temples from exertion and his grip was slightly slippery, but his fingers remained strong and supple as he pulled her back to him and dipped her in one fluid motion.

It was only then she realized it was silent, the only sound their breathing.

At the sound of a throat being cleared behind them, Violet scrambled to stand up straight, and even more heat suffused her cheeks.

Because it was Gregory DuPont, the record company's CEO.

Chapter Three

VIOLET SHIFTED HER WEIGHT AWAY from Henry—No. Mr. Parker—and put her hands on her hips. She saw that Mr. DuPont had plucked the record from the phonograph. He leaned against the record cabinet with one arm, his other hand on his hip, holding the disc of black vinyl between his fingers. He said nothing.

Violet watched Mr. Parker's eyes dart around the room. "Sir," he said, "I was wasting company time. I apologize because I know you always say—"

"Damn what I always say, Parker. You always had that talent of yours hidden away?" DuPont twirled the record between his fingers.

Mr. Parker's jaw looked in danger of falling open. Violet stifled a giggle.

Which turned into a gasp when DuPont

turned to her, his eyes narrowed. "You know, Miss Swanson, I kept thinking you seemed familiar. Now I know why."

Violet put a hand to her throat and took a step back, bumping into Mr. Parker, who clasped her elbow. "He's right," Mr. Parker murmured, his lips far too close to her ear. "I was thinking the same thing now that I've seen you dance."

Violet's gaze darted from one man to the other, and then to the door. Her hand at her throat clenched.

"Because you dance just like Gloria Dare in *Dancing At Midnight*."

Violet forced a light laugh. "I know!" But she breathed a sigh of relief. So they hadn't read that terrible write-up in *Silver Screen* magazine about her awful on-set accident. Yet.

"Which is perfect," DuPont continued. "Because I want the both of you to head-line this talent show idea that Parker's cooked up at The Blue Mirror Club. With a swing dance number. Something big and flashy."

"Sir, I didn't think you knew anything

about that. I was planning on telling you at the—"

"Word gets around, Parker."

"Sir, I—" Mr. Parker tried again. He shot Violet a look she couldn't quite read.

Violet pleated and un-pleated the fabric of her skirt between her fingers. She couldn't do this, could she? What if she screwed everything up for Golden Gate Records like she had for MGM?

DuPont's raised hand silenced Mr. Parker. "It'll be great. The audience will love it and it'll boost our record sales."

And maybe in this case, she wouldn't nearly burn the place down? She shook her head and grimaced, remembering: tripping over lighting, which lit the movie set curtains on fire, that somehow managed to shatter two movie cameras, before melting a master reel, injuring three cast members, causing thousands of dollars in expenses, and snarling everyone up in red tape for weeks afterward...

"The show's only a few weeks away. Miss Swanson, what do you say?"

Who knew? Maybe this would help her dance studio gain customers? Even if it meant she'd have to dance in public and risk being recognized.

This could be a way to keep a closer eye on Mr. Parker, too. See if he slipped up. Violet took a deep breath, then nodded. "All right. I'll do it."

"Good." DuPont nodded. "Now, you two had better get busy practicing."

♫

VIOLET SLIPPED OUT OF HER pale pink camisole and into the smooth satin of her favorite polka-dot pajamas. She sighed in relief. The day was finally over. She stretched and yawned. Who know sleuthing could make a gal so sleepy?

She sank down onto the vanity stool and picked up her hairbrush, its silver plating catching in the lamplight, the initials almost worn off.

She ran a fingertip across the letters; her initials had been Gran's, too. She plucked out her hairpins and began brush-

ing, the rhythmic motion slowing the beat of her heart. Had she really told the CEO of Golden Gate Records, and Mr. Parker today, that she'd do a talent show number? Yes, she had. Was that why she couldn't get Mr. Parker's blue eyes out of her mind even when he was acting suspect?

Her knuckles whitened on the brush handle and she felt her heartbeat speed up. She had to admit she liked dancing with him. No. She just liked dancing, not him.

She set aside those thoughts and set down the brush, her hair now glossy and sleek. She didn't bother to hide another huge yawn as she padded barefoot to the white wrought iron bed and crawled underneath the covers, then reached for the crime story on her nightstand.

Just then, the telephone rang.

She sat bolt upright. Good thing she wasn't all alone in the apartment or she might start to think this was a scene from *Sorry, Wrong Number*. The phone rang a second time. But she doubted it was a murderer on the other end of the line. Violet shuddered and made a dash for the ringing phone in the living room.

"Hello?"

"Miss Swanson? It's Henry Parker. Listen, I'm sorry if it's a bit late."

"This is my favorite time of day, actually. I was just in bed reading."

"Oh." Mr. Parker cleared his throat. "I'm a bit of a night owl myself, so I'm glad I didn't wake you up, then. I was just thinking about what DuPont said and I thought it'd be nice to go out to The Blue Mirror Club tomorrow."

Violet twisted the phone cord around her finger. Dance in public?

"Not really to practice," he continued, "but just to go see the layout, now that we both know we'll be dancing there."

Hmmm. He did have a point. "All right." Besides, this would be a perfect opportunity to see if Mr. Parker slipped up outside the office. "How about 7 p.m.?"

"I'll pick you up."

The next night, the doorman unhooked the velvet rope for Violet as Mr. Parker escorted her inside. Violet suddenly wished she'd worn her new red striped dress with the bias-cut skirt because when she put it on, she'd felt like Ginger Rogers.

Mr. Parker gestured to the parquet dance floor, now surrounded by round tables draped in white tablecloths. "Once those tables are taken away, the space is really pretty large. More than enough room for the talent show participants and spectators."

Violet gave a nervous laugh. "Of course, I forgot. What's a talent show without spectators?" She swallowed. "Well, let's go out on the floor, then, and see how things look from there."

Violet found herself slipping a gloved hand into the crook of Henry's—no—Mr. Parker's, elbow as they moved onto the polished parquet. Strictly out of politeness, of course.

She looked around. "We should have room for those aerials DuPont wants," she said, sizing up the space. "I think that'll be big and flashy enough for him."

Henry nodded.

Violet found herself tapping her fingers along with the snappy number performed on stage. "Oops. Sorry." She stilled her fingers when she realized she was using the hand on Henry's arm.

Henry chuckled. "It's a catchy song. This quartet's got talent."

Hmm. Henry did have good taste in music. She glanced at him out of the corner of her eye. So far, he hadn't made any slip-ups. In fact, he'd been downright nice. But it was only a matter of time until he did slip up. She straightened her shoulders. She had a mission. She couldn't let herself be drawn in.

But as the music changed tempo to a slow number and the dance floor started to fill, she couldn't help a soft sigh. This was one of her favorite songs.

Instead of stepping off the floor, though—after all, their number was a fast one—Henry offered her his hand, a question in his eyes. She hesitated a fraction of a second before she resolutely placed her hand in his and allowed him to slide his arm around her waist and pull her in.

She had no choice but to put her cheek on his chest and close her eyes; at least, that's what she told herself. Over the delicate twinkle of piano notes, she could hear his heartbeat and feel the softness of the lapel of his spring flannel suit jacket.

Her eyelids fluttered closed. She couldn't understand why she'd resisted dancing for so long. What had she been afraid of, after all? That some bogeyman would jump out at her and pull her down from where she stood, now?

No. She didn't need to be frightened any more. The past was the past. And now was now. And she could live with that.

"Miss Swanson?" Henry murmured, and Violet startled awake. *That* was the last time she'd stay up 'til 1 a.m. reading...

"Wha—Oh!" She pulled away from him. She hoped she didn't have red marks on her cheek from resting her head on his chest. But she had left a smeary patch of makeup on his lapel. She plucked the display handkerchief out of his breast pocket and began rubbing the spot away.

She glanced up at Henry. "Oh. Sorry." She cleared her throat and stuffed the handkerchief back in his pocket.

He inclined his head toward her and said in a conspiratorial tone, "Keep it. I can never figure out how to get stains out of them, so I just buy new ones all the time. I have packets and packets of hand-kerchiefs at home." He chuckled.

She blushed and tucked the handker-chief into her dress pocket.

AFTER WORK THE NEXT DAY, Violet saw the windows of her dance studio shining in the rays of the late afternoon sun as she strode down the sidewalk, swinging her handbag. Her grandmother's legacy would be safe. She'd see to it.

She tried to ignore the pinch of her new cherry-red T-strap heels. She just knew it'd been a bad idea to wear them all day, and wished for the first chance to take them off.

She also tried to ignore the giddy feeling in her stomach as she thought back to last night at the club. It had been rather wonderful. She smiled to herself, then frowned. Of course, that was only because she'd danced again, without pressures or expectations. It had nothing to do with Mr. Parker at all.

She reached for her purse to fish the key to the studio out of the inside pocket when she realized—she'd forgotten it.

She smacked a palm against her forehead.

"Are you all right?"

Violet jumped and looked around. Oh no. Her stomach tightened.

Mr. Parker pushed the brim of his fedora up on his head.

"Oh! Fine, fine. It's just that I forgot the key." She looked at her wristwatch. "It's after six and I, uh, wanted to um, practice... and finish up that painting and plastering before my first students come for classes. Which will be any day now," she finished in a rush. That wasn't exactly true, though. The studio was a long way from being open for business. But Mr. Parker didn't need to know that.

He leaned a shoulder against the door-frame of *her* studio. "You wouldn't have to worry about any of that if you simply sold to Golden Gate Records."

Yes, and if she did that, all the memories, all the history, and the last pieces of her grandmother's legacy would be gone forever. Last night had been nothing more than a ruse, then?

He obviously didn't care about history or family or anything else. Probably not even dancing. All he wanted was to do his job, to expand that big fancy corporation. "And then this studio would be gone forever." She glared at him. "I won't let you destroy the place where I first fell in love with swing dance."

"Now, wait just a second, Miss Swanson. You can't go around accusing me of

that when you know perfectly well you need the money Golden Gate is offering you for the studio." He folded his arms across his chest.

He thought money was the answer to everything, didn't he? "How dare you assume anything about me, Mr. Parker."

"Miss Swanson, do you know what I think?"

"I don't care what you think."

"Well, you're going to hear it anyway." He made a sweeping gesture. "I think that you don't even want that studio. I think..."

He leaned toward her, his blue eyes intense. "I think that you don't want a dance studio. You want a dance career. You want to be a dancer again."

"Oh, Mr. Parker. You have it all wrong."

"No, Miss Swanson." He snagged her wrist. "You want to feel the music again, to lose yourself in the lyrics, to meld yourself into the melody."

She pulled out of his grasp. "No, Mr. Parker. I think that's what *you* want." She leaned forward so they were nearly nose-to-nose. "Go on," she said. "Deny it."

Mr. Parker took a step back. "You don't know me."

"But I do know the way you dance," Violet said. "And that tells me every-thing."

Mr. Parker shifted his weight from one foot to the other. "Well," he said slowly, "there's a park across the way."

Violet cocked her head at him.

"If you want to practice, I mean."

Violet pursed her lips. "With you? I wouldn't dream of consorting with the enemy." She started to turn away. She hadn't meant to say those things out loud. Then again, she wasn't sorry. It was, after all, how she felt.

"That didn't seem to matter last night," Mr. Parker called out.

Her shoulders tensed. He had the nerve to bring that up now? Especially after she'd received that horrid letter—with Mr. Parker's signature—officially offering to buy out the studio. She'd torn it up. He wouldn't win. And neither would her

fears. She stopped and spun around. "All right, Mr. Parker. Even though I have no idea why you *just happen* to be here outside my studio..."

"If you must know, I was working late at the office. Which is right next door."

She eyed him. "Fine. Let's dance."

As they crossed the street to the park, Violet eyed the gray clouds scuttling across the sky, then buttoned the top button of her cardigan. She turned to face Mr. Parker, but he was now standing under a tree nearby, suit jacket slung over a low-hanging branch, fedora neatly stacked on top.

Violet's heart jumped. "O-on the grass I'm not sure my heels will do too well."

"So take them off." Mr. Parker began rolling up his shirtsleeves.

Violet swallowed. "My stockings would be ruined."

He leaned back against the tree. "You could always take off your stockings, too."

"What if I'm not wearing stockings at all?" Oh, why had she said that out loud?

Violet couldn't be sure at this distance but it looked like Mr. Parker's gaze flicked to her legs.

Well. Hadn't she just wished for a reason to take off her shoes? Violet sat on a nearby park bench and leaned forward to undo the buckles of her heels. As she did, she couldn't help glancing up through her lashes at Mr. Parker. He'd crossed his ankles and his arms as he leaned against the tree trunk, his gaze in her direction. She bit her lip as she slid off one shoe, and then the other.

Violet stuffed her shoes into her purse, then wished she'd painted her toenails.

But she strode over to Mr. Parker, her shoulders back, chin up; her stomach, though, quivered. She swallowed as she noticed the light filter through the leaves.

"Ready?" Henry's voice brought her eyes back to his face.

No. "Yes." Violet forced herself to begin humming a melody despite the fact that a few people had now paused in their strolling to watch. She swallowed nerv-

ously.

"Oof!" Henry said.

"Oh my goodness! I'm sorry." Violet stopped moving. "It's your *other* left foot, you know. Then I wouldn't be stepping on your toes."

"I thought you said this was the basic step." Mr. Parker frowned.

"It is. For West Coast swing."

"West Coast swing? I thought we're doing Lindy Hop. Why didn't you say that from the beginning?"

"That's what I did say. Only I don't know if you were listening," Violet said.

"Of course I was listening. I just—"

"Assumed you were right," Violet stated.

Henry winced.

"Let's start from the top," Violet said.

"Right." Mr. Parker smiled, though it was a little strained.

"Ow!" Now Violet let out a cry of discomfort.

Mr. Parker stopped moving. "I'm sorry. I was—"

"Trying to lead when I'm trying to show you the steps to the dance, which means *I'm* leading—at least for this measure."

The wind picked up. Violet glanced at the sky. The gray clouds had multiplied, as had the onlookers. "I'm not sure this is going to work out," she lied.

It was the perfect excuse. Violet's fingers gripped Mr. Parker's shoulder a little tighter than they had just moments before. She couldn't let him know the truth—that she hadn't wanted to dance with anyone in public since the on-set catastrophe. And yet, here she was, in a public park. But what about last night?

Last night, though, had been different. Last night she'd let herself dance because there were no pressures. No expectations. And best of all, no movie cameras. Violet lifted her chin. She was doing this for her grandmother, for the dance studio.

One raindrop splattered onto Violet's nose. Then three. Then ten.

Violet felt her skirt twist around her

legs as the wind grew stronger. The rain fell in earnest now.

Violet snatched at her skirt, then put one hand on her thigh to keep her skirt from flying up.

She hunched her shoulders against the downpour that had now begun. "I'm sorry to hear that you think this won't work out," Mr. Parker said, his hair and shirt getting damp. The onlookers had gone on their way.

Violet tried to smile but there were tears in her eyes. Gran. She would have loved this. Gran, who had taught her to dance, barefoot in the grass. Under a leafy green tree. Just like this. Gran, who had encouraged her hopes and dreams.

Violet glanced at Henry and her stomach clenched. Would he take that away from her? Everything she'd worked so hard for?

"Are you all right?" He reached up to place a hand on her shoulder.

"I'm fine." Violet blinked. "I think that's enough practice for today, don't you?"

She blinked again, and swallowed.

"Sorry," he mumbled, pulling his hand down quickly before shoving it into his pocket and taking a step back, away from her.

Mr. Parker's eyes shifted left, then right, before finally landing on her face again. "Can I give you a lift back to your place?"

"Oh, the trolley stop's just around the corner." Violet shivered. "Thank you though."

"You're soaking wet and you want me to leave you at a trolley stop?"

Violet bit her lip, but nodded.

"Well, suit yourself then." Mr. Parker gathered his things and, before Violet could say anything else, he walked away.

THE FOLLOWING TUESDAY EVENING, VIO-LET, with her nose in a book, jumped when the buzzer went off. She poked her head out the door and frowned. No one was in the hall. She was just about to shut the door when she heard, "Psssst!"

Had the cat escaped?

"Pssst!"

But no, it was Mr. Parker, crouched down and half-hidden by the potted palm next to her door.

"Mr. Parker? The landlady doesn't allow gentlemen callers up here."

"Then hadn't you better let me in?"

"What are you doing here?"

He held up her favorite hat. "You forgot it at the office."

"Oh." That was nice of him. "Thank you." She reached around the partially open door to take the bright blue hat.

"All right. Come in," Violet said. He darted inside before she shut the door behind them. "You're lucky she didn't spot you."

"That's why I climbed up the fire escape." He cleared his throat. "Miss Swanson, I have to admit, I had an ulterior motive for coming by."

Violet tensed. Was he about to admit to his illegal actions?

He fiddled with the brim of the fedora he held, then lifted his gaze to hers. "I got your suite number from your application form and came to see you because I think you're avoiding dance practices. It's been almost a week now and we've only gotten in a few."

Violet fiddled with her bracelet. "The talent show's great publicity for my dance studio, so I'm not avoiding it." She avoided Mr. Parker's gaze. "Uh, I can roll up the rug, so there should be enough room in the living room here to squeeze in a practice right now—" The door opened and Violet and Mr. Parker both turned.

"Molly, what on earth are you doing here?" Violet said.

"Well, don't look so shocked. I live here." Molly, who was standing in the doorway, lowered her voice. "Are you two practicing together *here?*" She came into the foyer and shut the door. "Well, don't worry. You won't even know I'm around. 'Scuse me." She started to move past them.

Violet pivoted toward Mr. Parker in the narrow foyer to let Molly go by. As she did, her hand brushed the sleeve of Mr. Parker's—oh!—he wasn't wearing a suit jacket, and she could feel the warmth of his skin underneath the pale blue cotton of his dress shirt.

She dropped her hand as if burned. Violet swallowed and walked into the living room, Mr. Parker behind her, while Molly plopped down on the couch with the latest issue of *Silver Screen.*

"So you didn't grow up around here, did you?" Henry leaned beside the mantel.

Violet's stomach lurched. Henry's elbow rested right by a framed photo. A photo of her and her twin sister in matching dance costumes, their arms around each other, on the back porch of their parents' house, nothing but cherry orchards behind them.

She hurried over to the gramophone and put on a Cab Calloway record, hoping to turn his attention from her personal life as Mr. Parker joined her by the record player. "Yes, well, no. I mean, no, I didn't. I grew up in rural Washington State. What about you?" she said, much too brightly.

"Born and raised California boy."

Violet turned her back on Mr. Parker and fiddled with the records again. "Now I was thinking," she said in her best professional tone, "we could start off slowly, just to get the feel of the steps and then speed things up from there. Minus the aerials, of course. There isn't enough room in here for that. What do you think?"

Henry looked up from pulling his handkerchief out of his pocket. He sneezed, then nodded.

They did the routine a few times before Violet turned to her roommate. "Molly, can you start the record over again?"

"Sure thing." Molly tossed aside her *Silver Screen* magazine and headed to the gramophone. Henry had turned to Molly and was saying something to her, and Violet saw her opportunity.

Violet snatched up the magazine and stuffed it underneath a couch cushion. She couldn't let Molly spot her among *Silver Screen's* pages. Not that she was in this edition, probably. But she couldn't be too careful.

Molly turned back around just as Violet was straightening back up. "Say, what did you do with my magazine this time, Violet?"

"I wasn't doing anything. The, er, couch cushions looked a little lumpy. I was just..." She cleared her throat. "...plumping them up."

"Uh-huh." Molly put her hands on her hips. "I swear, you're jumpier than a cat in a room full of rocking chairs with that magazine. We've been going back and forth about it for weeks. Every time I try to read it, you go and hide it."

"Yes, well...it's a trashy magazine."

Molly gave an exasperated sigh, then plopped back down on the couch and pulled out her nail file. "Guess I'll give myself a manicure instead."

Violet turned back to Henry with a sigh of relief. When the music swelled in the final phrase and Henry twirled her out, she felt herself spin and spin. And spin. Darn it. She shouldn't have polished the floor quite this much, perhaps.

Finally she put her arms out to stop her progress, nearly knocking over a beaded lamp in the process.

She shook her head, willing the room to stop spinning. "That was...great. I think that's enough for today." She gave Henry a weak smile. Or was it that his smile made her weak at the knees?

Violet couldn't help but notice that Molly was no longer even pretending to be engrossed in filing her nails. Instead, she openly eyed the two of them. Violet looked toward Henry—his slightly mussed hair, his askew tie; one button, she noticed, had come undone from his shirt—and she caught her breath when she noticed he was a little out of breath.

So was she.

She took a breath. "Um, would you like

a glass of water?"

Henry sank down onto the couch beside Molly, who didn't move over one iota. "That'd be swell. You're a great dancer, you know, Miss Swanson," he said. "I've never seen anyone move so flawlessly on the dance floor."

"Thank you. I'm such a klutz off the dance floor that I surprise even myself sometimes that I can dance at all."

Violet carefully made her way back to the living room from the eat-in kitchen, working hard to avoid meeting Henry's gaze. Though why, she didn't quite know.

But it might have had something to do with him being so nice—oh! She tripped over the edge of the rolled-up rug, sending the glass flying in Henry's direction. It arced into the air, water droplets flying every which way before they landed with a splat on Henry's dress shirt, making a large splotch on the expensive cotton. The glass landed harmlessly beside Henry on the couch.

"Oh my goodness! I'm sorry."

Henry jumped up, his shirt clinging to him as he dabbed at the wet patch with his handkerchief. "It's okay. I was needing a bit of a bath." He chuckled.

"I don't think I'm going to ask you if you want another glass," Violet said.

"Oh no?" There was a hint of challenge in his eyes now.

Violet suddenly found her nails fascinating; she needed a manicure, too. "No."

"Well, in that case, I'll take my leave."

"Then I'll show you to the door."

A sharp knock at the door froze the smile on Violet's face. "Rats." Violet's eyes widened.

The knock came again.

"Er," Violet's eyes darted around, "how about I show you to the window?"

Molly jumped up off the couch. "Quick! I'll answer the door. Pretend you're not here. Or hide him, or something." Molly sprinted to the door as the knock sounded a third time.

"Where are we going?" Henry narrowly avoided whacking his leg against the back

of the couch as Violet pulled him along behind her.

"The broom closet."

Henry stopped moving. "I would've preferred the window for a quick exit."

"Girls! I know you have someone in here." The landlady's voice drifted to Violet.

"Too late for that now," Violet hissed.

"I'm claustrophobic."

"You're—well, it's either that or me getting chucked out of this place. She doesn't abide second chances. And this is the only place I can afford right now."

"All right. I'll do it." Henry swallowed as they approached the tiny broom closet door. He tugged at his tie and paused again, but the sound of the landlady's footsteps in the entryway spurred him into action.

Beads of sweat, Violet could see, had broken out on his forehead. But he was actually doing it. For her? Her heart fluttered for a second. Maybe he wasn't as bad as she'd thought him to be...

Violet swung the door open for him and he wedged himself in just as the landlady rounded the corner into the living room.

Violet shut the door as quietly as she could and turned around to act nonchalant. But it was too late.

"Violet Swanson, what on earth are you up to?" The landlady put her hands on her hips.

"Just finishing some sweeping."

A muffled sneeze came from the broom closet.

The landlady's eyebrows rose and she opened her mouth to say something. Just then, the Siamese came sauntering around the corner. "Meeerrrruph?"

"Rats!" Violet said under her breath.

"What on earth is this cat doing in here? They aren't allowed either."

"Rats!" Violet said again. "We, er, brought him in here to get rid of the rats, er, mice." Violet twirled a lock of hair around her finger faster and faster, looking at the landlady without blinking.

"Oh, girls," the landlady said, shaking her head and chuckling. "You're lucky this isn't 1903." She wiped at the corner of her eyes with her handkerchief, still laughing. "I happen to think of myself as rather progressive, so you can tell your fellow he can come out of there. But he has to leave by ten p.m., and next time, please take him somewhere else. The cat, well, he can stay. I'm rather fond of them. But—" her eyes narrowed "—don't look a gift horse in the mouth." The landlady put her hands on her hips again. "I have a reputation to maintain, after all." And she winked.

HENRY TUCKED HIS RUMPLED HANDKER-CHIEF back into his coat pocket and rubbed the back of his neck. He'd gotten a crick in it from being jammed into that broom closet.

He turned up the collar of his coat against the chilly night breeze and made his way back to his parked car. What a fiasco.

A smile tugged at his lips. That gal was the furthest thing from boring. He couldn't help chuckling. Hadn't he hoped to be freed from his boredom?

There was just something so...appealing about Violet. Her quick remarks. Her independent nature. The way she smelled like Juicy Fruit and cherries, and how her nose scrunched up when she laughed. Her beautiful green eyes... The way her clothes had clung to her when they'd both gotten soaked that evening in the park. Even though she could be exasperating, she'd somehow gotten under his skin.

He raked a hand through his hair. But *why* did she look so familiar? Even though he'd been a Harvard man, sometimes he still felt like a dunce.

His mind strayed again, remembering how the light had caught her green eyes, and the worry he'd seen there, when they'd been out dancing in the rain. What had she been so afraid of? What was she not telling him? His hand froze on the door handle of his coupe. Wait. Her eyes.

That face. And the way she moved... Why hadn't he realized it before? No wonder Miss Swanson had looked familiar—she was Gloria Dare, star of *Dancing At Midnight*. After all, everyone knew that Gloria Dare was a stage name. No one knew her real name, though. But now he did.

Henry's pulse quickened as he got into his Mercury. But what was she doing up here in San Francisco? That movie had done so well... Shouldn't they be filming another one or something? He frowned. It didn't make any sense why she wasn't working. But maybe she was just taking a break between pictures?

He grinned. With Golden Gate Records providing the musicians, and with him and Gloria providing the opening dance number, well, the talent show was sure to be a success. He climbed into his Mercury and headed to The Blue Mirror. He could use a drink.

Henry sank down on the bar stool with a satisfied smile and ordered his usual martini.

He tapped his fingers on the bar in time with the snappy tune Nick Hart was performing onstage.

Wait a second... Henry's fingers stilled. That was it! He could simply take the talent show idea he'd been presenting to the movie studio executives the day after tomorrow, and have it play a key scene in a new swing dance picture. Starring Gloria Dare! It could even be a sequel of sorts to *Dancing At Midnight.* Henry could help her out, give her career a boost. She was too talented a dancer to waste her time as an office girl. So a new swing movie would not only give her an opportunity to shine again, but he'd also give his own dancing dream a chance, too.

And now that he knew Violet's secret, he could film the talent show here. Henry already knew most everyone at The Blue Mirror, so why not?

He dropped his chin into his hand.

But he couldn't tell Violet of his deliberate deception right now—she already seemed so skittish. He'd only withhold

the truth from her to protect her.

He would tell her the truth about the filming at The Blue Mirror—but only after it was completed. That way, everyone would win: Golden Gate Records, the movie studio, Gloria, er, Violet. And him.

Henry grinned to himself and signalled the bartender to bring him another martini.

Chapter Four

"READY TO PRACTICE?" MR. PARKER asked, closing the door to her dance studio behind him as he entered. "The show's only a week away now."

Violet turned and watched him approach, her mind running back through the time they'd danced in the park. She could have been a bit more civil. Maybe they didn't need to be enemies... She adjusted her hair barrette.

He came closer, and a floorboard creaked. She flinched. Here he was treading across her floorboards, taking up space in her studio. The same studio he wanted to take away from her. And all for what? To store some dusty old records? Her shoulders stiffened.

Why couldn't he be ugly? She felt a flicker of annoyance. A man was made of

more than his looks, as Gran used to say. Still, it'd be easier to dislike him if he weren't so good-looking. And nice.

But she let Henry take her right hand in his left. Violet let the warmth of his fingers close around hers with strength and firmness. She resisted the urge to pull her hand out because it was too late. The music had already begun. At least, that's what she told herself. And as inevitable as time itself, the beats tripped after themselves. One by one by one, until she felt as dizzy as that time in the back orchard under the cherry trees when she'd spun too much...

Violet found she couldn't lift her eyes to Henry's, could only look straight ahead at the tiny spot where his gray dress shirt was unbuttoned, and a small piece of skin showed.

She felt him pull her forward even as he stepped backward. She came closer to him and rested her left arm on top of his right. But she continued only to be able to look at that tiny patch of skin in which she could now see the pulse beating in his throat. At the point where his collarbone disappeared under his crisp cotton shirt.

Violet couldn't breathe, couldn't focus, couldn't do anything except obey the push and pull through every turn and whirl, the steps getting faster and faster and faster until she no longer remembered to feel dizzy; only free.

Sweat beaded on her forehead, her upper lip, and under the patch of skin where Henry's palm rested on her back. The heat from his hand seeped through the thin rayon of her flowered dress; his touch light, his hand strong yet guiding and gentle at the same time. She suddenly wished there were no barriers between them at all, wished that she could somehow, finally, be brave enough to face things squarely.

And then she tripped on her hair barrette, which had somehow worked its way free of her hair and fallen onto the floor.

"Steady there," Henry said, bringing his other hand down so that both his hands

spanned her waist. She felt her throat tighten.

She remained frozen in place, staring up into Henry's blue eyes. Neither she nor he blinked.

The singer on the phonograph, though, continued to wail about eating potato chips for lunch.

Henry hadn't released her, but she felt a giggle rising within her. Who sings about potato chips? She tried to stifle her laughter but it came out anyway.

Henry cocked his head, letting his hands slide off her waist and find their way to his trouser pockets.

"I-it's just—" she giggled, "—this s-song." Another peal of laughter. "Is so ridiculous. Potato chips? Who sings about potato chips?"

Henry chuckled. "You have to admit, though, it does have a good beat."

"Yes," she agreed, finally sinking into a chair by the half-open window, "it does." She reached up and pulled the needle off the record. Sudden silence filled the airy studio.

Henry rolled up his shirtsleeves as he moved to the window too. Violet could see his color was high. She jerked her gaze away from his, and stared out the window, her shoulders relaxing as she spotted the white sail of a boat on the bay, the sparkle of sunlight glinting off the smooth surface of the water.

Violet continued to stare out the window, but the scent of his expensive cologne and the sweet tangy salt air came to her anyway.

"I think we're pretty good," he said softly. "Don't you?"

THE DAY OF THE MEETING, Henry tucked the last crisp white typewritten page into the pocket of his brown leather briefcase and shut it with a smile. The latch clicked closed with a sharp snick.

He donned his brown fedora and stepped out into the entryway, only then realizing he'd forgotten his briefcase on

the kitchen table, so he went back in to get it.

While gripping the handle firmly this time with one hand, as if to prevent the case's escape, he locked the front door with the other hand before getting into his coupe.

As he motored over to Golden Gate Records, Henry turned on the radio and whistled along with the new Nick Hart tune that began playing. It had a lot of airtime these days and he was glad because it tied directly into the plan he would pitch for the film studio execs today. Everything was sure to go well—he had a good feeling about this.

He whistled a little louder and rolled down the window half a crank, the warm March wind ruffling his hair and reminding him that he wanted to go out to the beach sometime soon.

He finally arrived at Golden Gate Records, got out of the car, and headed to the building. When this talent show pitch went well, it would solve everything. He'd get out of here at last and pursue his dancing dreams. He strode into the lobby, with his suit jacket thrown over his shoulder, his shirtsleeves rolled up and the brim of his fedora pushed back.

"Morning, Doris," he said to the dour-faced receptionist. She didn't even acknowledge him.

He shrugged and made his way over to his office, where he hung up his suit jacket and fedora on the coat rack in the corner, then made his way to the conference room. He glanced at his Cartier wrist-watch—it had been a gift from his father. Might as well get things set up.

Henry opened the door to the confer-ence room and saw with satisfaction that not one of the film executives was there yet. Good.

He placed his briefcase on the table near the projector and began sorting out the copies of the charts and diagrams he would distribute.

ON HER WAY TO WORK Wednesday morning, Violet nearly walked through a red light, so distracted was she by the final few words of *The Glass Key*. How could it have ended already?

She stopped short on the curb and reached into her purse for a stick of Juicy Fruit—it tasted so much better than cigarettes. She shuddered—she didn't know how people could smoke those hateful things.

But just as Violet was about to shut the clasp on her purse and pop the piece of gum into her mouth, a blur of movement caught the corner of her eye.

She turned her head and realized it was her Siamese cat. He'd escaped after all. Mr. Mischievous started to trot over to her, tail in the air, when Violet noticed he was limping. She crouched down and stroked his head. "Molly must have left that window open too wide, huh?"

She set her still-open purse down on the sidewalk next to her and leaned forward to examine the cat's leg.

She checked her watch. She didn't have time to take him back to her place or to the vet now, but what if she took him on her lunch break? There was an empty record box by her desk that Mr. Parker had asked her to throw out—she could put the cat in there til lunchtime.

She looked up from her watch in time to see half the cat had disappeared into her handbag. He was after the tuna fish sandwich she'd packed for lunch. She reached in and plucked the waxed-paper packet from his sniffing nose and tucked it into her jacket pocket.

"Listen, Mr. Mischievous, I'll give you part of my sandwich if you come with me to the vet's."

Meorrrow.

She laughed. "Okay, but you'd better behave yourself at the office."

She reached in and lifted him up and out of her purse, but not before a wadded piece of paper came out, too. With the cat tucked under one arm, she picked up the piece of paper. Her gut tightened. Mr.

Parker's scribbled notes. She'd wondered where they'd gotten to.

What better time than this morning at that board meeting, to confront him? He'd have nowhere to run.

Violet strode through the doors of Golden Gate Records ten minutes later.

She suppressed a smile as she sailed by the receptionist, the cat still tucked under her arm, with her raincoat draped just so over top of him. She continued along the corridor and up the stairs. So far so good.

But when she got halfway down the hallway, she spotted Mr. Parker at exactly the same moment that she felt the cat nudge her arm and try to poke his head up to look around, which caused the raincoat to bunch and move.

"No," she hissed at the cat, just as Mr. Parker approached.

She stiffened.

"Good morning, Miss Swanson."

"Uh, good morning, Mr. Parker." She clamped her arm more tightly around the cat. "I'll start right away on those papers that you—"

Mr. Parker sneezed.

"Bless you!" Violet said, trying to edge around him and to her desk. She could feel the cat shifting around more insistently.

"Miss Swanson, I want you to—" Achoo! "—know that I'm glad you've decided to—" He cleared his throat. "A-a-choo! I mean, agree, to, well, practice more with me."

She just nodded, all the while inching past him and toward her workspace.

Mr. Parker sneezed once more, fumbling for his handkerchief before finally continuing down the hallway in the opposite direction.

Violet moved quickly to her desk and slid her coat off her arm. She deposited the cat into the record box, pulled on the lid and then slid the whole thing in the kneehole beneath her desk. Violet glanced around. Even though, she admitted, this might be a bad plan, she couldn't help grinning to herself. Real life was better than a crime novel.

VIOLET GLANCED AT THE CLOCK. The meeting would begin in five minutes. And those boys needed someone to serve them coffee, didn't they? She grinned. It would give her the perfect excuse to barge in on them and confront Henry—er, Mr. Parker.

She gave the record box one final check, and slipped in another sliver of tuna sandwich, for good measure, next to the sleeping cat. Then she got up, satisfied the cat wouldn't be going anywhere for awhile.

After telling the receptionist she was going to make the coffee for the meeting, Violet made her way back to the conference room directly opposite her desk and just down the hall from the reception area.

Taking a deep breath, she set the coffee tray on the cart. She pushed the cart to the closed conference room door, then propped the door open so she could easily shuttle the coffee things back and forth instead of cluttering up the conference room and making a general nuisance of herself.

She couldn't help glancing at Mr. Parker as she walked in holding the coffee carafe, with his condemning evidence in her skirt pocket.

"—because The Blue Mirror Club is the perfect location. And if you're on board with my idea, well," Mr. Parker said, as his eyes met Violet's for the briefest of seconds, "then we both win: Golden Gate Records gets more exposure for its musicians through the soundtracks, and you fellas would get top-notch music at a discounted price."

She silently passed out napkins and cups amongst the men, who were paying rapt attention to Mr. Parker. She bided her time. Her opportunity would come. She started pouring the coffee, but couldn't help sneaking another glance up at Mr. Parker through her lashes.

Oh, the blue of his pinstriped tie

matched perfectly with his eyes... No. She wrenched her gaze away, nearly spilling coffee on the fellow whose cup she was filling.

Then Henry began sneezing.

She poured fourth and fifth cups with trembling hands. Surely the cat was still asleep...? More sneezes from Henry.

He pulled out his handkerchief and continued. "As you can see," he said, starting to distribute a stack of papers that had been sitting in a neat pile near his end of the long table, "these figures show the projected income for both of us if a joint soundtrack venture is pursued. You can be assured we'll have plenty of room to house the master tracks for you, too, what with the new storage space we're working on acquiring." Mr. Parker's gaze flicked to Violet, then away.

Violet put down the coffee cup she'd just filled, the hot liquid sloshing around the rim, and spoke. "Mr. Parker, I have something to say." She planted her hands on her hips. "You're up to something.

First it was breaking records in the alley. Then it was staying at the office after hours to *dance.* And now it's setting up meetings to give bribes to officials so you can conduct an illegal property buyout!"

Mr. Parker crossed his arms. "Golden Gate Records has never conducted illegal—"

"Ouch!" Gregory DuPont bolted up out of his chair. "Something bit my ankle." His face began to turn red and he turned to Mr. Parker for an explanation.

But Mr. Parker looked just as bewildered.

Violet felt a flush creep up her neck. She ducked down behind one of the chairs to search for the cat.

"No!" she exclaimed, and made a move toward Mr. Mischievous. All heads in the room swivelled to her. But she was too late—the cat crouched and sprang off of an unoccupied chair opposite Violet and scrambled awkwardly up onto the conference table. He began meowing loudly as he limped up and down, his tail in the air, looking for all the world as if *he* were the CEO of Golden Gate Records.

No one made a sound. They all simply stared at the Siamese.

Violet darted forward to catch the cat, but he only eluded her, jostling coffee cups as he darted unsteadily toward the neat pile of papers next to Henry.

Violet, slightly out of breath, continued with her speech. "You're conducting an illegal buyout of *my* property. Golden Gate Records has been engaging in illegal activities from the very beginning. And this proves it!" Violet whipped out the crumpled paper from her pocket.

"What the hell is this?" DuPont exclaimed.

The cat jumped up onto the pile of papers and sent them flying in all directions before he sat down in the middle of the whole mess and promptly started to give himself a bath.

Mr. Parker eyed the cat. "Miss Swanson, I'll have you know that is not true. You're making false—Achoo!—accusations."

Seizing the opportunity, Violet snatched at the cat, her hair in disarray as she tried not to slosh coffee on her dotted-swiss blouse with its mother-of-pearl buttons.

The film studio executives shifted and muttered amongst themselves.

"Golden Gate Records acted according to the bylaws and the guidelines set out by city ordinances. Besides, those records you saw me breaking? That's policy; they were only played once. And those so-called bribes?" Mr. Parker clenched his jaw. "Are merely bid prices."

Henry paused, and then sneezed again, before looking at his boss.

"This is an outrage! Get this beast out of here, Parker," DuPont bellowed. "Or you'll be the one out of here!"

Sensing some sort of impending doom, the Siamese began yowling. Mr. Parker made a grab for the cat but missed.

"And that meeting?" Mr. Parker raised his voice to be heard over the caterwauling. "Well, that was in reference to today.

Because, Miss Swanson, I think *you're* the one hiding something." He made an expansive gesture, holding Violet's gaze. "I figured out your secret. You're Gloria Dare, the star of *Dancing At Midnight*. And this meeting was to discuss the talent show you've agreed to. Because these boys are all the way from Hollywood."

MISS SWANSON FLED THE ROOM, her face buried in her handkerchief.

Henry's heart sank.

"I apologize for the inconvenience, gentlemen, but...achoo!" He blew his nose. "But as you know, I spoke earlier about filming. Well, that fits in perfectly, because Miss Dare agreed to do a swing dance number with me as an opener for a talent show that Golden Gate Records is sponsoring at The Blue Mirror Club on the first of next month. So let's film it!"

Silence. Had he said something wrong?

Out of the corner of his eye, Henry saw some film executives stand. Some began sneezing. Most began hastily stuffing their papers into their briefcases.

The cat stopped yowling. And the film executives began drifting out the door behind Gregory DuPont.

Damn it. Henry balled his handkerchief into his hand.

He made a move for the cat, but the animal jumped up on top of the projector, leaving a trail of wet, coffee-colored paw prints all over the shiny surface, before it leapt down and out of sight.

Between sneezes, Henry knelt to see where the cat had gotten to. He began cursing under his breath as papers started raining down on him, and the coffee drip-drip-dripped off the table and onto his head.

"Parker! What are you doing on the floor? Get up. Get up. You're a genius!"

"But sir..." Henry swallowed, sneezed, and then started to crawl underneath the conference table to reach the cat.

Just a few more inches... The cat didn't move a muscle; it only blinked up at

Henry. Henry stretched out his hand, slowly, slowly...

The cat shot out from underneath the table and made a beeline for the door as Henry watched from his position between chair and table legs.

Henry clenched his teeth as he backed out from under the table.

"...Are you listening to a word I'm saying, Parker?"

"Sir, I—Ouch!" Henry banged the back of his head on the edge of the table as he tried to stand too soon.

"Sir, I'm so sorry. I didn't know—"

"It looks, Parker, like RKO loved the whole thing. The accusations. The coffee. Even the cat. That's why they want to double their offer price! They're already arranging the paperwork to get Gloria's studio to loan her to RKO."

"Mr. DuPont," Henry attempted to adjust his tie, which now had blotches of coffee all over it, "I don't know where that cat came from but it's not mine and I had nothing to do with its entry into this building..."

DuPont crossed his arms and tapped his foot.

Henry blinked and slowly straightened up. "Wait. What did you say?"

"They're doubling their offering price, Parker. They want Golden Gate Records to provide the whole soundtrack for the picture. Not only that, but they love your idea of filming Gloria Dare at the talent show! They want her in the starring role."

Chapter Five

FROM JUST INSIDE THE BLUE Mirror Club on the evening of the talent show, Henry sighed with relief. He watched Miss Swanson step out of the yellow cab and onto the curb after a second or two of fumbling with the door handle before she paid the cabbie.

Henry caught his breath. She looked ready for the silver screen tonight, wearing a filmy strapless lavender evening gown. Was he ready, though?

He felt a flicker of anger at himself for worrying if she'd jeopardized his chance of dancing on film. After all, their number was for the greater good of the talent show's success. Wasn't it? He frowned, and smoothed his tie.

He had to admit, the past few days had been hell. Not only had he been racked by guilt at withholding the truth from her, but he also hadn't heard from her at all. She hadn't even shown up at work. It was as if she'd gone into hiding. He'd been placating DuPont and all the studio executives with reassurances. After all, she hadn't found him and said she was backing out.

But even when he'd swung by her place, he'd been unable to track her down. He'd thought she'd be over the moon to have a second chance in Hollywood. Or at the very least, come yell at him for outing her secret. But he'd seen nothing of her. Until now.

He watched as she bit her lip and glanced around, the light catching the sparkle of her diamante hair comb. But she held her head high as she eased through the throng of onlookers who spilled out even onto the sidewalk in front of the club.

She squeezed her way into the club's foyer. He started to make his way toward her, smiling as she automatically moved

her head to the bright brass-infused beat while she scanned the crowd for—him? He touched her elbow.

Violet jumped, then smoothed down the chiffon folds of her floor-length gown. They made their way into the club and over to the dance floor.

A microphone crackled as the bright notes of Nick Hart's ensemble faded when Gregory DuPont stepped onto the stage.

"Violet," Henry whispered in her ear, as they maneuvered onto the dance floor. "I didn't mean to upset you or hurt you. I wanted to give your career a second chance and I tried to find you, before tonight, to explain everything. I'm sorry."

VIOLET THOUGHT SHE'D BEEN BRAVE, done the right thing, in coming out here to-night. But was she ridiculous for thinking that she'd ever be able to fix things? To hope that she could overcome her fear of performing in public, when all she'd done so far was gotten herself—and everyone around her—into a colossal mess?

She found herself looking up at Henry. He met her gaze; his eyes at first questioning, but then he smiled. Well, maybe she could allow herself to relax and enjoy the music, the melody, the moment.

And maybe she wouldn't make a mess of everything after all. Not with dancing. And not with Henry.

Violet felt the play of muscle in his arm as he turned her again, and again. "I forgive you, Henry, because I've made a mess of things for you. So I'm sorry, too," she said. "I have a knack for messing things up."

"Now, I don't think that's entirely true." Henry squeezed their joined hands as the buoyant, happy notes changed tempo.

"Yes, but it is."

The sound of trumpets and the crash of cymbals faded into the background as Violet looked into Henry's blue eyes, silently waiting for the downbeat, her body swaying in tune with his. She had to say it. And she had to say it now. She couldn't keep avoiding the truth. She owed it to him, and to herself. She stopped moving.

"Henry, I came here tonight to help out my studio. But also to confess. That's why you couldn't find me after the film studio meeting. You see, I was hiding."

Henry opened his mouth to say something but the pop of a flashbulb in their faces silenced them both. More flashbulbs went off as a circle of pressmen began to form around them. "Miss Dare, Miss Dare! This fellow your new co-star?"

"Over here, Miss Dare! Is this a new movie in the works for you now that *Dancing At Midnight* has wrapped?"

"Gloria! Gloria! Why are you here filming in San Francisco instead of L.A?"

"But I'm *not* Gloria Dare!" Violet blurted.

"You're not?" Henry's brow wrinkled.

"Oh sure, Gloria. There's no need to keep your identity a secret. We know all about that." One pressman laughed. Another popped a flashbulb in her face.

"I bet that's what your press agent told you to say," a third one called. "After all, that's why this whole scene at the club is being filmed right now, isn't it?"

Violet looked at Henry. "Is that true?"

Henry looked glum, but nodded.

Violet's mouth dropped open. "You're *filming* this?" She started backing away from him. "And you think you can just apologize in advance for something like that? You came waltzing in there asking me to do swing dance with you when all along you had this going on behind the scenes, behind my back?"

"That's what I was wanting to explain to you before tonight. But I couldn't find you." He crossed his arms.

"You tricked me into thinking that you actually wanted me to swing dance with you—"

"But you're the one who agreed to the idea in the first place!" Henry frowned.

"That's irrelevant!" Violet jabbed her finger closer to his chest. "The point is,"

she said through gritted teeth, "that you lied to me, you betrayed me."

"You're just as much to blame! You were the one who led me to believe you were Gloria Dare."

"Oh, no, you don't get to do that." Violet glared at Henry. "You don't get to tell me that I duped you, mister, when you and your fancy corporation were lying to me the whole time about the talent show. And that's besides your trying to steal my grandmother's legacy. Not only that, you told everyone about Gloria Dare!" Violet's stomach dropped.

"You want the truth?" she continued in a low voice. "The studio fired me because I was responsible for a huge accident that nearly ruined the set of the sequel to *Dancing At Midnight*. That's why I was scared to dance with you, scared to perform in public. Especially tonight." A lock of hair fell into her eye and she batted it away with a huff. "But I went ahead and did it. For myself. For the dance studio. And for you. But that was before I knew you were filming it. And now look what happened with this mess I made."

She fumbled for her handkerchief and blinked back tears, hoping her eyes didn't look too red and puffy. But she couldn't feel sorry for herself. It wouldn't get her anywhere.

"Come on, Gloria," one of the pressmen shouted, "now tell us what this picture's about."

"I'm *not* Gloria Dare," Violet repeated.

"She's telling the truth, boys, because she's not Gloria Dare. I am." A woman in a black dress stood off to the side of the dance floor, her hands on her hips.

"Rose?" Violet's eyes widened. "What are you doing here?"

"Word gets around in Hollywood, sis."

Henry looked back and forth between the two women. "Wait a minute. You two look just exactly alike."

Violet lifted her chin. "Because we're identical twins, I was the stand-in for my sister Rose—her stage name is Gloria Dare—in *Dancing At Midnight*. But after I

caused that awful mess on the set of the sequel and they fired me, Rose had to lay low for awhile. So I guess you made an assumption about who was who."

"Yes, but you could have told me in the first place."

Henry's jaw tightened and he strode away before Violet could explain further. From somewhere backstage, Violet heard Gregory DuPont yell, "—then turn off the cameras!"

Rose stepped directly in the path of the newspapermen. "Please leave my sister alone." Rose smiled, but there was steel behind the sparkle. With one last pop of a flashbulb, the horde of journalists finally backed away from Violet.

Rose put an arm around Violet. A sob built in Violet's throat but she swallowed it back. "You're always rescuing me, Rose. I thought I could help you out for once."

"Oh, Violet." Rose squeezed her sister's shoulder. "Don't worry about it. You and your fella go on, I'll keep 'em at bay."

"He's not my fella." Violet winced and

glanced at the space where Henry had stood only moments before. "And I don't think he ever will be now."

Chapter Six

VIOLET SAT ON THE APRICOT couch, picking absently at the upholstered buttons on its arm, and trying to distract herself by flipping through Molly's copy of *Silver Screen*. No need to keep it hidden now.

She sighed. The distraction wasn't working. And now she'd dripped tea all over Marlene Dietrich's face. She rubbed the spot off with her handkerchief but Marlene's face had now been warped.

Molly wouldn't like that too much.

Violet gnawed her lip and hated herself for continuing to glance over at the telephone, which hadn't rung in days. But at least Violet's dance studio had visitors stopping by every day saying they wanted to take lessons once she'd finished with the repairs. And RKO wanted Rose to make a new swing-dance picture set in

San Francisco.

Violet smiled, but it faltered. She had been such a ninny, allowing herself to hope that Henry would have—she winced as she allowed herself to acknowledge the fact—asked her to dinner. Or to the pictures. Or heck, she'd even settle for an ice cream cone.

But he hadn't done any of those things. Not that she'd really expected him to, what with their whole talent show number unravelling and her own behaviour. She sighed. Had she imagined the intensity of his crystal-blue eyes as they'd danced together? Had she made up the soft touch of his warm hand on her back as he guided her through each step?

She glared at the phone yet again. But that didn't make it ring.

She tossed aside Molly's magazine, then got up so suddenly that the Siamese, who had been peacefully napping beside her now that his leg was healing, jerked his head up and looked around with a sleepy *murrrumph*.

Violet marched over to the offending

machine. She was more annoyed at herself than anything else, for allowing herself to give in to hope and let herself dream, more than once, of being in Henry's embrace. And not just for dancing.

She picked up the heavy black telephone. She'd just decided to stuff it into the broom closet when she looked down and saw that the thick brown telephone cord was chewed clean through and was no longer attached to the telephone.

Did they actually have mice, after all? No, the cat should have—The cat! Violet didn't suppress the flare of hope that surged through her at the realization.

He must have chewed through the cord. It was a wonder he hadn't electrocuted himself. But after his record studio antics and his trip to the vet, Violet knew Mr. Mischievous had at least nine lives. Violet glanced at the sofa and began to laugh. The Siamese now had his head tucked upside down, between his paws, and was snoozing once more.

She shook her head and put the phone

back down. Her hands, though, were shaking, and she tucked them into the pockets of her gingham dress. Now she had the perfect reason to find Henry. But she bit her lip again. Had he actually tried to call her at all or was she just letting her imagination run away with her—again?

"I'M SORRY, SIR." THE SODA fountain attendant adjusted his white apron. "We're all out of that ice cream flavor right now. That tourist group," he waved a hand behind him, "took the last of it. The best I can offer you is strawberry." He glanced in Violet's direction. "Unless you want to share?"

Henry met Violet's eyes, his brows raised.

Violet blushed, then nodded.

After they'd found a table, and had eaten partway through the sundae between them, Violet spoke. "Listen, I want to apologize for my behavior, well, ever since I met you, actually. That's, um, part

of why I asked you to have ice cream with me."

"Only part?" Henry studied her, then took a bite of ice cream.

Oh boy. Violet scooped up a spoonful of whipped cream and took a deep breath.

"When I stopped by Golden Gate Records today to pick up my things, I didn't know if you'd even want to see me," Violet blurted as they finished off the sundae.

Instead of replying, Henry stood and offered her his arm. She took it. After she'd paid for their dessert, of course.

"Why did you come here?" Henry asked as they strode out into the sunshine and onto the pier.

"Because I like their ice cream. Oh. You mean to San Francisco. Well," she paused, leaning her elbows on the rough-hewn railing along the boardwalk. "I'd hoped to make things right. And to figure out what I really wanted instead of just following along with what everyone else thought I should do."

"I can understand," he said softly. "All those expectations that you have in your head." He pulled out the handkerchief from the pocket of his suit jacket and began fiddling with the red piping along the handkerchief's edge.

Violet noticed this one didn't have his initials on it, but she watched his fingers pleat and then un-pleat the stiffly starched fabric. "Have you seen the seals out on Pier 51? They're a real hoot."

He was studying her now, as if seeing her for the first time, and it seemed like he might be moving closer...

"The seals!" she practically shouted.

Henry took a step back.

"Oh, I mean, uh, we haven't seen the seals yet." Violet bit her lip.

"N-o, we haven't."

"Come on, it's not that far." Violet offered him her arm with a playful flourish.

He took it and they set off together, the sun shining down on them and the breeze buffeting their clothes, with tourists jostling them.

"So do you think you're going to leave?" But he addressed his question to the water. "After...after..." He swallowed. "Everything that's happened between us?"

Violet darted a glance toward him. "Over the last few days, I've had time to think things through. The thing is, I couldn't have told you at the very beginning about my sister and me, because it would've put her career in jeopardy. Rose was in the middle of re-shooting the sequel to *Dancing At Midnight*. And if word got out about the on-set accident, well, that wouldn't have helped box office sales any. Not to mention my own reputation was on the line because I wanted the dance studio to do well under my own name. So we both jumped to conclusions. I thought that you were out to get me." She bit her lip. "And you thought I was a movie star."

"I was to blame, too, so I was justly accused by you." He chuckled. "I just couldn't see it at the time, so I went off, made assumptions, and didn't bother to listen." He ducked his head. "I do that sometimes."

Violet reached a lace-gloved hand out and placed it on his forearm. "Me too."

Henry's gaze met hers. "Two peas in a pod, aren't we? Say, how's about we put aside our differences and all those misunderstandings and start again?"

Violet's heart pounded. "I'd like that."

"Good." The wind ruffled Henry's blond hair. "I needed a few days to sort things out in my head, too. Because back when I first got the talent show idea, well, I thought that I wanted to be in the movies, too. Maybe have a dance number or something in a swing-dance picture. Be like Fred Astaire."

"Oh." Violet blinked. "That's why you were pushing so hard for the talent show to be filmed."

Henry nodded. "I *do* love dancing and don't want to give it up. But after what happened at The Blue Mirror, I realized that I only want to dance...with you," he said softly, reaching for her hand.

They stood there for moments or minutes, Violet couldn't be sure. But the one thing she could be sure of—she felt a swell in her chest. She had found forgiveness.

"Miss Swanson—Violet," Henry said, and placed his hand on top of hers.

He said her name with such earnestness that she couldn't bear to look at him. But she did sneak a glance out of the corner of her eye.

"I screwed up too, you know. I should have been the one to ask you out for ice cream. I know these are just words, but I'm sorry. I'm sorry for the whole buyout situation. And I'm sorry for telling everyone you were Gloria Dare. You'll be happy to know Golden Gate Records has cleared out a few offices in the building we have and turned that into storage instead. But I want to make it up to you. Which is why I've quit my job."

"Whatever for?"

"Well, I haven't liked my job for awhile now, and seeing you stand up for what you believe in gave me the guts to finally leave. Besides, I want to help you out with your studio." Henry squeezed her hand. "And I want us to dance together."

He stopped by a park bench as seagulls dove and squabbled over pieces of popcorn left by earlier passers-by.

Violet felt her skin tingle as he leaned toward her. "I know that it's a little sudden." He ran a thumb across her knuckles. "For me, too. But I want to give things a try between us. And what better way to start than by dancing together? I have a feeling this time we'll get started on the right foot. So what do you say?" He leaned closer.

"Well," she said, leaning in too, "just as long as our fancy footwork doesn't get in the way of studio renovations." She wrapped her arms around his neck. "Then, Mr. Parker, it's a deal. Maybe we could even teach a class or two together." And she kissed him.

He kissed her back, his grip tightening around her waist as he spun her around in a circle. And as her feet left the ground, she knew she'd found her footing once again.

Acknowledgments

Karen Dale Harris – editor, who helped me smooth out the story so it could shine

Shannon Page – copyeditor, who had a great eye for detail, especially about San Francisco

Angela Waters – graphic designer, who gave me a beautiful and classy cover for the story

Sabrina Volman – friend and beta reader, who graciously read over my manuscript with a fresh set of eyes

My family – who graciously supported me with their love and kindness

SRW writing group – who helped me keep up my writer morale

Unspoken
Lyrics
A Novella
Jessica Eissfeldt

Unspoken Lyrics

A Novella

**The Sweethearts & Jazz Nights Series of Sweet
Historical Romance**

Jessica Eissfeldt

Chapter One

MOLLY EVANS DID HER BEST to ignore the faint but persistent melody that floated through her mind as she shifted in the stiff leather chair.

The head of TransContinental & Western Air's San Francisco office cleared his throat and continued. "You've been with TWA for two and a half years, Miss Evans."

"Yes, sir. You hired me in the autumn of '45 just after they closed the aircraft factory I worked at."

"And your stewardess record is commendable."

Molly smoothed the skirt of her yellow dotted-swiss dress and lifted her chin. "Thank you. I do love it so—that's why I took this job, for the travel and adventure."

"But there's something that's come up."

"Oh?" Molly swallowed the tremor in her voice and smiled.

"You see, we've been in talks with European airlines. Now that the war's over, all the airlines are in competition with each other. Which means that, well, in October of next year, we're going to be starting up something called the Sky Chief service. TWA already started an all-cargo service across the Atlantic earlier this year. But next year, we're looking at providing the first luxury passenger service to Europe."

"That's...wonderful."

"So." He shuffled some papers on his desk. "I've talked with your supervisor. And we've decided to give you a promotion."

"Really?" Molly thought she might jump up and hug him. She restrained herself.

"Yes." He smiled. "That means once you get back from this routine trip to New Orleans the day after tomorrow, we can have a training meeting for your new posting. Just think—soon you'll be head stewardess for our international division. You deserve it. You're one of our best."

"Oh, thank you, sir!" Molly grinned and got up to leave.

"One more thing."

Molly sat back down.

"The international route you'll be flying is New York to Paris. Which means you'd finish out this spring and summer in New York, just so you're familiar with how things are run out of that office. You leave three days from now."

RAYS OF EARLY AFTERNOON MAY sunshine glinted off San Francisco Bay and the Golden Gate Bridge as Molly glanced through one of the round windows in the small silver DC-3 airplane while she began preparing tea, coffee and milk in the tiny galley.

Task accomplished, she tugged at the hem of her blue gabardine TWA air hostess blazer with its matching skirt. Then,

after settling the hatpins of her blue-and-red cockade hat more firmly to her head, she stepped out into the airplane aisle.

"Now that the plane has reached its cruising altitude of nine thousand feet," she told the passengers, "you're free to smoke, and you can take off your seatbelts if you'd like. I'll be coming through the cabin momentarily to serve you coffee, tea or milk. Dinner will be in a few hours. But remember, no cigars inflight, please."

She checked her wristwatch—the only piece of jewelry the company would let her wear—and sighed in relief. The flight was on schedule.

By this time tomorrow, she'd be back in the City by the Bay and then on to her new adventure.

As she passed out Chiclets and then beverages to each of the six passengers, she couldn't help smiling to herself. The last time she'd been on this route, crooner Nick Hart had been aboard. She'd accidentally put Chiclets instead of ice cubes in his Scotch.

He'd been kind enough to laugh it off. That, after all, had been her first flight.

She grinned. Sometimes her job was straight out of the pages of *Silver Screen* magazine. More and more celebrities were making flights these days. Thank goodness she hadn't made that ice cube mix-up with Greta Garbo on her flight yesterday to Los Angeles.

A couple hours later, Molly started to prepare the three-course dinner in the tiny kitchen in the back. She smiled her thanks at the co-pilot, who'd come out of the cockpit to help her serve since she was the only stewardess aboard.

"Weather's holding?" Molly asked.

The co-pilot nodded. "Bit of a storm building over Louisiana. But it's nothing we can't handle."

Molly carefully balanced the last full cardboard tray as the plane shimmied slightly while she walked down the narrow aisle. The co-pilot returned to the cockpit.

Molly gave a warm, reassuring smile at

the passenger despite the pinch of her new navy blue pumps. "There you go, ma'am. Be careful, the tray's heavy. Just set your pillow across your lap and I'll put the tray on top of it."

As twilight faded to dusk, the passengers began nodding off. Molly made her way to the back of the plane, collecting and stacking the dishes.

Humming to herself, she put the soap in the warm water and felt a little thrill.

Despite the long hours, sore feet and back-to-back trips—in fact, the last time she'd flown this route, which wasn't often if she could help it, she'd been in and out of New Orleans so fast she hadn't seen any of the sights—she wouldn't trade this for the world. Not for anything.

She laughed softly to herself. Who was she kidding? She'd been given the world when she'd first walked through the doors of McConnell Air Hostess School in Minneapolis that glorious September day. Before the war had even started. And thanks to her wartime airplane factory job, her fascination with taking to the skies grew.

Freedom and adventure. She'd gotten both in spades when she'd been hired by TWA after the war. Like the time Rita Hayworth had asked her where the best glove shopping in San Francisco was. Or that first orchid lei draped around her neck on Waikiki Beach...

But she'd never had the courage, somehow, to sign up with the Women Airforce Service Pilots during the war. She hadn't had a pilot's license, so she couldn't have joined WASP anyway.

She frowned at a particularly stubborn piece of dried-on food on the white china plate she was scrubbing. But then again, she'd done her part working as an aviation mechanic in that factory...

She started humming again, the tune at first aimless and wandering, but as it always somehow seemed to do, it glided into a soft yet buoyant melody that stayed in her head for hours afterward.

Where the melody came from, she

didn't know. Only that it had always been with her, like a second heartbeat or a trusted friend.

Though she had to admit, as she dried the final dish and caught her balance at a slight bump of turbulence, she had neither the knowledge nor understanding of music to jot it down. Nor the ear for it, either.

She'd just settled into her jumpseat by the exit with her latest issue of *Silver Screen* when cups began rattling in their saucers and her flight bag fell sideways with a thud. Molly put down her magazine.

She moved into the aisle at the worried murmurs of passengers, helping to adjust pillows. Lightning flashed just beyond the windows. Thunder rumbled.

"What's going on here?" Diamonds winked on a young brunette woman's wrist as she snagged Molly's sleeve. "I don't like this one bit." She smoothed down her mink stole.

Molly flashed a warm, reassuring look

at the lady and called out to all the passengers, "Don't worry, folks. Just going a bit lower in altitude to get around that cloud patch. We should be nearly to New Orleans now—"

The plane jolted.

Molly caught her balance and repeated her reassurances to the other passengers who woke with all the jostling.

More thunder boomed and cracked. A child began crying. Lightning flashed in rapid succession outside the windows.

Turbulence made Molly stumble.

The plane jerked and bucked and some suitcases tumbled into the aisle from the overhead rack.

"Ladies and gentlemen, please stay in your seats and fasten your seatbelts. Don't worry, we're just going to alter our flight path."

But the wind picked up. The airplane stuttered and shimmed. Lightning flashed every few seconds.

Keep your chin up and your smile on, Molly chanted to herself. She grated her

teeth against a roil of airsickness.

Rain lashed at the propellers and the wind howled.

A hissing crackle and snap sounded. The cabin lights flickered.

Molly gave another reassuring smile to everyone. Then she ducked behind the partition separating the passengers from the cockpit to confirm their altered flight plan. She would not throw up.

But at the sight of the co-pilot sprawled semi-conscious in his seat, Molly's stomach did a loop-de-loop.

Several of the control panel's dials were spinning crazily. The lightning must have hit the entire navigation system.

Was the pilot—

"Miss Evans!" The pilot glanced over his shoulder at Molly. "I need you to help me land the plane."

Molly glanced at the co-pilot and bit the inside of her cheek. She checked him for a pulse. Faint but present.

"He's dazed and can't operate the controls. He hit his head on the control panel with that last bout of turbulence," the pilot said. "Careful when you move him."

She took a deep breath and helped the co-pilot ease out of the seat and onto the floor.

Nothing to panic about. She gave a shaky laugh. Just keep going. Focus. After all, they'd learned all about aircraft aerodynamics and flight procedures at McConnell's. In theory. How much different could it be from the drawings?

Besides, she'd put together lots of control panels in the airplane factory. So she knew what levers went where.

With trembling hands, she pressed the button on the mic. "Ladies and gentlemen, due to the sudden storm, we need to land." She suppressed the quaver in her tone. "This is just a routine precaution. We'll get you safely on the ground in no time."

Molly put the comm back.

"Check the chart," the pilot said. "We're sixty miles from New Orleans and need to find an airstrip to land on around

here."

Molly took the paper chart and scanned it. No commercial airports nearby. Military bases were too far away, too.

She checked the flight plan. Frowned. There was nothing around. Nowhere they could safely—wait.

She double-checked their coordinates. Yes. She scanned the chart again. A tiny grass airstrip, next to a large tract of land.

"It looks like there's a private landing strip ten miles from here."

"Good. Now I need you to watch the altimeter and let me know when we pass five thousand feet."

Molly nodded.

Beads of sweat formed on her forehead. She squeezed her eyes shut a second against the nausea before opening them and surveying the sea of gauges and dials in front of her.

Taking a deep breath, she confirmed their position. Checked the altimeter. Everything looked good so far. Level and—

More lightning flashed. The airplane jolted. Molly's stomach jumped. The props droned on, only marginally reassuring.

As the plane started to descend, Molly peered out into the gloom and could see nothing but darkness and lightning. Oh, why had she thought being a stewardess would be a lark and free her from responsibilities?

She gritted her teeth. "Five thousand feet."

"Start to lower the flaps," the pilot said.

She gradually began to slide that lever down. More lightning followed by a rumble of thunder. Rain slashed the windshield. "Three thousand feet," she said.

But the sudden swoop in her stomach wasn't a bout of airsickness. She was helping to fly. An airplane. Really and truly.

She slid the lever down further, looked up from the control panel and grinned.

But another roil of airsickness had her

clenching the lever, her knuckles white.

They broke through the cloud cover. Molly could see what she prayed was the strip next to a large open field—she couldn't tell for sure in the dark and pouring rain. At least the land looked like a field. She hoped it wasn't a swamp filled with alligators.

"One thousand feet," she said.

"Now extend the landing gear," the pilot said.

Molly flipped the switch that lowered the wheels.

With a bumping and jarring, the propellers droning, the plane finally touched solid ground. Molly let out a breath of relief. Maybe she would've made it in WASP after all?

But her job wasn't finished.

She peered through the darkness. About a quarter-mile away, she could see faint flickers of light from a large dark shape that must be a house.

"You stay here and tend to Jim," the pilot said. "I'll go get help."

Molly straightened her hat. "I'm part of this crew." She got up from the cockpit on shaky legs. "I can do it. I'll just go check on the passengers first."

The pilot studied her a second. "All right, go ahead then. I need to check the extent of the damage, anyway."

She walked back down the aisle. "Is everyone all right?" No one looked hurt. Just dazed.

"Well, ladies and gentlemen, it looks like we'll give you the scenic tour of rural Louisiana tonight."

"What's going on here? You almost got us killed! You don't even know how to do your job," a bald, spectacled man shouted.

"The plane has landed safely, but just not quite in the right spot." She smiled to cover her nerves. She wasn't going to let a little detour like this muddy up TWA's good name.

"And there's more good news—I spotted a house about a quarter mile from here we can take shelter at."

"I don't want to shelter anywhere. I

want my money back! This is horrible service." The yellow silk daisy petals on a middle-aged lady's hat fluttered as she looked up to glare at Molly.

"We'll get this all sorted out." Molly straightened her spine and fought off weariness. "For the time being, though, let's not panic. The pilot's tried radioing for help but the comm is knocked out. The rain doesn't look like it's stopping any time soon. Now, since you're still the responsibility of TWA, please stay here."

"I didn't pay nearly $100 to be stuck in backwater Louisiana at midnight and get pneumonia. I just might sue." The young brunette woman frowned and wrapped her mink stole more tightly around her shoulders.

"Let's not overreact," Molly said. "I'll go see if I can get some help at that house and then come back."

After putting on her stewardess jacket in signature TWA red, she shoved awkwardly at the door of the plane. Wind howled on the other side.

Finally she pushed it open, the near gale-force winds ripping it out of her grasp.

Molly teetered back and forth on the edge, her knuckles white on the door frame. Well, compared to that time in San Antonio when she'd had to refuel the plane in her high heels, this was a piece of cake. Right?

She ducked her head back into the cabin and straightened her shoulders. What would Amelia Earhart have done? Faced the alligators, of course.

Molly looked down. Then, before she could think a moment longer, she slipped off her heels and jumped. The fall felt forever in the pitch black.

Cold water and slimy mud squelched between her toes, ruining her silk stockings. But no alligators. Yet.

She lifted her chin and glanced around. She didn't think she was near a bayou.

Pure blackness surrounded her. She frowned. She could have sworn she'd seen a house light in the distance when she'd been back in the cockpit.

She blinked and swivelled her head. Yes. There it was. Faint but unmistakable.

She started moving forward, heels in one hand, mud sucking at her every step. The rain soon soaked through her jacket and then through her thin uniform; she shivered.

But, she supposed, stewardesses weren't meant to go slogging through muddy fields at midnight in the pouring rain. At least, not usually. She suppressed a wild giggle and kept walking.

LIGHTNING FLASHED, HIGHLIGHTING THE CURVES of the dust-covered Steinway grand piano that Tristan Lachaynais leaned against in the music room of Twisted Oaks.

Why had he even bothered to come into the music room tonight? He kept this door firmly locked. And everything in it untouched.

He rubbed his forehead. The candles

he'd lit, thanks to the power outage, guttered then sprang back to life. He'd come in here probably because the silence in his head had kept him awake. Yet again.

Thunder rumbled and boomed. Tristan glanced out one of the large casement window framed in heavy burgundy velvet brocade.

He frowned. Under the growling of the thunder a few minutes ago, he thought he'd heard the drone of—He cocked his head. An airplane? This late at night? That Honeycutt boy up the road a piece only flew in the daytime...

No. His ears must be playing tricks on him. Just like the rest of his artistic perceptions these days.

He had no music in his mind, so now he was pretending to hear things. Though he'd always had an ear for melodies, not airplanes. That was partly why he'd never served in the war...

Tristan continued to lean against the piano, its solid weight a comfort despite his not touching its keys in years.

He reached out a fingertip. He smoothed out the creased and torn piece of paper on top of a pile of sheet music. Just where she'd left it. Right here on top of the piano.

He studied the letter. His eyes moved automatically to the last few lines. The back-slanting l's, the not-quite-crossed t's. Her handwriting. His dead wife's.

Congratulations, Tristan! I'm so proud of you and so looking forward to your performance tonight. All my love, Charlotte.

The next flash of lightning lit up the field beyond the plantation house. Tristan glanced out the window again and squinted. Was that a flash of silver? Some sort of metal. He blinked but all was pitch black again.

He rubbed his temples. He needed to get out of this room.

Lightning flashed again. Yes. He blinked. It was an airplane. And not one of Honeycutt's bi-planes, either.

Had it crashed?

All the blood drained from his face. He reached out to steady himself. Whoever was out there might be hurt or injured or even...dead.

He swallowed.

He had to help them. And quickly.

His heart jumped. Maybe this was his opportunity to make things right...

Besides that, helping was what the Lachaynais family had been doing for generations around here. And now, he was the last of them. It was his duty to help.

He frowned. Even if the last thing he needed was an intrusion. An invasion of his privacy. But the least he could do was offer to help them...

He snuffed out the candles on top of the piano, then crossed the room in long strides to the mantel and snuffed out the candles there as well.

Then he headed to the kitchen and grabbed his rain slicker off its hook by the door and a lantern off a nearby shelf. He

lit it, then jammed his straw hat onto his head.

He'd just turned to double-check he'd locked the music room when a loud banging sounded at the front door.

Everyone knew to use the kitchen entrance. Besides, who would be out and about this late at night?

But he picked up his boots and made his way down the long hallway and into the marble foyer, lightning illuminating his path.

Chairs and hall tables stood silent sentry, covered in a fine layer of dust. Tristan felt a pang of guilt.

He jerked his gaze from the darkness and continued on to the large oak front door.

The banging sounded again, louder this time. Tristan thought of all the people who had come through that door over the centuries.

Governors. Lieutenants. Dignitaries. And, if the family pirate legends were to be believed, even Jean Lafitte himself.

But all those historical figures were un-important when he remembered how Charlotte had laughed and wrapped her arms around his neck as he'd picked her up and carried her across this very threshold on their wedding day four years ago.

Tristan grasped the crystal doorknob and gave it a tug.

Swollen slightly because of the rain, the door at last swung open. There on his wide verandah stood a woman.

Tristan froze.

Her pale blue outfit was wrinkled and mud-stained. And her short red curls clung to her forehead from underneath a drooping blue-and-red cockade hat, the silver wings pinned to the peak wet and heavy from the moisture.

Her stockings were torn. She held a pair of navy blue pumps in one of her neat and slim, though muddy, hands.

She had a smear of mud across her deli-cate cheekbones and he saw weariness mixed with a flash of wariness in her big

hazel eyes.

He couldn't breathe—not because she was the most beautiful woman he'd ever seen—but because she seemed to radiate warmth and sunshine.

He felt raw. Split open. As if all the nerves in his body had somehow been rubbed with sandpaper and then salt.

He blinked, his mind blank. Couldn't he even a form coherent sentence?

But she did. As the young woman gave him her warmest, brightest smile, she said, "Hello there, sir. I'm a TWA stewardess..."

Tristan saw her shiver. She needed to get in out of the wet or she'd catch a cold. Still wordless, he gestured for her to come in. How many others were on the plane?

With a muffled thud, his boots fell onto the hall rug and he scrambled to pick them up. This always happened. He always made himself a blamed fool in front of a pretty girl.

He darted a glance at her and held his breath, as if at any moment the stewardess might disappear. She was, in a word, gorgeous.

Then again, wasn't that a job requirement for stewardesses?

Damn it. This was an emergency. He couldn't be gawking at her.

She spoke again, her words tumbling over each other. "I'm the stewardess on Flight 38 en route to New Orleans. We've crash-landed. The co-pilot's hurt and the passengers are stranded. Radio's out, too."

His eyes widened. The nearest doctor was in New Orleans. His icebox was almost empty. The power could be out for days. And who knew what the roads would be like after this storm. But at least he could offer them all warm beds and something hot to drink.

He realized he'd said nothing to the young woman and tamped down a flicker of irritation at himself for remaining speechless.

He was glad for the darkness, which hid the flush that had no doubt crept up his neck and onto his cheeks. He cleared his throat and opened his mouth, but no words came out. He swallowed and tried again. "How c-can I help?"

"If you have a telephone, I'd love to use it."

"Um." He shifted his weight from one foot to the other, then realized he hadn't said anything else. He gestured, indicating she should come all the way inside. She did, tracking in mud and dirt onto the ancient Aubusson.

He flinched but didn't say anything more until he remembered she'd asked to use the telephone.

"T-telephone's out." Thunder rumbled as if to underscore his point.

"Oh." Her shoulders sagged. She plopped down on a wide bottom step of the curved double staircase and leaned against the ornately carved newel post.

A gust of wind slammed the door shut behind them.

"I have to—" the young woman hid a yawn "—go get the passengers and the pilot and co-pilot. There's only eight people on board besides me."

As Tristan darted a glance at the stewardess, she looked up at him. "I don't know what I would've done if no one had been here."

She blinked and he felt his heart lurch. "E-excuse me." He frowned. Damned nerves. They always made him stutter.

He needed to go get his Ford. Ferry the rest of the passengers over here. She was far too exhausted to be expected to do that herself.

And with that, he turned and abruptly walked out the door to his truck.

MOLLY HEAVED A HUGE YAWN as she finished her bath. It had been a long, difficult evening. For everyone.

She climbed into the bed covered with a hand-stitched, colorful quilt, grateful that everyone and their luggage were settled safely inside.

She wriggled her toes. Oh, it was glorious to be clean again. She'd even gotten all the mud from between her toes.

She shuddered, glad again there weren't any alligators where they'd ended up.

At least, not the scaly green kind.

Their host had said barely more than two words to her. Granted, they were polite, well-considered words. But still. For a Southerner, he certainly knew how to be rude. Well, maybe that was a tad unfair...

She could hardly blame him if he was a bit abrupt. An airplane had crash-landed in this fellow's backyard, after all. And so late at night, too.

She thought again of his soft drawl and frowned. The sooner she got out of the South, the better. Her father, wherever he was now, had been from the South. And her mother had lived to regret it.

Well, Molly certainly wasn't going to repeat her mother's mistake.

She recalled her mother crying in the kitchen late at night. And how Molly and her brother worked three jobs plus the newspaper route, just so they could pay the rent, after—that man—had left them.

She flopped an arm above her head and stared up at the water-stained ceiling in the semi-darkness. She had to get back to San Francisco. This detour wasn't going to stop her.

She closed her eyes and drifted off to sleep.

But somewhere in the middle of a dream about melting clocks, water-logged airplanes and frowning brown-eyed men with curly black hair, she awoke with a start.

Semi-darkness filtered in through the large windows framed by yellowing lace curtains. Worn but plump velvet pillows lay scattered on the wide sill. No wind, either. That must have been what woke her up, she realized.

The storm was over.

Her stomach rumbled. She hadn't eaten anything since dinnertime.

Molly sat up in the four-poster bed. Suddenly wide awake, she swung her legs over the edge of the mattress. The worn

Oriental rug underneath her feet felt dusty yet soft.

Molly flicked the lamp switch experimentally. Nothing. She rummaged around in the nightstand drawer, found some matches along with a candle stub in a saucer, and lit the wick.

After she picked up the hem of her long flower-print voile nightgown, candle in her other hand, Molly edged her way over to the door and slowly opened it.

He'd told the passengers to make themselves at home. Surely he wouldn't mind her poking around in the icebox for something to eat?

The door creaked loudly on its hinges. But no one stirred in the nearby rooms.

Gliding her hand along the polished handrail, Molly made her way, barefoot, down the bare wood stairs of the third floor.

She cocked her head. Was that piano music? The notes seemed to come from the first floor. Her stomach growled again.

A flicker of movement caught the corner of her eye as she reached the worn carpeting of the second-floor landing.

She turned. And gasped, startling backward, banging her bare heel against the edge of the stair tread.

But the ghostly figure had only been her own image in a dusty, mottled gilt mirror mounted on the cracked plaster wall.

She sneezed and continued down the flight of stairs to the first floor.

The wide double staircase curved back on itself in an unfurling of faded flowered carpeting and nicked mahogany balustrades. Fluted columns supported the high ceiling.

She descended to the marble foyer where she and the plantation house owner had stood earlier that evening.

Now where was the kitchen?

The piano notes started up again. She always had loved piano music.

She felt another hunger pang. Maybe that door at the end of the hall would lead her to the kitchen?

Moonlight filtered through the half-open casement windows, the night air heavy with the scent of magnolia blossoms and alive with the whirr and buzz of cicadas.

And above it all, the piano notes seemed to swirl, as if suspended somewhere between reality and imagination.

Molly could see the faintest bit of golden light seeping out from underneath the door at the end of the hall.

She reached out to turn the crystal doorknob. The door swung soundlessly open.

But it wasn't the kitchen.

And she wasn't the only one up.

He wore the same white cotton button-down dress shirt she'd first seen him in, but now it was untucked and rumpled. And his gray trousers were creased.

He sat at the piano bench, his face in profile, his black curly hair tousled as if he'd run his long fingers through it multiple times.

In the candlelight's flickering flame, she

saw his strong jaw clench. His hands tightened into fists where they rested at his sides on the piano bench as he tilted it forward onto two legs.

Suddenly she recalled the exact caramel shade of his eyes as she'd stood on the verandah. A clear, deep, rich hue that seemed to speak of a poet's soul.

She frowned. The lid of the piano was closed. And he stared down at its polished surface.

Molly blinked.

The piano notes weren't coming from the piano but from a small oval music box. Candlelight gleamed on the box's inlaid cherry-wood surface.

He moved his head to look out the window, his face now bathed in moonlight.

He placed the music box, still playing, on a stack of sheet music on top of the piano. He ran a single finger across the oval box's smooth surface.

Molly's stomach flipped.

She shook her head. She didn't need to

waste her time distracting herself with this Southerner's behaviors. Or his good looks. Neither made up for his personality.

Besides all that, she would never see him again after tomorrow anyway. After all, she had a flight to catch and a career about to take off. And then it was on to New York and the rest of her life.

She turned away from the door, suddenly no longer hungry.

AS GOLDEN MORNING LIGHT STREAMED through the kitchen, Tristan carefully knotted the crisp white apron around his waist and then dug in the pantry until he found what he was looking for—a cast iron skillet.

Moving it to the burner on the stove, he then opened the door of the icebox. A slightly wilted head of lettuce, three carrots, a dozen eggs and a hunk of Brie lay there.

It may be all he had to offer, but offer it

he would.

He grabbed the carton of eggs and the cheese and set about whipping up a couple of omelettes. A dash of garlic powder, some freshly chopped chives and a slice or two of cheese and all would be well.

A small smile lifted his lips from their usual frown.

He whisked the eggs a little harder. He hoped he hadn't come across as rude to that stewardess last night. He chewed his lip for a second.

Besides, he had no business even thinking about a woman as beautiful as that stewardess. She was leaving in a matter of hours anyway, what with the power having come back on earlier this morning.

He couldn't do that, could he? Let himself notice someone else? Not after Charlotte's death.

His long fingers tightened on the whisk as he poured the eggs into the skillet. He began chopping up chives; a shade of green that almost matched the flecks of green in the air hostess's hazel eyes.

He shook his head.

No woman had even glanced his way in the past few years. Not that he'd made it easy for them, out here shut up in this big run-down Antebellum mansion by himself for nearly two years.

He'd been glad for the quiet. Glad for the privacy. But, he had to admit, it'd been a little lonely. But that was just because he didn't have his music to keep him company.

He added a sprinkle of garlic powder to the eggs.

Tristan had just lifted the cutting board to scrape the chives into the skillet when he heard heels clicking on flagstones. He glanced over his shoulder.

And nearly dropped the cutting board.

After fumbling, he managed to put the cutting board on the counter and wiped his hands on his apron.

"Good morning," the air hostess said. He still hadn't learned her name.

"Good morning," he replied without turning around. Hopefully she could see he was busy and wouldn't bother him too long. He prodded the eggs with a spatula before turning his attention to slicing up a baguette he'd made yesterday.

Instead of retreating footsteps, though, the soft footfalls came closer. He clamped his lips together.

"Can I help? I'm not the best cook in the world but—"

"Thank you, but that won't be necessary." He cut a look in her direction and saw her shoulders droop. "You're a guest." Tristan softened his tone.

He heard her soft sigh and felt her slight hesitation. He waited.

She turned to face him again and he noticed the pale green of her striped seersucker dress. It was wrinkled but went beautifully with her fair skin.

"Are you a pianist?" she asked so softly he thought at first he'd misheard.

But he hadn't, he realized, as he glanced sideways at her and saw the expectant look in her hazel eyes.

He frowned. Why would she ask that?

His throat tightened. Had she somehow heard Charlotte's music box and thought it was him playing?

She blinked. He blinked.

Then he realized he hadn't answered her question. Perhaps he could simply ignore it and go back to the business of making breakfast.

But still she stood there. She wanted an answer. Well, he didn't have to give it to her. This was his house, after all. His life.

Tristan swore softly under his breath as he realized the eggs were getting over-cooked. He flipped them absently, but expertly, and wondered how to evade her question without seeming rude.

Not that he cared how he came across, but then again, perhaps he did. It had been a goodly amount of time since Charlotte—He jerked his thoughts back to the present and slid the first omelette onto a plate before handing the warm plate to the air hostess.

A flash of annoyance flitted across her face. "I'll tell the others breakfast is ready." She took the plate from him with rather more force than necessary.

He bit back a retort and returned his attention to the skillet. He didn't owe her an explanation. So why, then, did he feel as if he'd been slapped?

He cleared his throat and forced himself to look at her. "Is there anything else I can g-get you before you go?"

She blinked again, finally breaking eye contact with him. "You've done quite enough, thank you."

She turned and left the kitchen. Even though he stood in a beam of sunlight, it suddenly felt cold.

Chapter Two

AFTER BREAKFAST, MOLLY PACED BACK and forth between crumbling, ivy-choked Ionic columns on the wide verandah.

It was already past nine o'clock and her flight back to San Francisco, as a passenger on one of TWA's new Constellations, was in three hours.

And headquarters would have to be notified once she got to New Orleans, so that the DC-3 could be dealt with, since the telephone was still out here because the phone lines had blown down.

The co-pilot, who would be going to a doctor in the city, sat near the steps while the pilot spoke with a few of the passengers.

Everyone who had connecting flights would head directly to the airport to make up their missed connections.

But she couldn't help smiling as she looked around. If there was any place more romantically ramshackle than here, she couldn't find it.

If her friend Violet had been in Molly's place, no doubt she'd already have given their host the role of stoic but good-at-heart hero and herself the beautiful-but-distressed-miss in one of those Gothic novels Molly had given Violet when she'd run out of Dashiell Hammett books.

But Molly herself was not prone to too many flights of fancy.

Speaking of which, where was that man? He'd said he'd arranged with a neighbor to ferry everyone back to the city.

She frowned. Her father had always done that. Used hospitality to disguise his true feelings, often saying the very thing he didn't want to reveal with a backhanded compliment. No doubt their host was just the same.

She shook her head. She couldn't paint all Southern men with the same brush.

But she could try.

The beep of a horn made her jump and she looked up. Two vehicles pulled up into the carriage drive.

A man drove up in a large white panel van. And their host hopped out of a midnight-blue one-ton Ford pickup. The treads on the back tires looked a bit thin and, she noted, had more than one bald spot near the rims.

He gave her a nod as he caught Molly looking his way.

She retreated into the house to make sure everyone had been notified, before she could dwell any further on the way that his pale blue checked chambray shirt had fit his broad shoulders and lithe frame.

Or the way that his brown eyes had again turned a caramel color in the sunlight when he'd looked up at her.

The remaining passengers all filed outside, Molly behind them.

She saw their host lean against a fluted verandah column, arms casually crossed and the brim of his straw hat pushed back.

"Alrighty then," the neighbor said as he got out and swung open the back door of his van. "Why don't y'all come on over here with me and we'll get you back to New Orleans."

From force of long habit, Molly stood and waited while all six passengers got into the back of the van. The pilot and co-pilot sat on the bench seat in front beside the neighbor.

But that's when she realized her mistake.

With no room left in the panel van, she would have to ride with her host.

She forced a smile on her face. It would only be for a little while. She bent to pick up her bag but it was gone.

She looked up to see him holding it. "Oh...thank you."

He gave her a nod and stowed the case in the truck bed. Before she could move, he then opened the passenger door for her. She stepped up onto the running board and then settled onto the bench

seat.

He shut the passenger door with a thud.

She supposed she could forgive him his manners. After all, he didn't know she could very well take care of herself, thanks to the independence she'd gained during the war.

She straightened her skirt as he got in on the driver's side and put the truck in gear.

"I don't believe we've been properly introduced, ma'am. I'm Tristan Lachaynais."

"I'm Molly Evans." Molly fidgeted with her wristwatch. "How long will it take to get into town, Mr. Lachaynais?"

"About an hour, give or t-take."

"What do you mean?"

"Depends on the roads."

"The roads?"

"Might be a bridge wash-out. Or flooding."

"Oh."

Silence fell between them. Molly fidgeted with her wristwatch again.

"Have somewhere to be?" he drawled.

Southerners. Always asking about your business. As if they had some sort of right to know everything about you. Molly frowned. "I have an appointment."

His gaze slid to hers.

She turned her head and looked out the window instead.

"What time's your appointment?"

He chose now to be talkative? Molly withheld a sigh. "My appointment's at three p.m. Today. San Francisco time. And my flight leaves in—" She looked at her watch. "—Two and a half hours."

Mr. Lachaynais merely nodded. Silence fell again.

Molly stole a sideways glance at him as they bounced along the rutted dirt road.

Only an hour more in his company and then she'd be free of him at last.

He shifted gears and the Ford moved up a slight incline and onto the highway. The truck picked up speed.

Molly watched the scenery flash by out the window—nothing but swamps and

Spanish moss. And a few lumpy-looking logs that might have been alligators. Her father used to tease her about her fear of the reptiles.

She turned her gaze back to the straight piece of highway in front of them and reached for the radio dial.

Her fingers collided with Mr. Lachaynais'.

She smiled her best air hostess smile. "Go ahead."

He gave her a quick nod and flicked on the knob. A lively jazz tune floated out. He hastily turned the tuning dial and static erupted. Molly saw the small frown between his brows.

"Here. I can do that for you." She eyed the road. "You're driving, after all."

But he kept his fingers on the dial, twisting until another station came on. Also playing jazz.

He twirled the dial again. More static. Then more music, this time with what sounded like fiddles and accordions.

Mr. Lachaynais flicked his wrist again

and the radio went silent.

"Well, jazz didn't used to be my favorite, either," Molly said, hoping for a pleasant tone.

His hands tightened on the wheel.

Molly continued. "But if I did want to listen to jazz, I'd do it live. My friend Violet and I go to The Blue Mirror Club in San Francisco all the time. They have great jazz there. In fact, crooner Nick—"

"Hart?"

"Yes, Nick Hart. You know him? Is he a friend of yours?"

"I don't believe I said that."

"No, but it seems you might have implied it."

"Maybe."

Molly shifted in her seat and stared out the window again, grudgingly admiring the drape of Spanish moss along the gnarled trees that lined the road. "Have I done something to offend you?" she said at last.

The wheel jerked in Mr. Lachaynais' hands and Molly saw his grip tighten,

along with his jaw.

Molly continued. "I feel like every time I try to say something to you, or ask you about your personal life, you clam up."

Molly saw his shoulders stiffen. "My personal life is p-personal."

A beat of silence passed.

People always told her she was friendly and easy to talk to. Men even said this to her. All the time, in fact.

So what was wrong with her that she couldn't seem to put this man at ease?

Did he just think it was some sort of mask that she was wearing? When she'd tried so hard to be genuine and open and caring. That's why, for heaven's sake, she'd become a stewardess in the first place. Because she enjoyed people and taking care of them.

But it was as if this man had an impenetrable brick wall up around him that no amount of kindness could melt.

"Well, I apologize," Molly said through gritted teeth.

Silence fell once again.

Finally, Molly sighed. "Listen, I'm sorry. I'm not sure what I did to aggravate you but clearly you don't want to talk about it."

Molly tapped her unpainted nails against the doorframe. She'd done her part, at least. This little trip was almost over and then she'd—

Bang!

The steering wheel jumped in Mr. Lachaynais' grip again. He swallowed a curse and tried to jerk the wheel back under control. The tire had blown.

"Steer straight and take your foot off the gas!" Molly said, her eyes darting to his face. He'd gone pale. "Don't hit the brakes—just apply gentle pressure," she said in a calming tone.

The truck rolled to a halt at last by the shoulder. Mr. Lachaynais swore under his breath, then mumbled an apology with a look in her direction.

Molly gave a shaky laugh.

He put the truck into first, shut it off and got out.

Molly slid across to his side of the bench seat and stepped out onto the running board. "How bad is it?"

Tristan looked up from his crouch by the driver's-side back wheel and rubbed the back of his neck, leaving a greasy streak. "It's definitely flat." He gestured at the road ahead. "And it looks like the others have gone on ahead without us, so I'm sorry to say I think we're in a fix."

Molly jumped down onto the road and began pushing up the sleeves of her dress. "Mind if I take a look?"

Tristan stood. "Now, I don't think a lady such as yourself should go around getting her pretty dress all dirty for the sake of—"

"I spent the war building airplanes. I'm sure I can handle a little flat tire."

This was why she hadn't gotten involved with anyone. They always thought she was some sort of helpless female. Not to mention it interfered with her freedom.

"Be my guest, then." Mr. Lachaynais made an expansive gesture, then crossed his arms.

Molly crouched down. "I'll need to take off the hubcap and loosen the lug nuts. Where's your tire iron?"

"I'll go check under the seat."

Molly swallowed her growing unease. They'd be on their way soon enough again.

But he returned empty-handed and scuffed the toe of his loafer on the pavement.

"You don't have one?" She looked up at him with a flare of annoyance. "I don't suppose you have a spare tire either, what with rubber still in short supply?"

"That was the spare."

"In that case, we *are* in a fix." Molly wiped her hands on her handkerchief and straightened.

Cicadas hummed and a faint breeze stirred the curls on her forehead. "Looks like we'll be hitching a ride, then." Molly glanced up and down the highway.

It was empty.

TRISTAN HAD THE SUDDEN URGE to smooth those wayward curls off her face. She must be hot, and he wished he could offer her a glass of lemonade. Or some reassurances. But found he could produce neither.

His tongue seemed to be stuck to the roof of his mouth.

"Where did you learn to do that, anyhow?" He winced. That could have come out better. He frowned at himself.

She studied him a second before crossing her arms as she replied. "My father. He was a mechanic. And I worked in a Bay Area aircraft factory during the war. Found I had a knack for fixing the planes so I did some work as an airplane mechanic, too." She stuffed her handkerchief into her dress pocket.

"I wasn't in the Service," he blurted. "I'm sorry I couldn't be more help."

Miss Evans blinked at him.

He wasn't sure if he'd meant about the

war or about the blown tire. Maybe both.

"Well, we'll just have to wait." She took a seat on the running board.

He leaned against a front fender. "It'll get awful hot here pretty quick."

She fanned herself with one hand. Tristan couldn't help but notice the grease now under her fingernails and felt a twinge of guilt.

"Oh, I'm sure it won't be long," she replied. But she checked her watch again and gnawed her bottom lip.

The highway remained quiet.

Tristan scratched his head.

"Are there no cars in this desolate place?" Her tone was sharp.

Given her deadline, that was understandable. "Looks like it," Tristan said.

After what seemed like hours, but was only twenty minutes according to Miss Evans' wristwatch, a station wagon neared.

Tristan's heart lifted.

He jumped into action and waved an arm, giving the driver his best please-help look.

But Tristan's heart sank.

The red Chevy station wagon, with wood-panelled doors and out-of-state plates, had five kids squished in the back. The mother in the front seat held a road map, upside down. The father behind the wheel had a confused look on his face. A brown cocker spaniel had its head out one of the rear windows, tongue lolling. And bulging suitcases were tied firmly to the roof.

It sped on by.

MOLLY SWALLOWED AND WISHED FOR a bottle of Coke. Or some water. She'd even be happy with a glass of that ridiculously sweet tea everyone in the South seemed to drink by the gallon. They'd been sitting here over an hour now.

Cicadas droned. The sun grew hotter.

Mr. Lachaynais rolled up his shirt-sleeves and unbuttoned the top button of his chambray shirt.

Molly wished she'd packed a practical

sun hat instead of this minuscule but dressy one. And her hair, no doubt, was starting to frizz. But she straightened her shoulders and shifted her position on the running board.

She glanced over at Mr. Lachaynais, who still leaned against the front fender. His jaw was set and his expression seemed far away as he took off his straw hat and wiped his brow.

"I wasn't supposed to miss the flight," she said softly.

He swatted away a mosquito that buzzed near her ear. "You know, some people say that there's no amount of 'supposed to' in the world. That some things simply aren't," he gestured up to the bright blue sky, "written in the stars."

"You're a romantic?" She glanced at him, and she saw the flush creep up his neck.

He shrugged a shoulder. "In some things, yes. When it counts," he said softly.

Molly cleared her throat. "Mr.

Lachaynais, I'm sorry if I snapped at you back there. I just—" Molly sighed. "—I have a new job I'm supposed to be starting soon..."

Mr. Lachaynais sighed too. "Well, we're in this together. Might as well call me Tristan. And I wouldn't be a gentleman if I let you think like that because it's not your fault. It's mine. I—"

The sound of a vehicle approaching from behind had them both swivelling around.

Sunlight winked off the chrome bumper of a brand-new green Cadillac. The touring sedan came rumbling down the road.

Molly wavered a moment before she jumped up, extended her hand and gave her best smile.

The car came closer. Tristan stuck out his thumb.

White-walled tires crunched on some stray gravel as the car came nearer. And finally slowed.

A young man in a crisp white linen suit

and a Panama hat cranked down the driver's-side window. A young woman, with a pink polka-dot headscarf tied beneath her chin, leaned against the man's shoulder. Tristan explained their predicament.

"Sure thing. We'll get you-all to New Orleans in no time. Hop in back there."

♫

TRISTAN SCRAMBLED TO OPEN THE back door for Molly. Giving him a weary smile, she got in. Her flight was long gone now.

She straightened her shoulders. Well, if she could handle an emergency landing, she'd handle this too. She'd think of something. She always had, hadn't she?

She settled back more comfortably into the leather seat of the Cadillac.

The young woman twisted around, a blonde pin curl escaping from under her silk scarf. "So where y'all headed in town there?"

Molly replied, "Oh, um, the Hotel Monteleone." She'd stayed there last time she

was in New Orleans.

"It's a darlin' place! Are you just married too?" The woman glanced at the man in the driver's seat and chattered on without waiting for a reply. "We had our weddin' reception there, didn't we, dear?" She leaned over and kissed the man on the cheek. He took her hand and interlaced their fingers.

Molly shifted in her seat and began drumming her fingers on her suitcase.

How could she have let this happen? She should've said something about the tires. She frowned. She should've asked Mr. Lachaynais—*Tristan*—to drive a different vehicle. She should have—

"Sure did." The man grinned. "Only last week, too."

"Well, congratulations," Tristan said.

The young woman beamed. "Now we're off to our honeymoon—in Hawaii!"

"Make sure you go to the pink sand beaches," Molly said, then sighed. Thinking about what she should've done wouldn't change her present circumstances.

"You've been there?" The young woman powdered her nose, then shut her engraved silver compact with a snap.

"I'm an air hostess for TWA," Molly said. "But I'm not staying for long at the Monteleone. I'm heading back to San Francisco for a meeting with my supervisors tomorrow."

"Golly!"

Tristan cleared his throat. "Does your appointment have to do with your new job?"

Molly glanced over at him. That was observant of him. She supposed it wouldn't hurt to tell him a bit more about it now. Now that they were in this together. "I'm supposed to be at a meeting about the new Sky Chief service since I'm going to be head stewardess for the New York to Paris route TWA's unrolling next year." She paused. "Women really can do anything they set their minds to." She waited for the suppressed smirk. The sideways glance. The disbelief written all over his face.

But it didn't come.

In fact, he looked pleased. "Women these days should be able to do whatever they want. They did help win the war, after all."

Molly's eyes widened. She opened her mouth, closed it, then simply nodded.

"Don't forget to mention your ability to change a tire."

Was that a twinkle of good humor in his eyes? Her heart fluttered.

"Right," Molly said. None of the men she'd known before would ever have said anything like that. She smiled at him. "I'll be sure to mention it."

Tristan smiled back at her.

"Oh, my Walter here fixed all sorts of big machines during the war." The young woman in the front seat laced her arms around her husband's neck and put her head on his shoulder again. "What did you do during the war?" she asked Tristan.

Tristan fidgeted with the door handle. "Oh, I, um." He tugged at his earlobe and his eyes darted to and then away from her face. He lowered his voice. "Played piano at the New Orleans USO. Couldn't do anything else. I had a weak heart so I couldn't join up."

Molly found herself reaching across the seat and placing a hand on his arm.

Tristan's eyes met hers and she thought she saw gratitude there for a moment before he turned his attention out the window. Molly withdrew her hand.

Several more miles passed. The driver flicked on the radio as the New Orleans skyline drew nearer.

The newlyweds began humming along to *(I Love You) For Sentimental Reasons*, singing the chorus to each other.

Molly fiddled with the latch on her suitcase.

Tristan shifted in his seat.

Molly checked her wristwatch one last time. Yes, there was definitely no help for it now. She would simply have to call headquarters long-distance and let her boss know that things were out of her hands. No one could control the weather,

after all. Or a flat tire.

Despite her best intensions not to let her frustration show, she sighed and frowned as the Cadillac headed toward the French Quarter.

THE CADILLAC CRUISED ALONG PALM-LINED Canal Street but couldn't find a spot to park.

"Looks like I'll have to let you out here," the young man said. "But the hotel's only a block or two."

He pulled up next to a parked car just as a streetcar clanged a warning as it rattled by.

"Thank you." Tristan handed the man a wad of bills. "You've been very kind."

"Don't be silly." The young woman laughed, waving off the money. "You two just have a good time."

Tristan pocketed the bills again and got out. He rounded the car to open the door for Miss Evans, but she was already out, her small suitcase in hand.

"Here. I can carry that—"

Tristan glanced at her out of the corner of his eye. She bit her lip and blinked rapidly but tried to hide it as she shook her head.

He shut the door for her. The Cadillac left.

Tristan found himself fidgeting and tugging at the cuffs of his shirt.

If she had gone with the neighbor, he wouldn't have to see her beautiful face in distress. Or at least, in anger. Which was probably partly directed toward him.

Well, the least he could do was escort her to her hotel. Not that that would really make up for much. But still, it was worth the gesture.

"Well..." she said as they stepped onto the curb.

His heart pounded and he spoke before he lost his nerve. "T-the least I can do is escort you to the Monteleone." He ducked his head.

She studied him a moment.

He offered her his arm. She took it. His

heart beat a little faster.

They crossed Canal Street and headed left onto Royal Street.

"The Monteleone is just over here," he said. The sudden blare of a trumpet startled him and he turned his head, the glint of bright brass in the mid-afternoon sun catching his eye.

He swallowed.

Yes. He looked more closely. That was Gus. Tristan pulled the brim of his straw fedora lower over his eyes and increased his pace even as Miss Evans slowed her steps to turn and look at the trumpet player. "He's really good," she said, her steps slowing even further.

"'Lo there, ma'am," Tristan could hear Gus call out from behind him.

"Hello there," she replied.

He silently willed her to turn back around.

Finally, she did. The trumpet notes seemed to follow her as Tristan opened the hotel door for her and stepped aside to let her pass, then ducked inside himself.

He recalled with absolute clarity the last night he'd been at the Monteleone's Carousel Bar. When he'd finished playing, finished pouring his heart out.

He remembered the ringing silence and rapturous faces as everyone stared at him, mouths open. The way he'd looked out at the audience, and would've sworn he could almost leap over tall buildings and walk on water.

Miss Evans glanced at Tristan. "Thank you for your hospitality and your help. All the passengers, and crew, are grateful to you. Now if you'll excuse me, I need to use the payphone."

"Right over there," Tristan said, indicating the bank of payphones on the wall next to the reception area.

"Thank you. Well...goodbye then," Miss Evans said.

Tristan cleared his throat. "Goodbye."

He watched her walk over to a payphone on the end and take a seat on the plush blue cushioned stool.

He'd only intended to stay a minute,

just to see her safely inside. But he found himself rooted to the spot in the lobby, his eyes on Molly—*Miss Evans.*

The sun and all that walking had done a number on her appearance; but her disheveled state made her all the more beautiful. His gaze lingered on her as she crossed her legs while sitting, her back to him.

He took off his hat and took a seat on the plush blue circular seat nearby, being sure to sit facing away from the street. Not that Gus would come into a place like this. He was too fastidious for such hoity-toity nonsense, as he would say.

A small smile appeared at Tristan's lips but just as quickly vanished. How long had it been since he'd seen Gus? Or any of the boys? Too long. Far too long.

He crushed the straw brim of his hat between his fingers. He didn't have to hole himself up in that drafty old plantation house as penance forever, did he?

A few notes from the trumpet drifted in as more hotel guests wandered into the lobby from the street and Tristan winced. Yes, he did.

Too many ghosts of his past here. The best place to wrestle with them was in the safety of his plantation house, not on the stages of piano bars in town here.

"Oh, you're still here?" Miss Evans interrupted his thoughts and Tristan looked up. He felt his heart squeeze. She looked happy. That meant she was leaving.

But she sank down on the seat beside him. "They said I'm to come in tomorrow afternoon, so I'll catch the earliest morning flight I can." She studied her handkerchief. "I suppose a crew member at the TWA ticket counter in the airport helped my passengers with their necessary flight changes since they no doubt missed their original ones." She fiddled with the latch on her suitcase.

"You did the best you could, you know," he said, voice low.

She lifted her gaze to his, her hazel eyes widening for a moment. "Oh." She blinked, her lips slightly parted. "Thank you for saying that."

He swallowed and stood up. He needed to leave. He couldn't stay here. Yet he blurted out, "W-would you like to see the Quarter?" What was he saying? "Let me show you around."

Molly's eyes darted to him, to the street, then back to him. She studied him a second. "All right. Let me just check in. And buy postcards for my mother and brother."

She returned several minutes later, written postcards in hand.

They stepped back out onto Royal Street and took a right, deeper into the heart of the French Quarter.

Storefronts displayed rolled-up Orientals and gleaming writing tables, complete with sparkling chandeliers and twelve-place-setting Delft china.

In the alleys, metal trash cans leaned against each other as if remembering the night before, and bright bits of crumpled paper and broken bottles spilled out of their half-open lids.

But Tristan steered Molly—*Miss Evans*—past all that. Though he couldn't help but watch her face full of curiosity and delight as they continued walking.

Charlotte had wanted nothing to do with the Quarter—she thought it was all noisy clubs and brightly colored restaurants with nothing but tourists eating ice cream cones and snapping photos.

He didn't see it that way at all, when he looked around the Quarter...

He felt the rumbling purr of that tiny white kitten he'd rescued from a trash can on Chartres.

He heard the first, and last, time he tried playing trumpet—badly—with Gus at a little jazz club near Jackson Square.

He smelled the Mississippi shrouded in dawn mist as he'd sat on a park bench in Battery Park and wrote the music for one of the songs he'd then performed at the Carousel that night.

Tristan took Miss Evans' arm as they crossed Saint Louis Street and headed further into old New Orleans.

He grinned to himself, a spring in his step as they approached the striped umbrella of a street vendor.

"Say, you must be hungry. I'm sorry to say I couldn't offer much breakfast. How about a po' boy for lunch?"

She laughed. "You Southerners and food. My father used to make cornbread and okra when he—" She stopped abruptly, her mouth pinched.

"Southern comfort is more than just a bottle of whiskey. Food is, too."

"Mmm," Miss Evans said, eyeing the line that snaked down the block.

They joined the end of the line.

Five minutes later, they were at the front. The vendor, in a white apron and white hat, leaned against his cart. "What can I do you for?"

Tristan nodded at Molly. "Go ahead."

"Um, I'll have a braised beef po' boy."

"And I'll have your fried shrimp one."

"That'll be thirty cents for the both of 'em."

Before Tristan could pull out change,

Molly had put down a fifty-cent piece.

"They taste better when you eat them walking along seeing the sights. Shall we?"

Molly nodded and they continued along.

Miss Evans lifted a hand and fanned herself. Her red curls stuck to the nape of her neck, the faint breeze not doing much to temper the rising humidity.

"Sometimes it gets hot enough to fry an egg on the sidewalk," Tristan said.

"Well, today must be a two-egg day."

Their laughter mingled with the sudden riotous piano notes that seemed to come out of nowhere but more than likely came from the jazz club across the way.

Tristan tensed but then relaxed. Maybe he didn't have to be so tense around her. "Bon appetite," he said as Molly took a bite of her sandwich.

"So have you lived here long?"

"You could say that. My family's been here since before the Louisiana Purchase. They came over from France and settled in a house in town here in the 1700s. Still have the townhouse but it's rented out now. But when my great-great-granddad met a local girl, she insisted they move to the country. So they built Twisted Oaks right around 1801." He chuckled but stopped abruptly.

What was happening to him? The last time he'd laughed had been with Charlotte—His heart squeezed and a trickle of dread crawled down his spine.

He called up Charlotte's face in his mind's eye but discovered he couldn't quite remember the exact shade of her blue eyes.

He blinked.

He glanced at Molly's expression; she looked as if she was inviting him to sit down and tell her all his secrets. Well. He took a bite of his sandwich. He wasn't doing that. Ever again.

As they stepped across a bustling side street, the afternoon sun touched the lacy wrought iron adorning houses as they wandered onto Toulouse Street.

Tristan glanced at Miss Evans and noticed the frown lines between her brows.

"Did you enjoy your lunch?"

"Yes, thank you."

The frown remained.

Now he frowned too. "Do you think your chances are ruined now that you've missed your flight?"

"No." She shook her head. "You certainly don't sugarcoat things, do you?"

"Not if I can help it."

"I thought you Southerners liked to sugarcoat everything."

"That's deep-fry everything."

MOLLY AND TRISTAN STROLLED DOWN the narrow street. Pink jasmine, yellow snapdragons and purple-and-white striped petunias, which bloomed in terracotta pots, lined second-story balconettes. The blossoms spilled down and over the wrought iron railings.

Brightly painted shutters now stood half-open to let in the late afternoon breeze.

"Wasn't that trumpet player wonderful?" Molly glanced at Tristan and saw his shoulders tense.

"Sure, he was grand."

Molly pursed her lips. Nothing more than polite and hospitable. That was the trouble with Southern men. They hid their true feelings behind masks of common decency.

Dropping that subject, Molly tried again. "Where are we going?"

"Well, right now we're headed riverside. If we keep walking, we'll get to Pirate Alley near Jackson Square. In fact," his shoulders relaxed, "some of my ancestors had a few duels there. Family legend even says one of them was a pirate."

But instead of continuing on Toulouse, Tristan turned right, back onto Royal Street. "You know, the French Quarter has been here since 1717, and this street was one of the first. It also just happens to have one of the best beignet cafes in the whole Quarter."

Molly couldn't help smiling. That was

probably the most he'd said to her without her trying to pry information out of him.

"It started out as a carriage house in the 1800s. Some say that the ghost of a jilted lover lives upstairs."

"I don't believe in ghosts. Spent too much time during the war dealing with reality to waste much time in nonsense like that."

Tristan didn't reply.

"But there is a certain romance to it," she added.

As they continued along Royal Street, Molly noticed the lacy wrought iron fence that surrounded a gray stone church with crepe myrtle and magnolia trees planted side by side in the churchyard.

"What a picturesque little church," she said.

Tristan didn't answer. He quickened his steps past the church.

But he held the cafe door open for Molly.

The scent of powdered sugar wafted

over her and the sizzle of something frying made her mouth water.

She made her way past bent-wood chairs cuddled up to white marble-topped tables.

As she got in line, Tristan came to a stop just behind her. "Beignets are delicious," he said, leaning toward her, the faint scent of cedar and leather accompanying his words.

"Oh?" She willed her heartbeat to return to normal.

"Yes," he said, his lips curving ever so slightly into a smile. He had rather nice lips. Full and—She wrenched her gaze away from his mouth.

He nodded to the long wooden counter. "They're like donuts. Only, well," he shrugged, "better. In my opinion, anyway."

The man behind the counter cut dough into four squares with a knife, then carefully placed the pieces in boiling oil.

Once they were golden brown, he lifted them out with a long-handled metal spoon and drizzled them with honey. He sprinkled them with powdered sugar, then handed them on a paper plate to the customer in front of Molly.

"Little pillow," she said to herself. "That's what beignet means."

"Yes. You speak French?" Tristan asked. Was that appreciation in his expression?

"I'm fluent. That's part of why they selected me to fly the international route."

She licked her lips and turned away from him, to the man at the counter. "A plate of beignets, please."

"Fifteen cents."

She began fishing in her purse for some change but before she could collect her coins, Tristan had already placed a nickel and dime on the worn wooden counter.

"I could have—" She blinked. Realizing that she wouldn't win if she argued in the face of Southern hospitality, she simply nodded and said, "Thank you."

"The pleasure's all mine," he replied, his brown eyes meeting hers. She sucked in her breath.

But she ignored the flutter of disappointment in her stomach. He was just talking about the food.

Tristan took the grease-spotted plate that the man behind the counter handed him and turned to Molly. "Where would you like to sit?"

"It looks so shady and cool out there in the courtyard."

His eyes darted to the patio door and the church beyond. His lips compressed for a fraction of a second before he nodded. Once. Then silently pushed the patio door open for her.

Molly stepped out into the dappled shade of the cobblestone courtyard and breathed a sigh of relief. A breeze ruffled the potted palms.

She spotted a table at the far corner and headed to it, Tristan behind her.

Tristan set the plate in front of her. "I'm going to order a cafe au lait. Would you like one?"

Molly shook her head.

When he returned, he settled himself onto the seat across from her, adjusting his chair so that he faced away from the church and its small graveyard.

She couldn't help but notice the mossy, water-stained white marble of the above-ground tombs.

"Why aren't the graves in the ground?"

Tristan shifted in his chair. Molly saw a flicker of pain in his dark eyes.

She looked past his shoulder. Ivy and vines twined themselves together over stone angels and under chiselled remembrances.

"The low water table." Tristan fiddled with his straw.

Her gaze lingered on the churchyard. Did he have bad memories of the place? She felt a pinch in her chest. The faint notes of a saxophone solo carried on the breeze. Or was he simply uncomfortable around graveyards in general? Fuchsia and white blossoms lay strewn across the curved tomb-tops. Was *that* why he'd been reluctant to talk just now? Then

again, he didn't seem to say too much, in general.

"They're best if you eat them hot." Tristan handed her a napkin before taking one for himself.

Molly glanced at him. The breeze buffeted his hair and sent a lock tumbling onto his forehead. Of course he was only doing all this as a courtesy.

To distract herself, Molly quickly reached for the nearest beignet and took a bite.

The sweet crispness melted on her tongue and mingled with the powdered sugar. She closed her eyes and took another bite; it tasted like honey and cinnamon.

Before she knew it, she'd completely polished off three of the four beignets liberally sprinkled with powdered sugar.

"I can see you're enjoying them," Tristan drawled.

Only then did she look up. He was leaning back in his seat, his eyes half-closed, his arms crossed, his expression unreadable.

She blushed as she saw his gaze flick to her mouth, then to the almost-empty plate. "Oh!" Molly straightened. "Go ahead." She indicated the plate. "Have the last one."

Tristan wrapped his long fingers around the white porcelain mug of cafe au lait he'd ordered and shook his head. "Finish it."

Molly felt warmth spread through her and fixed her gaze determinedly on the plate. This was all utter nonsense. She was leaving in the morning.

So she picked up the last beignet, taking small, careful bites and using her napkin quite liberally.

Just then, the wind gusted, dusting her dress with powdered sugar.

She grabbed another napkin from the dispenser and proceeded to wipe it off as best she could.

Tristan extended a fistful of napkins to her.

"Thanks." She smiled wryly and continued to brush off her dress until it was clean.

He nodded, then leaned forward suddenly, his face cast part in shadow, part in sunlight.

Her heart sped up.

He hesitated, then reached out a hand, "There's a little..."

Her own hand flew up. "Do I have something on my face?"

"Just on your left, right above your...here." His thumb lightly touched her cheek.

Her skin tingled as he gently brushed off the stray bits of powdered sugar.

She hadn't realized she'd been holding her breath until she let it out.

She flushed and twisted her napkin in her lap. Since when was she the shy and blushing one? She opened her mouth to say something but no words came out.

Tristan snatched his hand away and stood, grabbing up the plate with stiff, jerky motions before striding over to the trash can in the opposite corner of the courtyard and tossing it in.

She stood too and collected her hat and purse.

A trickle of guilt worked its way into her mind, followed by a flare of anger.

Why did she feel like she was constantly doing something wrong? Upsetting him?

She walked over to him. He silently turned and led the way out of the cafe and back out onto the street.

Turning to him, she said, "Thank you for the beignets, they were delicious."

"You're welcome," he said, but this time, he didn't offer her his arm.

THE LIGHT BREEZE OF LATE afternoon had cooled some as the sun sank behind the buildings. Molly sighed. It certainly was a charming place.

She ignored the ping of disappointment mixed with relief at Tristan's hands shoved in his pockets and the silence that stretched between them.

She lifted her chin. He'd probably forget all about her anyway by this time tomorrow.

The memory of him sitting at the piano in that moonlit room came back to her and she felt her heart squeeze. What had happened to him?

She shrugged. It was none of her business anyway.

The bright bursts of conversation and occasional peals of laughter from passers-by surrounded them as they wandered, accented by the occasional trill of violin notes or unrolling of a horn melody.

Molly looked up, admiring the way a fern trailed down from a second-story window shutter, when she felt a hand on her arm.

"Oh!"

Tristan had reached out to take her arm but just as quickly dropped his hand. "Careful there."

"What is it?"

"You were about to run into that balconette pole with a *garde depris*."

"With a...what?"

He nodded. "With a garde depris. Spikes. Back in the old days, suitors tried to shimmy up these poles here to be with their lady loves. But supposedly, fathers had spikes installed to prevent such...shenanigans." He glanced over at her.

She laughed. "This is why I love to travel. There are so many new and interesting things to see. So many stories. So much history."

The sound of a burbling fountain caught Molly's ear and she glanced through an archway.

She felt Tristan follow behind her as she walked across cobblestones that opened out into a sun-splashed courtyard with a low stone fountain in the middle and shade trees lining the perimeter.

A lone trombonist lolled against a wooden park bench opposite. The shiny brass of his trombone bell glinted in the orange and rose of the sunset. A pork-pie hat sat at a jaunty angle on his head.

The trombonist jumped up and headed straight for them. "Tristan. Tristan! It's good to see you!"

Tristan veered around the fountain.

But Molly slowed and glanced at Tristan. There was a tic in his jaw.

She glanced back at the man, who was getting closer. "Seems like he wants to talk to you."

Tristan increased his pace. "I know." He swung around to head back out onto the street.

But Molly waved. "Hello there! He's right here."

Tristan froze mid-step, his eyes sliding over to meet Molly's. His eyes darkened, a fierce light in their depths. And all at once, Molly just knew those Lachaynais family legends were true.

But she raised her chin. "He wants to talk to you. I don't think you should just ignore him, do you?"

Every muscle in his body rigid, Tristan slowly turned toward the other man. "Hello, Elliot."

"How have you been keeping?"

"I think you know how I've been keeping, Elliot."

A shadowed look passed over the other man's face. "Yessiree. But that shouldn't stop you. It's a beautiful evening. And," he winked at Molly, "you're with a beautiful gal."

Elliot spread his arms wide, as if to encompass the whole Crescent City. "That's why you should enjoy it all with a little jazz, man."

Tristan frowned. "Listen—"

"I won't hear any of your protests, Tristan. Just so happens we could use an extra musician for tonight. Now that's one coincidence you don't mess with." He chuckled, a deep rumbling sound.

Tristan crossed his arms and glanced at Molly before he pulled the brim of his straw hat lower over his eyes. "N-no."

"Aww, come on." Elliot blew a note or two into his horn. He waggled his eyebrows in Molly's direction. She grinned.

"I don't believe I've had the pleasure of

your acquaintance," Elliot said, making a hint of a bow in Molly's direction. "The name's Elliot Zachary Taylor McPherson III, but my friends call me Elliot."

Molly extended her hand and he shook it. "Pleased to meet you, Elliot. I'm Molly Evans."

"Tristan's new lady friend, I hope?"

"No," Tristan cut in.

"I was only playin,' Tris." Elliot turned to Molly. "Now normally we play every night at nine at the Carousel Bar. But not tonight. There's a sweet little spot up on Bourbon. Oldest bar in the country. Or so they say. You'd love it, I'm sure."

"You're wasting your breath, Elliot. I'm not playing tonight. Or any night."

"Well, now what kind of hospitality is that for your guest?" He nudged Tristan in the ribs. "At the very least, I'm sure Miss Molly here would love to stop and hear the music."

"Yes I would," Molly said. "Which way is Bourbon Street?"

Elliot chuckled. "Just follow the

crowds. But come on, I'll go with y'all. I'm heading there now."

Molly turned to follow Elliot, and for a moment, she thought that Tristan wouldn't come.

But finally, he did, after glancing upward at the rapidly darkening sky.

In a few minutes, they'd arrived on Bourbon Street, the raucous melodies and crush of the crowds leaving Molly breathless.

A firm hand closed over her elbow. Molly glanced around.

Tristan.

He steered her through the revellers until the crowd thinned some as they continued walking to the far end of Bourbon.

His expression was shuttered and she swallowed back her words of thanks.

The place looked just exactly like a house. A very old house, Molly saw. Had Tristan's ancestors sought entertainment here after months on the open ocean?

They entered the small building. It was

packed with people but the buzz of conversation fell away as Tristan stepped through the low doorway.

She glanced at Tristan. His face was pale.

Molly frowned.

Elliot indicated a table near the stage as he headed over to talk with his bandmates.

Molly studied Tristan in the dim candlelight as they sat down.

She followed his gaze to the baby grand piano sitting on the edge of the stage. Tristan's hands balled into fists and his eyes darkened.

The crackle of a microphone silenced the audience. "'Scuse me, ladies and gents. But we have a special guest in the house tonight. Mr. Tristan Lachaynais! Now what do you say he comes up here and tickles the ivories?"

A cheer went up.

"Come on up, Mr. Tristan."

But he didn't move.

Molly leaned in and whispered, "I'd

love to hear you play."

He shoved back his chair.

The crowd silently parted for him as he made his way to the stage.

He settled onto the piano bench. Candles dotted the shiny surface, throwing his features into shadow, but as he looked up, straight at Molly, his eyes glinted in the golden glow of the flickering flames.

Molly caught her breath.

♫

TRISTAN CAUGHT THE LOOK ON Molly's face, her eyes so eager and filled with anticipation.

His stomach clenched and his fingers trembled. Oh God. He bowed his head.

How could he have let himself get into a bind like this?

Anger simmered to the surface of his mind like beans left too long to boil.

How dare Elliot ask him, so blithely, if he'd play something.

As if it were easy. As if he'd actually want to play. As if he had some sort of

well to draw from in order for the music to flow out of him. But maybe it could?

He barely resisted the urge to bang his fist onto the keyboard.

No. He'd tried. And he was completely dried up. A barren musician with not even an inkling of inspiration to source himself from.

Even the memory of music was a distant dream.

Something that he'd loved so very much and had brought him so much pleasure in the past, had now turned and betrayed him.

He swallowed and looked out into the crowd.

He'd never expected it to be like this. He thought he would recover from the pain.

It had been more than two years since Charlotte's death. But the passage of time hadn't served to heal any wounds or allow him to play again.

He swallowed again, his fingers itching to play. But there was nothing. Nothing inside him to express. He had nothing left. And how would anyone else understand that?

Certainly not Elliot, who never had an off day in his life. And for sure not Gus, who'd always been a street musician and lived and breathed music.

He closed his eyes. Felt his eyelids quiver. Had he been fated to stay in his music-less hell for the rest of his life? It appeared so.

He forced his eyes open and cleared his throat. "I'm sorry," he addressed the audience, "but Elliot here seems to have been mistaken. I'll let you enjoy his show."

Tristan very carefully pushed in the piano bench, stood, and walked out of the room, careful to avoid even looking over in Molly's direction.

Tristan let out a sigh of relief as the balmy night air greeted him and his footsteps echoed into the dark. He wasn't going to put himself on the line for her or anyone else. Not now. Not ever.

But then guilt slunk in. He'd just *left* Molly there.

His shoulders tensed as the click of heels sounded on pavement behind him.

"Tristan?"

Molly.

Tristan shoved his hands deep into his trouser pockets. He kept walking. He didn't have the strength to face her.

But Tristan could tell, from the rustle of fabric in the dark, that she'd reached out to try to grab his arm. He simply increased his speed.

"I'm sorry for leaving you so abruptly. But I'm f-fine."

"No, you're not fine. What happened back there—stage fright?"

"I *said* I was fine." He made an effort to soften his voice. "Please. Leave me be."

He heard the click of her heels increase in pace to match his.

"But that piano music I heard last night at the plantation was so beautiful that—"

"That wasn't me, all right?" He winced. So she had heard Charlotte's music box.

"That was a music box. I haven't played a lick since…well, long enough," he said, his shoulders hunched.

"What do you mean? Can't you play?"

"Please," Tristan said again, his voice rougher than before, "leave me be."

"But I want to help you. Did you forget the music you were supposed to play?"

He made an impatient sound. "I remembered far too much." His mouth twisted.

"You're not talking sense."

"You think that just because you're some sort of gorgeous air hostess that you can fix everyone's problems. Well, not everyone lives up there with their feet on clouds. So please. Leave. Me. Be." He abruptly turned a corner onto Chartres Street and blinked back the sting of tears. That was horrendously rude of him. He needed to go back and apologize. He needed to—Damn it.

He needed to stop being so beholden to duty and honor. But he needed to honor his own feelings, too.

Though that didn't mean at the expense of being rude to others. His hands balled into fists.

He needed to hail a cab for Molly—*Miss Evans*. Make sure she got back to the hotel safely even if he didn't escort her personally. Besides that, he'd leave the poor young lady in tears if he didn't apologize.

He pivoted and started walking back in the direction he'd come. He looked up. And nearly ran smack into her.

Molly—Miss Evans. His heart pounded. His hands came up automatically to steady her as he saw her teeter slightly on her high heels. Charlotte's face rose in his mind's eye even as he grasped Molly's bare arms.

He looked down into Molly's upturned face lit by the light of the crowded piano bar across the street, laughter and ragged melodies streaming through its open windows. He blinked.

Again, words were stolen from him, his mind a perfect blank. He looked into her big hazel eyes, fringed, he noticed now, with long red-gold lashes. He could see the tiniest of moles right by her left temple.

He took a jagged breath. Why could he barely speak when he was around her? It was as if not only had he to endure this music wasteland in his mind but also had to look like a blamed fool in her eyes just by his being in her presence.

Under his grip, he could feel Molly's soft, smooth skin. And underneath that, her pulse, racing. Probably frightened he might hurt her.

He released her and hailed her a cab. Then he hung his head, turned and strode away.

Chapter Three

"THE KEY TO ROOM 401, please," Molly said, before taking it from the desk clerk and heading upstairs to go to bed.

She tried to ignore the pinch of hurt in her heart as she slipped into her white flowered nightgown. For a moment, she wished for a candle stub and a rainstorm...

She shrugged a slim shoulder as she belted the matching robe around her waist and begin brushing her teeth. His life wasn't, as Tristan made abundantly clear, any of her business.

She glanced out the hotel room window at the city lights. But she saw instead Tristan's troubled brown eyes. Was music somehow connected to his haunted look?

Something must have hurt him badly for him to just run away like that. From the jazz club. And from her questions. But who? What? And why?

She shook her head. Why did she even care at all? He'd been nothing but rude to her leading up to those moments in the Quarter.

But she'd felt that way too sometimes... When she'd say things she didn't really mean in order to protect herself from how she'd felt inside.

She put on cold cream and slid between the sheets. But loopy, meandering melodies and almost slapstick, happy harmonies floated in through the open window.

This music bore little resemblance to the jazz she'd listened to at The Blue Mirror, but she had to admit that this type of music *did* something to her. So did Tristan.

She rolled over and put the pillow over her head.

♫

AS DAWN TURNED THE SKY to pink and gold, Molly sat up. Today was the day.

She grinned. At least she had one good thing to count on—her promotion. A little while in New York and Paris and then she'd forget all about Mr. Tristan Lachaynais.

Molly jumped out of bed and put on the least wrinkled of the three dresses she'd brought along. A white rayon one with navy blue polka dots, a rusched bodice, cap sleeves and a narrow belt that cinched at her waist.

She ran a comb through her rather tangled curls and put on some lipstick. Then she picked up her small case and headed down to the lobby.

"I'd like to check out. And can you please have a cab sent to this address? I need to go to the airport."

THAT SAME MORNING, TRISTAN STOOD at the edge of the tarmac at Moisant Field, his shoulders sagging.

He clenched his hands into fists as he shoved them deep into his pockets. He'd completely ruined things, hadn't he?

He huffed in irritation. He was always doing that. Why couldn't he express himself?

He couldn't talk to women. And he couldn't play the piano, either. And he couldn't remember the tone of Charlotte's laugh anymore. Or the name of that perfume she used to wear...

He swallowed. Cocked his head. Had he been clinging to the past?

All during the time he'd spent with Molly yesterday...had he simply been lying to himself that he wasn't through grieving Charlotte?

His eyes widened.

Yes. Because he was scared.

He'd used Charlotte's memory, and her death, as a way to protect himself from new possibilities...with Molly.

And Molly was so full of life. He could remember exactly the sound of Molly's voice as she said his name. The way she'd looked up at him when he'd told her she'd done the best she could. Her curiosity as

he'd shown her around the Quarter.

A clamminess broke out on his palms and he rubbed his hands together.

Could he choose new possibilities, after all?

The sound of the airplane engines whining made him glance up. The silver Constellation with the red TWA logo glinted in the sun and started to roll down the runway.

But had that chance for new possibilities slipped right through his fingers?

Birds wheeled in the sky amongst a few puffy clouds as he pushed up the brim of his straw hat to watch Molly's flight taxi and then take off.

She was beautiful. And so accomplished and had, no doubt, traveled the world several times over.

She even knew how to change a tire.

He grinned. He had done none of those things. His parents had insisted on raising him genteelly. No changing tires or getting dirt underneath his fingernails.

Becoming a classical pianist had been

their sole aim for their only child, and that had certainly been accomplished. He knew his way around a piece of Mozart or Bach better than he knew his way around women.

Why couldn't he at least have gotten her phone number? Her address? Said something to her that wouldn't make her frown?

A furrow formed between his own brows. He took off his hat and raked a hand through his hair.

He watched the plane get smaller and smaller until it was a mere speck in the vast blue sky.

He'd never see her again. His heart clenched.

He'd had all those opportunities to say something to Molly, and yet...and yet he couldn't. Or wouldn't?

He cringed as he thought back to the dark street last night. A wave of panic rolled through him, followed by the heat of shame.

How could he have let her see him like

that? Weak and so goddamn vulnerable?

She had no business even wasting one iota of time or compassion for him. She thought, no doubt, that he was pathetic. And rude, on top of that.

He nudged at a stray pebble with his toe before he abruptly turned and made his way back inside the terminal.

Now what was he going to do? He couldn't just lolly-gag around town here.

She was gone. There was nothing he could do about it. Hell, he didn't even know if she was interested in him.

She was nothing more than friendly. It was, after all, her job. She got paid to be nice.

Damn it. Beating himself about it wasn't going to do any good.

He might as well head home. Tow the Ford back to the house. Learn how to change that tire.

While he was at it, he might as well buy Elliot a meal or three. He figured he owed him, not the least for his attempts at kindness last night.

He headed out the front doors and hailed a cab.

After hopping in the nearest one, Tristan rolled down the window and rested his arm along the edge, his shirt sleeve buffeted by the stiff breeze.

How could he fix this? How could he get out of this self-imposed desert he'd created for himself? Not just in his music. But in his life. Because when the music had dried up, so had his life, hadn't it?

He drummed his fingers on his hat brim.

Sitting down and forcing himself to compose a melody wouldn't result in much of anything.

He'd tried that one too many times. But sitting in silence in the tomb-like stillness of his house wouldn't accomplish anything, either.

He cocked his head. Maybe, just maybe, spending some more time here in the city would actually do him some good?

It was certainly better than sitting at home ruminating about the past. The past, which he couldn't change. The past, which he couldn't bring anyone back from. The past, which he'd been clinging to. It needed to be buried and put to rest at last.

Maybe if he simply went to a jazz club or two tonight and listened for a change, instead of trying to produce something, it would work and the floodgates of music would open up again.

It was worth a shot, he decided.

WITHOUT WARNING, THAT SOFT YET buoyant melody started drifting through Molly's mind. She shook her head and pushed open the door to the TWA office in San Francisco at three p.m. Friday.

"Go right on in, Miss Evans," the secretary said. "He's expecting you."

Her boss looked up from some paperwork without smiling and cleared his throat. "Miss Evans. Have a seat."

Molly removed her gloves and sank into the chair, her posture perfect, a confident smile on her face. But her heart was pounding. "I'm eager to start my training."

"Let's talk about your trip to New Orleans for a minute." He leaned his elbows on the desk. "The good news is the plane was retrieved and fixed. But that emergency landing, I have to say, well..."

Molly smiled. "Well, sir, my previous experiences came in handy, I'd say."

The melody hummed along, underneath her words. She shook her head ever so slightly to try and dislodge the notes, but they stuck. If anything, they got louder. More insistent.

"But that's not what a couple of Flight 38's passengers are saying." He paused. "Are you all right, Miss Evans?"

"Oh, yes. Of course. I'm sorry, sir. I'm just a little...I'm fine." She straightened her posture. "Go on. Please."

"Now, granted, it was an emergency landing. But some passengers—our richest customers, actually—are threatening to sue TWA. For neglect and bodily harm. I

even got a call from Mr. Howard Hughes. He doesn't like how this could reflect on his airline. And I don't like how this could reflect on me."

"Sir, I took care of those passengers. They all made it safely to New Orleans and seemed just fine."

"Multiple people complained about the abysmal service. The poor housing choice. Not to mention the missed flight connections. Miss Evans, I'm sorry."

"Wait. What are you saying?" Molly's heart pounded.

"I'm saying you're a liability to this company. Irate customers. Lawsuits. We can't have you jeopardizing our growing business."

"Sir, with all due respect," she took a deep breath, "I followed all the rules. I did everything we're trained to do. I don't see why you're doing this."

He frowned. "Nevertheless. This is what the chain of command has determined. As I've said, the customers aren't happy. Hughes isn't happy. Who's to say how this would've reflected on the company had this been an international flight?" He shook his head. "It could've damaged TWA's reputation beyond repair."

"But I've shown you very clearly that I'm competent at my job." Molly's stomach clenched and she ground her teeth. "It was an emergency. I went above and beyond my duties."

"You should have let the pilot—a man—handle the landing."

"Sir, he asked me to assist him. Yes, I did volunteer to go get help when we'd safely landed. But in the war, I—"

"We're not at war now, are we?"

Molly opened her mouth but just as abruptly closed it.

This man was letting office politics rule his decision. He only cared about the bottom line, not about the right and wrong of the situation.

He wouldn't listen to any argument she made, no matter how clear. No matter how many examples of her competence and excellence she gave, he would continue to offer only excuses and platitudes. And there was nothing, Molly realized, she could do about it.

"Goodbye, Miss Evans."

A falling sensation in her stomach forced her to get up. "Well, then, sir, I guess we have nothing left to say to each other. Goodbye."

For a moment, Molly wished the war was still on. Maybe then, that man would have listened to reason and seen—She sighed. She doubted he would have listened to reason if it had jumped up and bit him.

She pulled her gloves back on with stiff, jerky motions as she stepped out of the building and onto the curb in the late afternoon May sunlight.

She glanced up the street and saw a streetcar headed toward her. She hopped on without looking which direction it was headed.

The rattle and lurching had a soothing effect on her nerves.

If they wouldn't listen to her, perhaps some other airline would. Perhaps—But she knew in her heart that no one would.

Except Tristan would've listened to her... What?

She shook her head.

Her reputation as a stewardess had been forever tarnished. Hadn't it? She sighed. Word would spread. She swallowed and blinked back tears. Her wings of freedom had been clipped.

She took a breath of the salt-scented air. What was she going to do now?

Tristan's brown eyes flitted through her mind and she recalled his comments in the Cadillac. He'd believed in her abilities. She remembered the look on his face as he'd told her she'd done the best she could, in the hotel lobby.

For half a second, she wished he was here. Even if he said nothing to her, at least she'd have his company. His presence.

The streetcar rattled its way downtown, the steep incline as it headed down

Powell Street making her slip a few inches in her seat. She grabbed the brass handrail more firmly.

She couldn't face going back to her apartment. Molly wished Violet still lived there. But Violet and her cat had moved out earlier that month when she and her fiancé Henry had gotten married.

Molly stepped off the streetcar. She started walking, the early evening warm breeze filling her with a longing she couldn't quite place.

She blinked back tears. It didn't seem fair. Then again, was life ever fair, really? Her father taught her that, what with his leaving. Her mother had been inconsolable. And that's when Molly had sworn she'd never fall for a Southerner. Or become so dependent on a man she couldn't do anything on her own.

She sighed, then shook her head at her rather grim thoughts.

She needed to be grateful. She had the skills. She could do something else. She squared her shoulders.

Well, since she was in the neighborhood, maybe some jazz would take her mind off things...

She made her way to the entrance of The Blue Mirror, the streets quiet. Last night, she'd been surrounded by music.

But tonight, the silence only made her want to hear the notes that Tristan never played...

Molly found a seat at one of the booths along the far edge of the dance floor.

This early in the evening, not too many people were there. But Nick Hart and his ensemble warmed up onstage.

She ordered a yellow cab martini and settled back into the plush seat.

At least she could enjoy the show tonight. It would take her mind off her next step. Maybe, just maybe, getting fired wasn't a bad thing? She'd have time now to dream a little bigger. Figure out exactly what kind of future she wanted in the airline industry...

She smiled to herself. She'd really helped land that plane, hadn't she?

As more people filed in and the ensemble finished warming up, she felt herself relax. She would think of something—she always had.

As the music flowed from snappy numbers to more mellow melodies, Molly couldn't help remembering that expression on Tristan's face as he'd sat at that piano. He'd looked so...lost.

And scared, too, she realized. And now he was angry; the way his eyes had blazed there on that dark street... But maybe he actually wasn't angry at her. Maybe he was angry at...what? Who?

She turned her attention back to Nick Hart and saw the joy on his face.

Tristan deserved to look that happy, too, Molly realized. And suddenly, an idea took hold.

THE HEADLIGHTS CUT A SWATH through the darkness, illuminating the creeping ivy on the crumbling red brick.

Home at last.

Though he'd intended to go to bed, Tristan's feet led him past the sweeping double staircase and down the long, dark hall to the locked door at the end.

He fit the skeleton key into the lock and jiggled the handle. The door creaked as he pushed it open.

Moonlight streamed in through the high windows, bathing the Steinway and the pile of sheet music on its closed lid. Exactly as Charlotte had left it all.

His footsteps echoed on the dusty parquet floor. His gut tightened.

Nothing had happened. There was no epiphany. No revelation. No spark that had re-ignited him.

Going to those jazz clubs earlier tonight had only been an exercise in torture.

His jaw clenched as his mind flitted back to last night at Elliot's show.

Why was this happening to him? Why couldn't he play anymore? And why was he allowing himself to wallow in the pain and misery? He needed to stop it.

He let out a noise somewhere between

a snarl and a growl, and stalked over to the pile of sheet music.

He snatched up the first page. Mozart.

For a moment he only stared at it, every muscle in his body rigid as he stood there, looking at something he'd loved so much. Gave himself to in every spare moment he had.

And now?

His fingers bit into the page.

Now? Nothing. It had given nothing in return now, for all these long years.

His head dropped to his chest and warm drops splattered onto the page, blurring the notes so that they started to run together.

His chest heaved. With a roar of rage, he ripped the page in half, his hands shaking.

Blindly, he reached for the next piece of sheet music, neither knowing nor caring what it was.

It had to go. It had to go. There was noting left within him to give, so this music, this love of his life, it had to go.

Maybe then the pain would end and this parched desert would somehow fill up with...what, he didn't know.

He snatched up page after page, shredding each one, his chest tight, his vision blurred around the edges.

Bernini. Bach.

Joplin. Jolson.

All those hours of practice and more practice. Charlotte's soft, encouraging words.

All the summer days he'd given up when he'd longed to be outside in the sunshine, lying in the long grass with Charlotte or out fishing on the bayou.

All for nothing now. Because they were both dead. The music. And Charlotte.

He tore more pages in half, and in half again, shredding and crumpling piece after piece until nothing was left but a pile of tiny white confetti.

He blinked rapidly, his chest still heaving, as he looked around and saw what he had done.

He fell to his knees.

The tiny torn pieces fluttered around him helplessly like wounded butterflies, the moonlight glimmering and glittering as he scooped up the pieces and let them fall through his fingers like sand.

Like his desert.

Like this god-forsaken place he'd somehow stumbled into and could no longer even hope to get out of.

He let his arms fall to his sides and, suddenly exhausted, buried his face in his hands.

That's when he let the rest of his tears fall at last.

♫

"SAY, MR. HART, DO YOU have a minute?" Molly called out to the crooner as he walked backstage.

He turned, a ready smile on his face. "Sure thing. How can I help you?"

"Well, actually, Mr. Hart, I was hoping—great show, by the way—you could give me some..." Molly tapped her finger against her chin. "Insight, I think is the right word."

"All right." Nick leaned against the wall and struck a match to light his cigarette. "I'm listening."

"I went down to New Orleans."

"That's a great city. I bet you heard some swell music." Nick grinned.

Molly nodded. "And I met, well," she spread her fingers wide, "someone who I think is a talented jazz pianist. But the thing is, he won't play. At all. And I think he's stuck in some sort of...oh, I don't know. That's the thing, Mr. Hart. I'm not sure what to do. And I thought you might be able to give me some insight into, well, the musician's mind."

Nick chuckled. "Can't say I can do that for you, but I can try." He smoked his Lucky Strike in silence for a minute. "What did you say his name was?"

"Tristan Lachaynais."

"Hmmm." Nick tapped ash off the ciga-rette. His eyes narrowed, and he cocked his head, looking off into the distance beyond Molly.

"Lachaynais, you say?"

Molly nodded.

"You know," Nick blew out a stream of smoke, "I think I do know that fella."

"Oh?" Molly realized she was holding her breath, so she exhaled.

Nick nodded slowly. "I was down in New Orleans a few years ago, cutting a demo album with a friend of mine." Nick smiled, then cleared his throat. "And we happened to go to the Carousel Bar one night for a show. Friend of a friend, see?"

Molly nodded.

Nick continued, "So after the opening act, there was this amazing, just amazing, pianist that came on next. The man was absolutely superb. Made me think about taking up playing. But only for a minute." Nick finished his cigarette. "He played in such a...haunting way.

"Anyway," he went on, "if he is who I think he is, then after awhile, he got so as every place in that city wanted him to play. Night after night. And he'd do it, too. New Orleans pianists, see, they play something like five hours straight. He got quite well known quite quickly."

Nick paused.

"He had this great opportunity come up at what couldn't have been a worse time for him. See, on the night that he was supposed to perform at the biggest venue in the city, he got word that his wife and his parents died in a car crash."

Molly pressed a hand to her heart.

Nick nodded. "Likely, he's tormented by that. And sometimes that makes you blocked creatively." The crooner shook his head. "Sometimes, well, people become bogged down in something inside their head so that they don't quite know which way is up."

Nick fiddled with a matchbook with the Blue Mirror logo. "I can attest to that myself."

He continued. "You're sort of...stuck in this desert where you can't go back to the material you'd been working on, but you can't move ahead either. Frankly, it's hell."

"So what do you do about it? How can someone help him?"

"Unfortunately, the only person who can get him unblocked is himself."

Molly nodded and turned to go. "Thank you, Mr. Hart."

"You're welcome, miss. And good luck."

Molly headed outside. So much for trying to help Tristan. But could she go back there anyway?

Give herself a day or two in New Orleans to explore more? It'd be almost like a vacation...

She'd go to the Garden District. And walk along the Mississippi. Maybe even take a paddle boat cruise.

While she was there, she could also find Tristan and...what? Force him to become unblocked?

When she wasn't even sure he wanted to see her again or even cared about her at all?

But she did have that melody... The one that had been with her for so long. She wasn't a musician. She couldn't do any-thing with it.

So maybe if she just talked to Tristan and told him about it, that would take care of it...

And then, she decided, he could do what he liked with the tune. Her obliga-tion to the melody would be complete then.

Besides, maybe by helping Tristan, she'd feel a bit better about her own situation.

And, yes, maybe a small part of her wanted to see that Southerner again. But only a small part.

Besides, this was a completely different situation than her mother's. Molly was in charge.

And Tristan, even though he'd gotten stuck, had actually made an effort with something he cared about. Unlike her father.

No, Molly wasn't sitting around wring-ing her hands like her mother had, weeping about not knowing what to do.

She was giving herself a little vacation. And Tristan a solution.

With her chin up, she headed to her apartment to pack.

Chapter Four

MOLLY MADE HER WAY UP the line of idling cabs at New Orleans' Moisant Field airport the next afternoon.

"Battery Park, please. I want to see the paddle boats on the Mississippi."

As the cab slipped into traffic, Molly smiled and settled back into her seat.

But her driver didn't know where Twisted Oaks was, nor had he heard of the Lachaynais name.

She bit her lip and tapped her foot. Wait a minute. She was here to enjoy herself.

The cab pulled up at Battery Park. She got out and walked along the gravel path on the river's edge.

Molly adjusted her veiled hat. A bi-plane zoomed low and then flew off, and she thought for a moment again about the

exhilaration she'd felt at the controls of the DC-3.

Was getting fired from TWA the push she needed to follow her bigger dream? She thought again about sitting in the airplane cockpit. A dream she could barely admit to herself?

Her thoughts flitted back to Tristan. Had that dream stalled out too?

Tristan.

How he'd looked out for her. Her pulse quickened. Listened to her. She smiled. And shown her his heart—even though he hadn't known it.

She recalled that night when she'd first seen him, the pain and hurt and vulnerability in his eyes even as he'd avoided her gaze.

The secrets he had been holding onto that were obviously such painful ones that they shone through his eyes and straight into her heart.

She paused and closed her eyes, lifting her face to the sunshine.

She yawned. She hadn't slept well in

awhile. Too many thoughts about her job. And Tristan.

She couldn't help but remember again Tristan's supportive words in the back of that Cadillac.

So unlike her father's ideas. He never thought she'd make anything of herself. And believed women should mostly spend time in the kitchen.

She laughed. What would he think of Tristan dicing chives? *She* thought it rather nice. And even though Tristan didn't say a lot, he felt a lot. She'd always liked men who weren't afraid of their emotions.

She bought herself an ice cream cone and sat on a park bench to eat it.

That driver might not have known how to get to Tristan's, but Elliot did—and it was nearly showtime now. Surely he'd be playing tonight.

She started walking toward the Monteleone.

Molly shook her head. Who was she kidding? She wasn't here to give Tristan some melody. She was here to see if he liked her.

How was that for ridiculous? Though Violet would probably think it was so romantic. Molly smiled. That didn't make it any easier.

The bellman opened the door of the hotel for Molly with a flourish.

She walked into the hotel's Carousel Bar. Just in time. A band was warming up onstage. Molly approached. But it wasn't Elliot's band.

She made an impatient noise and swung around to the concierge desk.

"Can I help you, ma'am?"

"Yes, please. I'm hoping you might be able to tell me the way to Twisted Oaks Plantation. Jazz pianist Tristan Lachaynais lives there. He's also played in the Carousel Bar here in the past."

The concierge tapped his chin. "I'm afraid I haven't heard of him or that place. I just started working here a few months ago. But the manager has worked here for years. Let me ask him."

A few minutes later, the concierge came back. "You're in luck. The manager knew right away who I meant." He handed Molly a piece of paper. "Give these directions to the cabbie out front. He'll get you there. It's a bit of a drive, though."

He had a point. She could make a fresh start of it tomorrow morning. In the meantime, she'd see the Garden District.

MID-MORNING THE NEXT DAY, THE cab swung onto the long curving driveway that lead to the familiar columned house.

The car pulled up by the verandah. "Thank you ever so much," Molly said as she got out.

"You're welcome, ma'am. Want me to wait?"

Molly nodded and shut the door. Birds chirped. Leaves rustled.

She crossed the gravel driveway and headed up the steps. She lifted the brass door knocker and let it fall, her stomach in knots.

One minute passed.

Then three.

She tried the knocker again, her heart pounding. Still nothing.

After fifteen minutes, Molly chewed her lip. How could he not be here?

Her heart lurched.

Tristan had helped her to see a different view. A different way of being. Whereas before, she thought she only needed freedom.

Now, she could see that Tristan, with his sense of place and home, had shown her that being so free sometimes meant you had no sense of home.

She went around to the back, but the windows were all dark there.

She circled the house again and checked the grounds. No signs of him anywhere.

"Can you take me back into town, please?" She gave the cabbie an extra tip.

It was too late. She wouldn't find Tristan. But at least she knew now: without that sense of home, sense of place, sometimes you had nowhere to go.

Right after lunch, the cab rolled up to the curb of the Monteleone. She paid the fare and got out. She'd need to eat something before heading back to the airport.

Molly made her way to the Carousel Bar to get a sandwich and sank onto a stool there. She picked up the menu.

"Well, if it isn't Miss Molly."

She looked up.

A broad grin split Elliot's face. "Couldn't stay away, could you?"

"No, I guess not."

"Why so glum?"

"Well, I couldn't find Tristan. There's, uh, I mean, I have something I wanted to tell him. Give him... Are you doing a show here tonight?"

"Yes. But first I'm eating lunch. Then got a meeting with the manager here." Elliot settled onto the stool beside hers. "What were you going to give Tristan?"

Molly flushed. "A piece of music. Well, not even that, actually. I've..." Molly glanced out the window. "I've had this melody floating around my head for a long time. I didn't know what to do with it because I'm not a musician. But well, seeing as how Tristan's blocked, I thought maybe a melody would do him good."

Elliot shot her a knowing look. "I see you picked up on what was botherin' Tristan."

THE SAN FRANCISCO TAXI WEAVED through traffic. Tristan glanced out the window.

The cab coasted up and then down hills lined with Victorian row houses. Art Deco brick facades. Flashing neon. And soaring seagulls.

This wasn't like New Orleans much, now, was it? The cab cruised through downtown.

And yet, it had its similarities. The busy sidewalks. Palm trees. The streetcars. Jazz.

"I'll get out here, please," Tristan said. The cab slowed at the edge of Union Square.

The scent of salt air greeted Tristan as

he opened the cab door and stepped out into the late afternoon sunshine.

He pulled the brim of his straw fedora down over his forehead and took a deep breath.

Even the air was different here. He felt a giddy jump in his chest. His fingers curled around the return airline ticket.

He might as well stay in town a little while. Have a vacation of sorts. He'd even write postcards to Elliot and Gus when he got back to his room at the Whitcomb Hotel.

He smiled, remembering how happy Molly had been when she'd dropped those penny postcards in the mailbox by the Monteleone for her mother and brother.

Hours later, he found himself nearing The Blue Mirror Club.

He swallowed.

This was a crazy idea. He wasn't normally prone to crazy ideas, to acting on impulse. Had he really flown over 2,000 miles just to try and track Molly down?

No.

And yes.

Not that he had any reason to believe that she would be interested in him. Which made this idea even crazier. But he wanted to pursue his growing feelings for her.

Even if she'd not given him any sort of hint. But he wasn't going to let that stop him.

He was tired of holding himself back, tired of letting his fears rule his head and his heart.

And tired of not speaking the words of his heart at the time when it mattered most.

He'd lost the opportunity to do that with his family, with Charlotte.

But he wasn't going to lose the opportunity to say it to Molly.

After all, Charlotte would've wanted him to live, to love, again. He'd realized that as he'd sobbed amid the sheet music.

He pushed open the door of The Blue Mirror after nodding a hello at the doorman and handing him a nickel.

Cigarette smoke and the lazy meanderings of a saxophone working through some scales greeted him as he strolled over to the bar and sat down.

"Say," Tristan said to the bartender after he'd ordered a bourbon, "do you know what time the show starts?"

"About twenty minutes," the man said.

Tristan looked but didn't see Nick Hart among the group of musicians who glanced in his direction. Must not be Nick's show tonight. Tristan gave the group a wary nod.

Surely they had no idea who he was? He'd never made much of a name for himself up North here.

Tristan's mind wandered back to the night before last when he'd sobbed amid the shredded sheet music.

Yesterday morning he'd woken up with the rain pounding on the roof. But he'd felt lighter inside, somehow. Cleaner.

As if the rain somehow had gotten inside him.

He let his eyes close.

The Blue Mirror Club. Hmmm. What rhymed with blue? You? I do?

He didn't know if it was the surroundings or just the fact that he was in a city where no one knew him and there were no pressures or expectations, but suddenly, he could hear lyrics in his head.

The kind of joyful noise that he never thought he'd hear.

He laughed aloud.

Then again, they did sound quite a bit like music. He cocked his head.

He could hear the hum and flow of them. Consonants. Vowels. Syllables.

Just when he'd come here looking for a woman and a tune, he'd found words.

Tristan fumbled for the return airline ticket in his jacket's inner pocket and flipped it over, exposing the plain white surface.

"Quick," he said to the bartender, "do you have a pencil I can borrow?"

"What do you think this place is, an office?"

Tristan blinked.

But the man pulled a pencil from a pocket of his apron, then continued mixing a martini for another customer.

Before the words could drift away, Tristan started scribbling the lyrics that wound through his mind.

> *Knew it was you*
> *Even when I was blue*
> *There wasn't a thing I could do*
> *When I started to*
> *Fall for you*

Tristan's pencil moved faster and the tip of his tongue protruded from between his teeth as a furrow formed between his brows.

> *Oh it had to be you*
> *Yes it had to be you*
> *Even when I was blue*
> *It had to be you*

A smile tugged at his lips.

He continued to write, line after line flying from his pencil and onto the airline

ticket.

A surge of joy burst through him, washing away all the rage, all the fear and all the resentment that had been chained around his heart.

That's what being blocked had done to him.

Closed off his heart.

Because music was how he expressed these feelings of his heart. And now he could speak again, he could speak the language of his heart, to Molly, with these lyrics.

He did know what he was doing. He did, he did, he did. He wasn't some two-bit hack after all.

He grinned and completed the song. He sighed in satisfaction and took a long pull of his bourbon.

But he found himself glancing around. He didn't spot any redheads anywhere.

"Excuse me," he turned to the bartender. "Do you know if a Miss Molly Evans comes here often?"

"Never heard of her."

Tristan took a sip of his drink and tried to pretend he wasn't disappointed.

Was he going to give up that easily?

No.

And yes.

He didn't know what else he could do to find her. He didn't know her address. He didn't know her phone number. He didn't know any of her friends...The Blue Mirror had been his only lead.

Perhaps this *had* been a crazy idea.

But maybe he could ask at the TWA ticket counter?

He sighed. The trip had been a long shot. He knew that from the beginning. And if he was honest with himself, he'd loved the romantic notion of coming to find her...

But now it looked like going back to New Orleans was his only option. At least he'd tried. At least he had some lyrics now, even if he could never tell Molly how he felt. At least he'd written it down and written it out.

And maybe some day she'd be in a pi-

ano bar somewhere and hear that song and think of him.

He turned to watch the show.

Hours later, the night fog swirled around Tristan as he stepped out of The Blue Mirror.

He had no reason to stay in this town. But he couldn't make himself leave. Not yet.

He started walking.

What was he going to do with these lyrics now?

He passed a shuttered storefront with a hand-lettered sign that read Swanson's School of Dance. He smiled at the photos of twirling couples taped to the large plate glass window.

The streetlamps glowed.

Well, first he'd need some music for them. To start, anyway. And maybe Gus and Elliot would want to write themselves in on the number.

He walked on. Past an alley with stacks of crates stencilled with Golden Gate Records next to a tall brick office building with glass doors etched with the same name.

And on.

Up and down hills. Trolleys clanged. Street lights changed.

Could he even use this as a show opener? Maybe he'd invite Nick and his ensemble down to the Crescent City for a collaboration of sorts...

He found himself in a residential district. He spied red clay roof tiles. Curling wrought iron. Pointed turrets.

Did Molly live in one of these places?

He could go by the TWA ticket counter tomorrow morning and—Look a fool trying to track down a pretty face like no doubt hundreds of other male passengers had.

He grinned.

He wouldn't be a true Lachaynais if he didn't take a foolish risk every now and again, now would he?

♪

"SAY NOW, MISS MOLLY." A gleam came

into Elliot's eyes. "Can I hear a bit of this little tune you're talking about?"

"What? Oh! I'm not very good at humming."

He waved a hand. "Go on."

Molly hummed a few bars.

"Yessiree. I could think of a few songs with those notes you've been humming."

"Oh, I'm sure." Molly fidgeted with her cocktail napkin. "It's just a silly little melody that's been rolling through my head for what seems like ages. The thing is," she put her hands into her striped green dress pockets, "I don't even know where it came from."

Elliot laughed. "That's the way of music. Ain't no one sure jus' exactly where it comes from." He shot her a speculative look.

Molly shook her head. "I'm not a musician. And I sure can't compose anything."

"Don't you worry about that," Elliot said. "Things'll work out. I have a feeling. Now, if you'll excuse me, I have that meeting to attend to. A pleasure to see you again. All the best." He tipped his hat at her and walked out of the bar.

She checked her wristwatch. She'd better leave too.

A little while later, Molly opened the taxi door and got out at the airport. She sighed.

She'd even tried calling Tristan's number the hotel manager had given her after she'd come back from the plantation. But his phone line was still out.

All this searching had been for nothing. There came a point when you had to choose to let go. She blinked rapidly and swallowed. And now was that time.

TRISTAN STEPPED OFF THE AMERICAN Airlines flight and down onto the tarmac in New Orleans.

It'd been the same airline he'd taken to San Francisco.

Heading to California, he hadn't wanted to wait for an outbound TWA. So he'd hopped on the earliest California connection available, which was with American Airlines.

Not that it mattered now.

A gust of wind lifted his straw hat right off his head. He barely noticed.

Before he'd left San Francisco, he'd even gone to TWA headquarters and found out that she no longer worked there. And they wouldn't give him her address, either.

Apparently, it wasn't meant to be, no matter how much he wanted it to be.

He turned and bent to retrieve his hat, but another gust of wind sent it rolling along the tarmac in front of him.

He walked faster, trying to keep up but the hat tumbled on, just out of reach. Kind of like Molly.

He'd never see her again, now would he?

He was just about to cut his losses when he managed to snag a finger under the brim.

Tristan snatched up the hat.

As he placed the hat back on his head,

he spotted a glint of sunlight on red-gold curls. And a striped green dress some ways away.

He blinked. His mouth went dry.

But Tristan was already walking across the tarmac, dodging luggage, porters and passengers.

Well now, that green dress did look rather fetching on her, didn't it? Tristan couldn't help but admire her retreating form.

He increased his pace. "Miss Evans! Miss Evans!" He raised his voice.

She didn't turn around, though a few other women did. He gave them an apologetic look. "Miss Evans!" he tried again, louder, just as the propellers cut in.

"Molly!" he yelled, this time disregarding all sense of propriety.

But it was no good. She had started to climb the airplane steps.

He followed.

"Molly!" he tried again as loud as he dared.

At last, she turned at the sound of her

name. But she caught her heel on the stair rung.

"Careful," Tristan said, reaching out a hand to steady her.

"Tristan?" Molly's eyes widened. "What are you—? I have a flight to catch."

"I know."

"Then aren't you going to let me catch it?"

Tristan reached out and gently clasped her upper arm. "You can always catch the next one. I have something to say to you."

Tristan caught a look of panic mixed with relief cross Molly's face.

Mutterings from passengers behind them seemed to shake Molly out of herself. "I have something to say, er, give to you, too."

She descended the stairs behind Tristan.

His heart sped up. Did she have any idea how he felt about her?

A surge of heat washed through him and he paused just beyond the propellors' whirring.

"I don't think this is the best place to talk," Molly yelled over the noise.

The scent of her lily of the valley perfume filled his head as he leaned forward and spoke near her ear. "Then hows about Twisted Oaks?"

Chapter Five

A GRAY LINCOLN SEDAN WITH wide fenders and chrome detailing idled at the curb. Tristan held open the passenger door for Molly.

"But I thought you—"

"Always drove around in a truck with bald tires?"

Molly blushed as she got in. He shut the door and got in on the driver's side. "Nope."

Molly watched as palm trees and pedestrians zipped by. The sedan merged onto the open highway.

Tristan glanced at Molly. "So why are you back in New Orleans?"

Molly slid a sidelong look toward Tristan. "A little vacation. It's so charming I just had to come back." She tapped her fingers on the doorframe. "I had the time, you see. Now that I got fired from TWA."

Tristan nodded. "So I heard."

"How did you find that out?"

"Happened to talk with some TWA employees."

"TWA didn't find me competent at my job."

"I don't agree with them." Tristan paused. "You did a great service for the company and the passengers."

Her heart fluttered. "But where were you?"

Tristan's fingers curled around the steering wheel. "Oh, I took a little trip, myself. And," he continued, "I was hoping to make things up to you. I was rather r-rude last time we saw each other."

Molly felt her heart soften. "That's very kind of you, but you don't have to apologize. I wasn't so stellar myself. Which is something I usually pride myself on." She glanced at Tristan.

"That makes two of us."

Molly shifted in her seat.

"Don't worry," Tristan said, "I thor-

oughly checked this car's tires."

"Oh good." She leaned her head back against the seat and felt her eyelids growing heavy.

She stifled a yawn. Maybe she'd close her eyes for a little while...

Lulled by the warmth of the sun and the smooth hum as the car headed down the highway, she felt herself drift off to sleep.

She cuddled into the warmth. Her shoulders relaxed and she sighed, wishing she could stay like this forever. So warm. Safe. Happy. At home. Home?

The scent of cedar and leather drifted to her.

"We're here." Tristan's voice, soft and low, was filled with a warmth she'd never heard before.

Her eyes flew open. She was leaning against his shoulder.

He turned his head, his warm breath fanning her cheek.

She looked up at him, their faces mere millimeters apart.

Her stomach flipped and she hastily sat up.

Tristan didn't make eye contact as he said, "You go on in. I'll park the car."

She could see the familiar row of oaks on her left as she walked the length of the verandah and opened the big front door.

Could she have been wrong? That he was interested in her after all?

She made her way into the entryway and then down the long runner on the first floor, her tiredness replaced by a sense of curiosity. In the light of day the place didn't look scary at all. Merely old.

And dusty.

She ran a finger along an ornately carved hall table, disturbing the thick layer of dust on its inlaid surface.

She continued on to the door at the end of the hall and slowly turned the crystal doorknob.

It swung inward on its hinges.

Molly pushed the door all the way open and walked across the faded Oriental carpet to where the grand piano sat in the corner.

She took a seat on the piano bench. It creaked slightly.

As if impelled by some unseen force, she raised the lid on the keys and gently placed a single fingertip on one of the white keys, then closed her eyes.

She pressed down and held her breath as the rich mellow tone issued from the piano.

She placed her hand fully on the piano and experimented with a few more keys.

She became so engrossed she didn't notice that she'd knocked a piece of paper onto the floor.

She smiled softly to herself as a few more mellow tones sounded out into the silence.

Then she placed her other hand on the keyboard and pressed some more keys. It didn't sound like much of anything, but it was kind of fun. Her soft smile widened to a grin.

She hummed the melody to herself as she continued plonking keys. She glanced around. Where had Tristan gone? She looked toward the door. Should she go find him?

A tattered page lying on the floor caught her attention. She noticed the distinctive feminine handwriting. Was it a letter? She picked it up.

Sunlight began stretching across the rug and crept upward until the piano was bathed in the golden light of late afternoon.

A floorboard creaked.

She whirled around, heart pounding, the tattered letter falling out of her grasp and onto the floor again.

Tristan.

HE CROSSED THE ROOM IN a few long strides.

She stood. Reached out. Placed a hand on the side of his face and whispered, "I understand."

Tristan closed his eyes, Molly's hand on his face, her warm fingers all he could think about.

"And I wanted to give you...this melody." She began humming a tune under her breath as she continued to simply stand there. In the golden light. With him. His throat tightened and he opened his eyes.

She half-turned away from him, the sound dying on her lips.

He placed a hand on her shoulder and gently turned her back toward him.

He looked into her eyes, listening to the silence echoing between them.

Her hair was lit by rays of sunshine, changing the coppery curls to a burnished gold and outlining her in a golden glow.

He took a step nearer.

She took a step nearer.

He smiled. So did she.

But then he froze in place as notes began nudging at the edges of his mind, clear and distinct and ringing with joy, building upon the melody Molly had hummed.

Without a moment's hesitation, he swiftly sat at the piano and closed his eyes, raised his arms.

And began playing.

Softly at first and then louder, as the notes tumbled out over each other in a rush of desire for expression.

He grasped at the rapidly-forming melody, his fingers jumping across the keyboard as his head tilted back, his heartbeat speeding up, as he gave himself over to the sweet rush of music spilling through him once again.

The sweet, stirring ballad he conjured filled him with such an ache it nearly took his breath away.

Yet he continued playing, almost unable to stop.

He felt perspiration bead on his forehead, but still he played, brow furrowed, heart pounding, the notes surging to a crescendo inside of him and spilling out into the air around him.

His fingers finally stilled and he took a jagged breath, his chest heaving.

Slowly, slowly, he opened his eyes.

Molly was staring at him, her eyes wide, a delicate pink across her cheeks.

He felt his own face flush as warmth

spread through him and he met her gaze in the golden rays of sunlight.

But that was okay. Better than okay. In fact, he'd never felt better in his life.

He jumped up, and took her hands in his. "When I was thirteen, I had my first concert performance. I fell in love with performing and knew some day I'd become a concert pianist. My parents wholeheartedly encouraged me and supported me every step of the way. They had complete and utter faith in me, and as a result, I had that same faith in myself. So I decided on jazz as the outlet for my passion for music. But..."

He paused, swallowed, and then continued, meeting Molly's gaze. "That's when I met Charlotte. We fell in love. In between gigs and bottles of bourbon and riverside strolls...I had gig after gig night after night in the French Quarter and she was there, every night, for every one of them. Even if sometimes I'd play for six hours straight. The audience loved it. I loved it. But on the night of my biggest performance, there was a huge storm. My wife and my parents, who are buried in that graveyard on Royal Street, were coming to see me perform. They all died that night. Their car crashed into a tree that had fallen across the road. I'd been eaten up with guilt. And blocked musically. Ever since." He swallowed. "And I didn't realize just how much that had held me back. Until," he squeezed her hands, "I met you."

He let out a long, deep sigh, his shoulders sagging and his head dropping towards his chest.

He was barely aware of Molly coming to sit beside him until she rested a hand lightly on his forearm, the warmth of her fingers spread all the way into his heart.

He dared a glance up at her face.

"Thank you," she murmured.

"For what?"

"For being brave enough to share your true self with me."

His tongue stuck to the roof of his mouth, but he spoke. "Have a picnic with me this evening? I know the perfect spot."

His heart stuttered. And after that, then what? Now that she'd given him the melody, she'd have to go. Wouldn't she?

♫

THE GRASS TICKLED MOLLY'S BARE feet as she walked through it, her sandals dangling from one hand as she walked alongside Tristan down a sun-dappled path.

Molly's heart pounded. They approached some twisted oaks clustered together where the green grass grew with wild abandon.

Shade and sunlight splashed across Tristan's plaid shirt, and Molly's gaze rested on his broad shoulders and the play of muscles of his upper arm as he carried the wicker picnic basket.

"How about over there?" Tristan nodded to a shady spot where tree roots and grass intertwined and the land gently curved.

Molly blinked rapidly. "That looks just fine."

He put down the picnic basket and then knelt to shake out the old, but still brightly colored, quilt that he'd had draped over his other arm.

It floated gently down onto the grass, and Molly couldn't help but remember how it'd covered the bed she'd slept in the night of the storm.

"—or fried chicken?" Tristan said.

Molly blushed and tore her eyes away from the quilt. "Oh, either."

Tristan raised a brow. "You weren't paying attention, were you?"

"Of course I was. Here, I'll help you lay out the food." Molly knelt beside Tristan and she could smell, underneath the scent of warm grass and fried chicken, his cedar-and-leather scent.

She felt her pulse beat in her throat and her hands shook slightly as she poured them both tall glasses of sweet tea and handed Tristan one, the moisture beading and slowly running down the side of the glass.

She took a sip and felt her tension ease.

They were just having a picnic. That was all.

Tristan filled two plates and handed her one. "There you go. Fried chicken with all the fixin's."

Their fingertips brushed as he handed her the plate, a warm look in his eyes.

He had more than a picnic on his mind. A shiver went down her spine. She tried to hide it as she leaned back against the rough, solid tree trunk, then tucked her legs underneath her and straightened her skirt.

"So," Tristan said, and leaned back against the tree too.

"This fried chicken is delicious," Molly said.

"I'm glad you're enjoying it," he said softly, meeting her gaze, his eyes lingering on her lips.

Self-conscious, she dabbed her linen napkin to her lips as she finished the drumstick she'd been eating. She gave a nervous laugh. "Do I have any crumbs on my face?"

Tristan leaned forward, and a curl fell over his forehead.

"Just one here," he said, slowly raising his hand and ever so gently using the pad of his thumb to slide along the edge of her bottom lip.

Her eyes fluttered closed and a soft sigh escaped. Mortified, she jerked back and opened her eyes. "Thank you," she said.

"You're welcome."

She darted a glance at him and watched him take the last few bites of his chicken and cornbread.

He was nothing like her father, was he? A smile touched her lips. No. He was completely his own person. A *real* Southern gentleman.

Neither of them spoke, but the buzz of cicadas was a constant thrum, becoming more insistent and then fading away.

Molly took another sip of her sweet tea and spoke. "So, that melody... You know, it's been with me for so long. I can't even remember a time when I didn't have it in my head. But now it'll be on paper."

"Yes," Tristan said, his voice low. "And thank you for taking the risk. For sharing that part of yourself with me." Tristan studied her, his eyes the color of warm caramel.

"But what about the lyrics?"

Tristan glanced at her, a question in his eyes, as he started to stack the dishes and put them into the wicker basket.

Automatically, she reached out to help him and waited for him to say something.

Moments passed. He still didn't speak.

It was only when all the dishes and food remains had been neatly placed inside and the picnic basket closed, that Tristan spoke. "Lyrics came to me in San Francisco. That's where I came back from today. Looking for you. At The Blue Mirror Club."

Molly's pulse jumped. "For me?"

Tristan nodded.

Molly plucked up a blade of grass, trailing it along the back of her other hand. "That's why I came back to New Orleans.

To look for you."

He took her hand. "Really?"

She nodded.

He spoke again. "In those moments when I was writing the lyrics, I realized something. Do you know what that was?"

He turned and looked at her, his brown eyes serious.

Molly shook her head.

He reached into his pocket and pulled out a rather wrinkled airline ticket.

He handed it to her.

She looked down at the ticket, the last few lines jumping out at her:

> *Knew it was you*
> *Even when I was blue*
> *There wasn't a thing I could do*
> *When I started to*
> *Fall for you*
>
> *Oh it had to be you*
> *Yes it had to be you*
> *Even when I was blue*
> *It had to be you*

Her heart pounded a little faster and she looked up, meeting Tristan's gaze, which had now shifted from serious to intense. He leaned forward, as if to take the ticket from her.

But she closed her fingers around it. Could this be true? Thoughts tumbled one after the other, in her mind.

So all his hospitality, his formality, hadn't been a facade? He'd actually...he did actually...she felt a smile pull the corners of her mouth up...like her? And more, was saying he had feelings for her?

She opened her mouth to tell him of her own feelings, but the drone of a bi-plane flying by overhead caught her attention. "Remember when I told you I got fired? Well, I realized that was the best thing that could've happened. Because I discovered I actually want to be a pilot. I want to fly my own plane. And if I'd clung to that stewardess job, well, I wouldn't have found that out at all."

Tristan followed her gaze. "I think that's a great idea," he said softly.

Molly met his eyes. "I could have the freedom to work for myself, not some big airline. Give people rides all around the countryside."

This was such a beautiful, peaceful place. She'd never felt like she'd had a sense of *home*. That's why she'd taken to the skies. Because it felt like home.

She'd never felt that sense of home with any man. But with Tristan? Her heart fluttered, then soared. She did.

Her smiled widened as her gaze returned to the lyrics.

"Yes," she said, to Tristan's unspoken question, the silent lines on the paper doing all the talking she needed to hear.

Molly laughed. "I'm beginning to like Louisiana quite a lot." The same exhilaration she'd felt at the airplane's controls filled her now as she looked into Tristan's eyes. "And you, too." She pressed a hand to her heart, still holding onto the ticket.

Tristan spoke softly. "I could put on shows in each city and town you're in. Fix up this place, too. It's been neglected far

too long. Kind of like my heart."

The airplane's rumble faded. The hum and whirr of the cicadas grew louder, more insistent, mingled with the scent of magnolia mixed with honeysuckle.

Tristan continued. "Molly, you showed me exactly what I needed to see, and you healed me in ways I never dared dream were possible. You're the sunlight to the dark cracks in my heart."

"Oh, Tristan."

Yes. She could definitely see herself here. In Tristan's arms.

He leaned forward. So did she.

In the quiet evening stillness, the cicadas humming softly to themselves, Molly melted into him, into the warmth and softness of his mouth.

She placed a hand on his chest, felt the beat of his heart through the lightweight material, and threaded the fingers of her other hand through his dark curls.

He slid a hand around her waist in response, pulling her nearer to him.

And as he did so, she could feel the unspoken lyrics singing between them, floating out into the warm spring evening air.

Yes. She could keep her freedom and discover the possibility of love, too.

Thanks for reading! Want more sweet historical romance? Turn the page to meet Alessandra Velocchi in *Beneath A Venetian Moon*. It's the first in my *Love By Moonlight* series.

Now, read on for an excerpt from
Alessandra Velocchi's story,
Beneath A Venetian Moon:
Love By Moonlight, #1

Chapter One

THE MOONLIGHT SLIPPED THROUGH THE partially open window as Alessandra Velocchi smoothed her amethyst gown. If only her own escape could be so easy. But the binding ties of duty wound around her more tightly than the velvet-trimmed silver mask she wore as she stepped out of her chamber, down the stairs, and out into the waiting gondola.

She gasped as the chill waters of the Venetian canal splashed at her hem like greedy fingers trying to reclaim their prize. She shuddered, putting the childhood near-drowning experience from her mind, focusing firmly on the festivities ahead at the Doge's birthday celebration.

"Does the Contessa have an escort?" The doorman addressed Alessandra at the palace entrance.

Lifting her chin, she shook her head. "Tonight, I am a free woman." She felt her heart swell with gladness. No father to watch her, no boring escort to hinder her. Pure, clear freedom. Just the way she liked it.

Candlelight sparkled off cut crystal chandeliers as she took a goblet of wine from a side table. Winding her way amongst mingling revelers, she spotted familiar faces all around. Laughter and accented voices drifted past her as the pull of duty pushed her to the front of the ballroom where the Doge stood.

As she approached, the Doge's ministers bowed, acknowledging her as the daughter of Venice's most powerful palace advisor.

"Before the Doge begins his own speech," stated one of the officials, "he expects to hear the address your father entrusted you with." He nodded toward Alessandra. "You have prepared?"

"Of course." As she brought her goblet to her lips to calm her nerves, a sudden shadow flickered in her peripheral vision. She glanced sideways. Now nothing. Closing her eyes for a brief second to gather her thoughts, she savored the drink's heady sweetness.

Alessandra took another sip of wine, fiddling with the stem of the goblet, watching the carved facets glimmer in the light. And again, the shadow flickered in her vision, this time closer.

She frowned. Looked around. Returned her attention to the Doge, waiting for him to give her the nod. But just then, the shadow appeared again – this time taking on a form – that of a man. With a black silk mask tied around his glossy dark hair and a velvet doublet trimmed in the same midnight shade.

This time, she openly stared at him. Watched while his furtive glances around the room displayed fear. Watched while his fluid movements wound him between guests. Watched while his steps led him closer and closer to her.

She forgot all about her staid speech as

she searched the planes of his face. He was not part of the court. Or the Doge's administration. Or even a member of the Venetian aristocratic circles she'd known all her life. Though he certainly was attractive. And certainly not a boring escort. Her lips curved into a smile.

She continued to admire him, noticing that by now he stood only a few paces from her. But protocol and privilege forced her to turn away, forced her to acknowledge the Doge, who now beckoned to her.

She raised her chin and straightened her spine, pivoting to face the assemblage. As the guests' final murmurs died away, she inhaled, about to speak.

But in that brief hesitation, the masked man leapt toward her. As she startled, stepping back, her name tumbled from his lips. "Contessa Velocchi."

His eyes held hers even as he collapsed at her feet, gasping, his hand pressed to his side. And that's when she saw it. Blood. Seeping crimson onto the polished parquet floor.

She knelt, one look into that sea-green gaze telling her she had nothing to fear. Her heart filled with concern at his wound and she pulled out a handkerchief, leaning forward.

His breath warm in her ear, he whispered low, frantic. "Please...I beg of you...help me. They...want me dead."

Acknowledgments

Karen Dale Harris – editor, who helped me smooth out the story so it could shine

Shannon Page – copyeditor, who had a great eye for detail, especially about San Francisco

Angela Waters – graphic designer, who gave me a beautiful and classy cover for the story

Sabrina Volman – friend and beta reader, who graciously read over my manuscript with a fresh set of eyes

My family – who graciously supported me with their love and kindness

SRW writing group – who helped me keep up my writer morale

Author's note: In historical fact, the Carousel Bar came into existence in 1949, not 1947 as I have portrayed in this story. However, I thought it such a compelling place, I decided to take poetic license and move its opening back a few years. –J.E.